"Owl Goingback remains one of our most accomplished writers of horror fiction."
—Terry Brooks

Praise for the Bram Stoker Award–winning novel *Crota*

"How could you resist a book written by someone named Owl Goingback? *Crota* is not a tale to be read late at night. It's a chiller." —*San Francisco Examiner*

"Goingback keeps the action brisk." —*Publishers Weekly*

"Engrossing . . . Goingback proves he has a talent for creating heart-stopping scenes that meld realism and fantasy. . . . Claustrophobically frightening . . . Goingback utilizes his heritage well as he turns an Indian myth into a monster of a tale." —*Sun-Sentinel* (Fort Lauderdale)

"An extraordinary visionary novel."
—*Anniston Star* (Anniston, Alabama)

"One of the best un-put-downable novels that has passed through my hands in a long time. Goingback has excelled. Excitement on every page." —Andre Norton

"Wow! I devoured *Crota*. What a terrific read."
—*Halifax* magazine

"Owl Goingback is one of the most interesting new writers working today. A natural storyteller who will be spinning his tales for a long time to come."
—Martin H. Greenberg

Darker Than Night

"A chilling tale . . . Mr. Goingback creates a story line that rivals the best of the genre's masters. . . . One of the year's best horror novels." —Harriet Klausner

"Owl Goingback writes . . . the elemental scare, the campfire tale, that's all too rare these days." —Gothic.net

Also by Owl Goingback

Darker Than Night

Crota

Evil Whispers

Owl Goingback

A SIGNET BOOK

SIGNET
Published by New American Library, a division of
Penguin Putnam Inc., 375 Hudson Street,
New York, New York 10014, U.S.A.
Penguin Books Ltd, 27 Wrights Lane,
London W8 5TZ, England
Penguin Books Australia Ltd, Ringwood,
Victoria, Australia
Penguin Books Canada Ltd, 10 Alcorn Avenue,
Toronto, Ontario, Canada M4V 3B2
Penguin Books (N.Z.) Ltd, 182–190 Wairau Road,
Auckland 10, New Zealand

Penguin Books Ltd, Registered Offices:
Harmondsworth, Middlesex, England

First published by Signet, an imprint of New American Library,
a division of Penguin Putnam Inc.

First Printing, May 2001
10 9 8 7 6 5 4 3 2 1

Printed in the United States of America

For Jason, Beth, and Brianna

ACKNOWLEDGMENTS

Special thanks go to my editor, Joseph Pittman, and my agent, Andrew Zack, for all their hard work and dedication.

Prologue

July 23, 1831.

The smell of fear hung heavy on the air inside the tiny wooden cabin. A pungent, spicy odor. Sharp to the nostrils and metallic on the tongue, like the razored blade of a well-honed knife. It scented the room, mixing in with the aromas of fragrant oils, herbs, sweat and fresh blood.

Mansa Du Paul inhaled deeply, savoring the fragrances that were his gifts to the *Petro Loas,* the dark gods he served. They would be pleased with his offerings. In return they would answer his summons, coming to him with gifts of knowledge and spiritual power. Gifts that only a *bokor,* a voodoo sorcerer, such as himself, could use.

He lit a black candle and set it on the wooden table before him. Several others had already been lit. Along with them, the table was cluttered with numerous plates and bowls, filled with offerings of food and drink to the gods. On one of those plates lay the body of a black chicken whose neck he had just cut. The pewter bowl next to the plate held the chicken's blood, which was still warm to the touch.

Fresh blood for the *Loas,* gods who demanded gifts of sacrifice from those who served them. Gifts of wine and food, and offerings of flesh and blood. Usually that of animal, or fowl, but sometimes the flesh and blood were human.

On the opposite side of the table from Mansa kneeled a half dozen men and women, their ebony skin reflecting the glow from the flickering candles. They were his servants, waiting to do whatever he would ask of them, fearful of making any mistake that might offend him. They knew of his power and feared it. Feared him.

Like the sorcerer they now served, the others in the room had also been slaves of the white man. But they too had escaped the plantations and chains, following Mansa to the humid forests of central Florida. Together, along with twenty other runaway slaves, they had built a small village along the banks of the tiny Wekiva River, naming the settlement Blackwater.

The village was Mansa's, and these were his people. They had come to him for his help, seeking safety from the hounds and slavers that hunted them. In return for his help, they became his devoted subjects, doing anything and everything that he asked. They were loyal, without question, for to be otherwise would result in a punishment far more severe than any plantation owner could ever administer. After all, there were things in the world far worse than whips and chains: there were the unholy spirits that Mansa paid homage to, and then there was the sorcerer himself.

Mansa Du Paul had been born into slavery on a farm just south of Atlanta, Georgia, in the fall of 1801.

When he was old enough to walk on his own, he had been put to work picking cotton alongside his mother. He didn't remember much about his mother, other than that she had been beautiful, her skin two shades lighter than his own. She had died when he was only ten, bitten by a rattlesnake while working in the field. The snake had bitten him too, but he had not sickened and died like his mother. Even then he had the power.

He might have had a hard time after his mother's death, because there was no sympathy among the other slaves for the weak or orphaned. But Mansa was taken in by an old, one-eyed woman named Maggie. The other slaves were scared of Maggie, for she was a master of voodoo, a priestess from the island of Haiti.

Maggie had seen the snake bite Mansa and his mother, and knew that Dramballah, the Supreme Mystery, was pointing the boy out to her. The *Loa* had taken Mansa's mother, leaving the boy in the care of one who would teach him how to work powerful magic.

Even under the old woman's protection, Mansa's youth had not been a happy one. In the daytime there were fields to plow and cotton to be picked, and by night he was pressed to remember ancient ceremonies and formulas, learning the ways and wants of each and every *Loa*. He was a quick learner, and soon he was assisting the old woman in her magical rituals, allowing the gods to enter his body in order to obtain power and knowledge.

But Mansa was not content with the limitations the old priestess put on him. He wanted to learn more of voodoo than what she was offering to teach. He thought it was foolish to learn how to heal the sick and help others. Instead, he wanted knowledge that would give him power over others, knowledge that would allow him to hurt or kill his enemies. So Mansa had embraced the darkness, promising to faithfully serve the *Petro Loas* in return for the power they could give him. He had learned all of Maggie's secrets and then he had killed her, offering her blood to the dark gods in a ritual sacrifice.

He shed the bonds of slavery shortly after taking the old woman's life, fleeing to central Florida. Other escaped slaves followed him, seeking the protection of his voodoo powers. Together they built a tiny village of eight cabins deep in the forest. Mansa ruled over the people of his village with an iron fist, through fear and intimidation, and with the use of black magic. In addition to offering blood sacrifices in his evil ceremonies, the sorcerer was extremely fond of eating the flesh of small children.

Mansa smiled, his gaze traveling to the large, ornately carved wooden post in the center of the room. The post, decorated with carvings of circles, rainbows, and snakes, was sacred to Legba, guardian of the passage between this world and that of the spirits. It was Legba who would throw open the passageway, allowing the other *Loas* to come sliding down the post into the world of the living.

Tied to the post were two young children, a boy and a girl. Brother and sister. They were Indian children, taken the previous evening from a neighboring Seminole village. Mansa would have preferred white children, but there were no whites living in the area, and the flesh of an Indian child was almost as tasty. Almost.

Mansa smiled. "Soon, little ones. Soon it will be time for you to die. Ye*sss* . . . time to die."

He picked up his *asson,* a gourd rattle filled with pebbles, snake bones, earth from a cemetery, and magical powders, from the table before him. The rattle had once belonged to Maggie, but he had stolen it after taking the old woman's life. There was powerful magic in the rattle; with it he could command the dead and control the cemetery *Loas*.

Shaking the rattle with a slow, steady beat, he circled the wooden table and crossed the room. His servants moved out of the way to let him pass, making sure to avoid eye contact. They knew better than to look directly into the eyes of the voodoo sorcerer, for such a gesture would be considered a challenge that would invoke his wrath.

The children, however, though afraid, did not avert their eyes. They watched him as he approached, the boy straining at the knotted cords that held him fast to the ornate post.

"Ye*sss*, that's it. Struggle little man. Struggle all you want. You shall not get away. Not from Mansa Du Paul. I will offer your life to the *Loas,* then I will set your blood outside for the witches that pass in the night.

"Have you ever seen the witches, little man? They pass through the night like fireflies. They are very fond of blood, especially the blood of children. They will be pleased by my offering, very pleased.

"The witches will have your blood, and the *Loas* will have your life, but your soul will be mine. I will steal your soul from the top of your head, and I will keep it in a clay jar upon the shelf. There."

Mansa turned and pointed to the far end of the room, where a crude plank shelf ran the length of the wall. Upon the shelf were bottles, plates, wooden bowls, gourds, stones of various size, and several small clay jars. The jars were called "spirit jars," and contained the souls of other victims he had sacrificed to the dark gods.

"See. There. That is where I will keep you and your sister. That is where I will keep your souls. Your souls I will keep, your blood I will set outside in big bowls, and your flesh I will eat."

The sorcerer licked his lips and turned back to look at the Indian boy. The boy was dressed in a long cloth shirt, which was gathered at the waist with a belt of woven yarn. His legs and feet were bare, and, unlike his sister, he wore no jewelry of any kind. The girl was dressed in a long cotton skirt, also gathered at the waist, and a short blouse that left her midriff exposed. Her feet were bare, but around her neck hung numerous necklaces of colored glass beads.

Even though they were young, both children were skilled in the ways of the forest. Had they not been tied to the post, they would have quickly escaped back to their village. But they were both firmly tied, so there would be no escape for them. Only pain, and death.

Mansa stopped in front of the children, shaking his rattle three times at each of them. Wetting a fingertip with his tongue, he slowly ran his finger down the left cheek of the girl. He again licked his fingertip, tasting the saltiness of her flesh.

He started to do the same thing to her brother, but the boy bared his teeth in a threatening gesture.

Mansa smiled. The boy would, no doubt, bite the hand that touched him. Even though he was still young, he had already been learning the warrior ways of his people and would put up a fight to the very end. His blood would be salty. Spicy. A fitting offering to gods and witches. And his flesh would make a fine stew for the voodoo sorcerer.

Shaking the rattle, Mansa slowly circled the post to start the ceremony that would call upon the dark Loas. He had just circled behind the children, when, outside the cabin, a scream of pain split the night. Another scream sounded, followed by shouts of anger.

Alarmed, Mansa turned and started back across the room. He had only taken three steps, however, when the door to his cabin was kicked open and several painted warriors entered the room. The men were Seminoles. No doubt they were from the neighboring village, and had come to rescue the children. They were armed with bows and arrows, spears, knives, and even a rifle or two.

Mansa was unarmed, for he had never felt the need for common weapons. His magic had always protected him, but it took time to work spells of magic. And time was something he no longer had. The warriors had attacked the village by surprise, slipping past the guards who watched the outer edges of the settlement. There was no time for magic, and he had no real weapons, other than the ceremonial knife that lay upon the wooden table.

Grabbing the knife off the table, he turned to his servants that awaited his command. "Stop them," he said, pointing at the Seminole warriors that were pouring into the room. There was a moment's hesitation, and then the six men and women rushed forward to defend their leader.

But the Seminoles were determined, and they would not be stopped. They attacked the black men and women with a frenzy usually seen only in animals. Swinging knives and tomahawks, they cut through Mansa's servants with ease, leaving their lifeless bodies to cool in spreading pools of blood.

Mansa tried to reach the children, determined to end their miserable little lives. He never made it. Tackled from behind, he was dragged forcibly from his cabin.

Outside, chaos had descended upon the village of Blackwater. Most of the inhabitants had already been killed; the rest had fled and were being hunted by the Seminole warriors. From the darkness of the surrounding forest came shouts and war cries, and the occasional scream of pain and death.

Someone had set fire to several of the cabins. Bright flames shot from thatched roofs, casting a flickering orange glow over the surrounding area. Thick black smoke rolled toward the night sky, blocking out the stars and the silvery glow of a full moon.

Mansa took in the surrounding images of carnage with but a single glance, for he cared nothing at all about the fate of those who served him, or the dwellings they lived in. He cared only for himself.

Still, Mansa Du Paul was not afraid to die. He knew that his spirit was too strong to be killed outright. He was a man of voodoo, gaining the protection of gods far more powerful than those served by the heathen Seminoles. Even as several warriors tied him to a cypress tree at the edge of the river, Mansa felt no fear.

"I am immortal." He laughed, staring down the men who stood before him. "You cannot kill me. My spirit will live forever."

His laugh turned into a cry of pain as a slender cane arrow struck his body, burying itself deep into his right thigh. His spirit might be immortal, but his body was mere flesh. They could not kill his spirit, but they could kill his body. And the death of the flesh could be extremely painful.

Lifting his gaze to the night sky, he whispered a prayer to the dark gods he had so faithfully served during his lifetime. It was a prayer for strength and courage, but mostly it was a prayer for revenge.

A second arrow struck him in the stomach, just above his left hip. A third arrow struck two inches higher than the second. More arrows buried their heads deep into his flesh, but none of them hit vital areas. The Seminoles were making a game of his death, punishing him for the two children he had stolen from their village the previous evening, and for the others he had taken in the past. Over the years he had taken eight children, being careful never to take more than two in any one year. Still, the Indians knew where their children had gone, and they wanted revenge for the lives lost.

The arrows flew like leaves in the wind. Tiny cane arrows specially made for a slow death. Mansa gritted his teeth as a fiery pain ebbed through him. He felt his blood flowing from his body in a dozen places, running wet and warm down his arms and legs. The blood dripped to the ground and ran in tiny rivulets to the black waters of the Wekiva River.

With the blood went Mansa's spirit, soaking into

the sandy soil and swirling away with the water. He felt himself becoming one with the land, and the river, but not dying. No. Not dying. For while the sorcerer's body slumped lifeless against the cypress tree, his evil spirit continued to live.

Part I

Chapter One

Few tourists ever get to see the real Florida. Most never make it beyond the boundaries of what many locals call the Kingdom of the Rat: the theme parks, hotels, and restaurants ruled by a giant mouse in white gloves, named Mickey. Those who do manage to break free from the land of Disney usually head due east to the space coast and the fabled beaches of Daytona and Cocoa, or they drive west to Tampa and the calmer waters of the gulf.

Robert and Janet Patterson cared nothing for the theme parks and tourist traps of central Florida. Nor were they overly fond of the sun and sand worshipers that gathered at the beaches like flocks of nesting seagulls. Instead, they wanted to spend their vacation away from the tourist meccas, enjoying a week of blissful peace and quiet, fishing, camping, and canoeing in one of the few remaining patches of Florida wilderness.

Of course, they had to promise their ten-year-old daughter, Krissy, that they would spend at least one day at Walt Disney World before heading back home to a bleak and dreary November in their hometown of St. Louis, Missouri. And they had to buy her a

Minnie Mouse T-shirt when they got off the plane at Orlando International Airport, at a gift shop where T-shirts cost three times what a normal shirt should cost.

Loading their luggage into the trunk of a rented car, they took Highway 436 north from Orlando to Apopka. Robert could tell that his daughter was disappointed that they hadn't passed at least one theme park during the trip, but all the major attractions were located south of Orlando. Krissy would soon have her chance to experience a theme park in all of its overcrowded glory, however, because Robert and Janet had already decided to spend at least two days at Disney World before going home. In fact, they had already bought the tickets through AAA. They had not told Krissy because they didn't want to spoil the surprise.

Reaching Apopka, they turned north onto a narrow blacktop road that wound its way past numerous nurseries and orange groves. Twenty miles later they passed through the tiny town of Blackwater. The town was little more than a clustering of weather-beaten houses, a small white church that sported both an American and a Confederate flag, and a couple of convenience stores. Two miles later they arrived at their destination.

The Blackwater Fish Camp & Campgrounds had been in operation since the early seventies. Located along a narrow section of the Wekiva River, the camp featured a dozen one- and two-bedroom cabins, a bait and tackle shop, a restaurant/lounge combination, and enough rental canoes and flat-bottomed fishing boats to supply a small army of tourists and Boy Scouts.

Since it was the middle of November, the off-season, the camp was mostly empty, with only a couple of the cabins rented. At least that was what the camp's owner, Ross Sanders, had told Robert when he spoke with him on the phone earlier in the week.

Pulling off the road, Robert parked in a space reserved for overnight guests. Switching off the ignition, he climbed out of the car. Janet and Krissy followed him.

It was a little after sundown, but the temperature was still in the upper sixties, a far cry warmer than what they had left behind in Missouri. In fact, it was much too hot for long sleeves, so Robert decided to leave his jacket in the car. Closing the door, he turned to look over the camp. He also took a deep breath, intrigued by a flowery smell that hung heavy on the air. He wasn't sure if it was the scent of magnolia or orange blossom, but it was extremely pleasant.

"Mmmm . . . that smells good," Krissy said, obviously smelling the same thing Robert did. "What is that?"

Robert shook his head. "I'm not sure. Maybe a magnolia tree. Or orange blossoms."

"It's night-blooming jasmine," said a voice from behind them. "We've got a patch of it growing behind the restaurant."

The three of them turned to see an older man coming out of the closest cabin. He stood about five eight and probably weighed a little over two hundred pounds, his skin wrinkled and tan from long years spent in the hot Florida sun. He wore a pale blue fishing cap and sported a neatly trimmed white beard. On his arms were several tattoos that spoke of military service, probably in the navy. The man looked to be in his early sixties, but he might have been older. It was hard to tell the age of someone who had spent the better part of his life outdoors.

"You must be the Pattersons," the man said as he approached them.

"That's us," Robert replied. "I'm Robert. This is my wife, Janet, and our daughter, Krissy."

"Pleased to meet you." The man nodded to Janet and Krissy, and shook hands with Robert. "I'm Ross Sanders. We spoke on the phone. Welcome to Blackwater Fish Camp. We've got a cabin all ready for you."

"That's great." Robert smiled.

"I just need to get the keys out of the office, and have you sign a registration form. The restaurant's still open, if any of you are hungry. And the lounge doesn't close until midnight."

"I'm starving," Janet said.

"Me too," Krissy added.

Ross smiled. "Well, then you're in luck. The food's not fancy, but it's good. And there's plenty of it. If you like old-fashioned country cooking, you won't be disappointed. My wife, Mary, is an excellent cook." To prove his point, Ross placed both his palms on his midsection and shook his ample stomach. "See what I mean? I wouldn't be so fat if it wasn't good."

Krissy giggled.

Ross smiled at the girl. "Think that's funny? Just you wait. You'll be this big after you eat. That's a promise."

"No, I won't."

"Sure you will," Ross teased. "You like catfish? We

have them fresh from the river. I believe Mary also cooked up a meat loaf. And there's always fried chicken, or hamburgers."

"Sounds good to me," Robert said. "I haven't had fresh catfish in a long time."

"Then you're in for a treat." Ross smiled. "Mary serves them up with French fries and homemade hushpuppies."

They followed Ross into the office, which was nothing more than a side room in the bait and tackle shop. Robert filled out the registration form and was handed two keys to cabin number seven. He was also given a brochure about the camp and a map of the river.

"If you need to rent any fishing gear, then come see me in the morning. We've also got plenty of canoes and flat-bottomed boats. Since you're staying with us, you get a fifty percent discount on everything you rent. Everything except bait. You have to buy that."

He looked down at Krissy. "What do you like to fish with, darling? Crickets, night crawlers, or minnows?"

"Worms," Krissy answered. "Rubber ones."

Ross laughed. "Good choice. Rubber worms aren't nearly as messy as the real things, and the bass seem to love them. Now, if you get bored with fishing and want to take a hike, there's a nature trail that starts on the back side of the camp."

"That sounds like fun," Janet said. "It would be nice to take a walk after breakfast."

"Morning is the best time for walking," Ross agreed. "Nice and cool then. Though it won't really get all that hot this time of year. There's also more critters out and about in the morning than there are in the afternoon: raccoons, deer, eagles, hawks. If you're lucky you might even see an alligator, or a black bear."

"You have bears?" Janet asked, concerned. "Are they dangerous?"

"Not as long as you don't try to feed them," Ross answered. "If you do take the trail, follow the signs. Part of the boardwalk caught fire and burned a few years ago, and we just haven't had time to repair the damage, so a few sections of the trail are now closed to the public."

"I'll be sure to follow the signs," Janet reassured him.

"You'll also want to keep a sharp eye on your little one," he said, smiling at Krissy. "It's a pretty big forest, and you wouldn't want her wandering around in it by herself."

"Don't worry. We'll keep an eye on her," Robert replied, patting Krissy on the head.

Ross nodded. "Now, let's see about getting you folks something to eat."

They followed Ross out of the bait and tackle shop to the very next building, which housed a small restaurant and an even smaller lounge, the two being separated by an interior wall. Ross explained that a lot of the fishermen liked to have a beer or two when they came in off the river, and he didn't want their tall tales and cigarette smoke to offend the dinner crowds, so he kept the two establishments separate, even if they were in the same building.

Sitting by the front door of the restaurant was a large black Labrador who sported an equally black eye patch over his left eye. The dog stood up and wagged his tail when he spotted Ross and the Pattersons approaching the restaurant.

"You waiting for a handout, boy?" Ross asked, causing the dog to wag his tail even harder. "Don't let Mary catch you sitting here. You know she doesn't like you bothering the customers."

Ross patted the dog on the head and turned to the others. "This here is Patch. He's the official camp dog. Don't worry, he doesn't bite. But he will become your devoted servant if you give him food. We call him Patch, because of the eye patch he wears. He lost his eye in a fight with a raccoon several years ago."

"Poor thing," Janet said, stepping forward to pet the dog.

"Oh, it don't bother him much," Ross said, "but he does sometimes run into trees if he's not being careful."

Ross gave his dog a final pat on the head, and then opened the restaurant's door and ushered them inside. The restaurant was small and cozy, featuring a narrow counter and about a dozen tables. The walls were covered in wood paneling, decorated with enlarged photographs of scenic areas along the Wekiva River. Several of the photographs featured waterbirds and wildlife; others showed people enjoying a day of fishing, canoeing, and hiking. In addition to the photographs, several mounted game fish hung on the walls. There was also a large alligator head sitting on a shelf behind the counter.

Following Ross into the restaurant, they were shown to a table beneath one of the mounted fish. Despite being the dinner hour, there were only three other customers in the restaurant: two at a table along the opposite wall, and one sitting at the counter.

"I'll let Mary know that she has some hungry customers," Ross said, handing each of them a menu. "I'll also get you good people something to drink. What would you like?"

Robert and Janet ordered ice teas. Krissy ordered a Sprite. Ross repeated the selections, then hurried off to get his wife.

Mary Sanders appeared a few moments later from the kitchen. She was a tall, stout woman with striking black hair and an infectious smile. She greeted each of the Pattersons warmly, and then frowned. "My husband didn't get you any drinks yet? Not even water? That lazy old man. I swear, I don't know why I keep him around. He's about as useless as his dog." She smiled, letting them know that her words were only in jest.

As if on cue, Ross appeared from the kitchen carrying a tray of drinks. "You talking about me, dear?"

Mary turned toward her husband, still smiling. "You bet I am. I was just telling these folks how useless you are."

"Useless, but lovable." Ross grinned. He set the drinks on the table and then stepped back. "I've got to get over to the bar to check on the drunks, I mean the customers. I've got old Charlie McGee watching the place, but Charlie's too generous for his own good. Everyone is probably drinking for free."

He turned to Robert. "You and the missus stop on by later on, if you have a mind to. We've got the coldest draught beer around. Also serve soft drinks, if you don't like alcohol. It would be a good way to pick up some fishing tips from the locals. Find out where the hot spots are."

"I might just do that, after we get unpacked," Robert said.

"Good." Ross nodded. "I'll see you then." He returned the drink tray to the kitchen and left the restaurant, leaving the three of them in his wife's care.

"What can I get for you tonight?" Mary asked.

"What's good?" Robert asked, teasing.

Mary laughed. "Honey, it's all good. Just ask the regulars."

Robert opted for the "all you can eat" catfish plate, liking the thought of having something for dinner that was caught locally. He knew the Wekiva River was still fairly unpolluted, so he wasn't worried about pesticides. Janet chose the meat loaf, and Krissy went for chicken fingers and French fries. Janet suggested that she also choose a vegetable with her meal, but Robert intervened by saying that vegetables could be skipped on the first day of vacation.

Taking their orders, Mary returned to the kitchen to supervise the cooking. While she did most of the cooking by herself, she did have two other people working in the kitchen to help out in case things got too hectic.

While they waited for their food, the Pattersons discussed plans for their stay at the fish camp. Robert wanted to go fishing first thing in the morning, but he was outvoted by the girls, who wanted to take a canoe trip down the river.

Krissy had been fishing several times with her father, but she had never been in a canoe. The thought of taking a canoe trip down the Wekiva River excited her, even though she did become a little worried when Robert commented that they might get to see a real alligator or two. The little girl turned to look at the gator head displayed on the shelf behind the counter, wondering if they would see any alligators that big.

Janet reassured her daughter that alligators in the wild usually stayed away from people. The ones kept in captivity were actually more dangerous than the wild ones, because people had been feeding them, so the alligators associated people with food. She also told Krissy that, if they did see a big alligator, her father would just put his foot in the water and scare it off with the smell.

Krissy laughed at the joke, nearly blowing Sprite out of her nose. Robert faked a frown, reassuring his daughter that his feet did not smell that bad.

Their food arrived a few minutes later, smelling wonderful and looking just as good. It had been a hectic day: awaking early to get ready, hurrying to the airport to catch their flight, renting a car, and then driving through traffic to reach their destination, so they hadn't had time to do more than snack. This was their first real meal of the day, and it was a wonderful way to unwind and put the tension of the trip behind them.

Ross was right: Mary was a wonderful cook. The catfish was some of the best Robert had ever tasted, and the meat loaf was an absolute delight. So were the chicken fingers, at least according to Krissy. Each of them thoroughly enjoyed their meal and ate every bite, leaving no room for dessert.

Thanking Mary for a wonderful meal, they paid their bill, leaving a generous tip, and headed back to get their luggage. All three of them walked slowly, their bellies full, none of them in a hurry to carry bags or unpack. Night had already fallen, and the first stars of the evening were poking their heads through a sea of purple. Around them the forest had come alive with the shrill cries of crickets and tree frogs.

They took a short detour before going to the car, wanting to see the river. The Wekiva River flowed dark and cold behind the wooden cabins. Formed from underground springs, the Wekiva twisted its way through old growth forests, joining up with the larger St. John's River just north of Sanford.

According to the brochure Robert had been given, you could canoe down the Wekiva all the way to the St. John's, if you had a mind to, but it was a trip much farther than he was willing to make. Because if you paddled down the river, you also had to paddle back up it to get home.

There was a park bench sitting by the river's edge, but Robert and Janet chose not to sit on it. They still had to get settled in and knew if they sat down they would be in no hurry to stand back up again. The rushing water of the Wekiva was hypnotizing, even at night, and they could easily spend hours watching it flow by. Work came first; they could always come back later, after Krissy had gone to bed.

Grabbing their suitcases out of the car, they followed a narrow path to cabin number seven. The cabin they rented was rustic, dusty, and smelled slightly of fish. Two small bedrooms were attached to a somewhat larger sitting room, which came furnished with a pair of oversized chairs, a small wooden table with two folding chairs, an electric coffee maker, a stack of chipped coffee cups, and a tiny refrigerator. Two single beds and a wooden dresser crowded each of the bedrooms, while the bathroom came complete with a sink, toilet, shower, and a medicine cabinet with a cracked mirror.

Krissy claimed the bedroom to the left of the sitting room, because the curtains covering the window had printed ponies on them. Setting her suitcase on the floor, she was startled when a large bug shot out from under one of the beds and raced past her feet.

"Cockroach!" she screamed, jumping back.

The bug didn't get far before it was squashed by Robert's well-aimed stomp. "They call them palmetto bugs down here, because they live in palmetto trees."

"Yuck. Gross," Krissy said, shivering at the sound of the bug being squashed under her father's shoe. She looked nervously under the bed closest to her. "I hope there aren't any more around here."

"Probably not," Robert said, lifting his shoe to make sure the bug was dead. "But that's the price you sometimes have to pay for being in the forest: bugs, spiders, snakes, hungry alligators that eat little girls."

Krissy smiled, realizing her father was teasing her. "I'm not afraid of alligators, or bugs. I just don't like cockroaches."

"A cockroach is a bug," Janet said.

Krissy nodded. "But it's a big, ugly, crunchy bug. Especially that one."

Robert kicked the palmetto bug out the front door with the toe of his shoe. "Well, that one won't be bothering you anymore tonight. I just hope he didn't tell his friends that a sweet young girl is living in cabin number seven."

Krissy looked around the room, searching for more bugs. "You're not funny, Daddy."

Not wanting her daughter to find another bug, Janet carefully inspected the bathroom, kitchen, and the dresser drawers. Fortunately there were no more creepy crawlers to be found. Opening the suitcases, she put their clothes in the dressers and then stacked the empty cases in the corner of the rooms.

Finished with the unpacking, she suggested that Krissy take a shower and slip into her pajamas. They had gotten up early, and the little girl was already showing signs of being sleepy. Krissy argued that she wasn't tired, but agreed to get ready for bed when reminded that they would be getting up early in the morning to go canoeing.

Robert was also tired, but he wasn't ready to go to bed so early in the evening. Instead he wanted to go over to the lounge to have a beer or two, maybe strike up a conversation with Ross or one of the locals. Promising Janet that he wouldn't stay out too late, he waited for Krissy to start her shower and then slipped out of the cabin.

The lounge was about half the size of the restaurant; it too was decorated with photographs of the Wekiva River area and mounted game fish. There were also a few neon signs and an old jukebox sitting in the corner of the room. The jukebox was playing a country song, but the sound had been turned down so the music was little more than background noise.

Robert spotted Ross talking to three men sitting at the bar. They were the only customers in the place. Judging by the way they were dressed, they had probably spent the day fishing on the river. All three men turned to look at Robert as he entered the lounge.

"Glad you could make it." Ross smiled, motioning for Robert to join them. "How's the cabin?"

"The cabin's just fine," Robert answered. "But my daughter did get to meet her very first palmetto bug."

Ross grinned. "Sorry about that. It must have slipped in when I was cleaning. We do grow them big down here; I hope it didn't put too much of a scare into your little girl."

"Naw. She's okay. I told her bugs were just a part of being in the woods."

Ross nodded. He turned to the other men seated at the bar. "Gentlemen, this here is Robert Patterson. He and his family are down visiting from St. Louis. They're going to be spending a week with us."

"Pleased to meet you," Robert said.

Ross continued the introductions, naming each of the three men seated at the bar. "This is Mike Walters, and his brother, Scott. They're both regulars here, been fishing this river since God was a pup. If it's fishing secrets you're looking for, then these are the guys you want to talk to. They know all the best places for catching the big ones. As a matter of fact, all the fish you see mounted on the walls were caught by them."

Robert turned to look at the big-mouth bass mounted on the far wall. "It looks like you've already got all the big ones. I might as well pack up and go home."

Mike laughed. "Oh, I think we might have left one or two for you."

"And this is Charlie McGee," Ross said, nodding

toward the elderly man sitting at the end of the bar. "Charlie's not much of a fisherman, but he can damn sure fill your ears with useless facts about Florida. He used to be a newspaperman, but he's been retired for almost twenty years."

"Howdy," Charlie said, nodding.

"Nice to meet you," Robert replied. "What paper did you write for?"

"The *Miami Herald*," answered Charlie. "But I got sick of living in the city, and tired of putting up with stupid editors, so I quit and moved up here."

"Please, don't get Charlie talking about the newspaper business," Ross teased. "We'll never get him to shut up."

"I don't talk that much," Charlie protested.

"Yes, you do," Mike and Scott said in unison.

"What can I get you to drink?" Ross asked Robert, laughing.

"Do you have Michelob Light?"

"Afraid not." Ross shook his head. "Not much call for it around here."

"How about Budweiser?"

"Supporting the home town brewery, are we? Budweiser, we have. Bottle, can, or draught?"

"Bottle," Robert said.

Ross opened a bottle of beer and set it on the bar in front of Robert. "Welcome to Florida. First one's on the house."

Robert lifted the bottle and took a sip, allowing the icy cold beer to flow slowly down his throat. He wished Janet would have joined him, but knew his wife would not leave Krissy alone in a strange cabin at night. Maybe he would bring a beer back for her.

Janet wasn't much of a drinker, but she did enjoy a light beer now and then.

The conversation at the bar turned to local events. Robert listened but didn't say much, offering a comment only when a question was directed his way. For the most part he was happy to just sit there and quietly sip his beer. The day's travel had been hectic, and he was starting to experience the first signs of jet lag.

He was halfway through his second beer when he looked at the clock on the wall, then glanced at his watch, realizing that he had lost an hour in his travels by crossing a time zone. It was later than he thought, and he was starting to get sleepy.

He paid for the beer, then bid Ross and the others a good night. He decided not to buy a beer for Janet because she was probably just as tired as he was and might already be in bed. Leaving the bar, he walked slowly across the campgrounds toward their cabin. He was halfway back when he spotted a large owl sitting on the sign that marked the beginning of the nature trail. The sight of such a large bird sitting there, watching him, startled Robert and caused him to stop dead in his tracks.

Even though it was nighttime, there was enough moonlight to see the bird clearly. The owl was definitely watching him. Robert could also see the blood that dripped dark red from the bird's claws, running in tiny rivulets down the sign it perched atop. The owl must have just made a kill moments earlier.

A chill marched up and down Robert's back, for the owl had all the surreal quality of an evil omen. Maybe it was the jet lag, or the beer talking, but he suddenly felt the bird was a messenger, and that something bad was about to happen to him or a member of his family.

Robert heard one of the customers leaving the bar and turned his head in that direction. When he looked back the owl had vanished.

Chapter Two

Robert had set the alarm clock to ring at 7:00 A.M., but the mockingbird perched in a tree outside their cabin window went off earlier than that. Knowing that sleep was now out of the question, he decided to get up to take a quick shower and shave. He tried not to make any noise, but his movements caused the bed to squeak, awakening Janet.

"What time is it?" she asked, rubbing her eyes.

He turned to look at the alarm clock, which he had placed on top of the dresser. "It's six-thirty."

"Why are you up so early?"

"Not my choice," he replied. "That stupid mockingbird outside wouldn't shut up. Since I can't sleep, I figured I'd go ahead and take a shower and shave."

"Use the unscented soap," she warned. "Otherwise you'll draw mosquitoes. And don't use aftershave. I'll make coffee while you're taking a shower."

"They serve breakfast at the restaurant. You want to get something to eat before we go canoeing?"

Janet thought about it for a moment, then shook her head. "I'm not in the mood for a big breakfast. I brought a box of Pop-Tarts. That's enough. Krissy doesn't eat much in the morning anyway."

"Okay then, Pop-Tarts and coffee for breakfast. Sounds like a winner." Robert grabbed a towel and a change of clothes from out of the dresser and headed for the shower. While he was getting cleaned up, Janet used the coffee maker to heat up some water for instant coffee. They always carried a small jar of instant coffee with them when traveling, and snacks, even when staying in the finest hotels. There was nothing worse than no caffeine and a hungry child.

Krissy was also up when Robert came out of the bathroom. The little girl shared a folding chair with her mother at the small table in the sitting room, leaving the other chair for him. A box of strawberry Pop-Tarts sat in the middle of the table, flanked by several chipped ceramic coffee mugs.

"Your coffee's ready," Janet said, gesturing toward the cup on the opposite side of the table.

"Great," Robert said. He gave Krissy a smile. "Good morning, bright-eyes. What are you drinking?"

"Good morning, Daddy. I'm drinking hot cocoa."

"With strawberry Pop-Tarts? Mmmm . . . yummy."

He sat down on the empty chair and took a sip of his coffee. He also helped himself to one of the toaster pastries, even though he wasn't a big fan of strawberries. As they ate breakfast, Janet and Robert discussed their plans about the canoe trip they were about to take. They decided to make their first trip a short one, paddling downstream for a mile or so before turning around to head back.

Both of them had been canoeing before, but they were unfamiliar with the Wekiva River and wanted to test the waters on a short trip before embarking on an all day journey. A short trip would also allow plenty of exercise without the risk of straining muscles unaccustomed to using a paddle. It would be foolish to do too much on the first day and risk a pulled muscle or sore back. Such things could put a real damper on their vacation fun.

Finished with breakfast, Robert rinsed out the coffee cups while the girls got ready for the trip. All three of them dressed in lightweight cotton shorts and T-shirts, selecting older items of apparel rather than their best stuff. Canoes had a nasty habit of flipping over from time to time, even with the most experienced paddler. No sense in ruining their good clothing when they had older items to wear. All three of them would also be wearing Teva sandals and inexpensive sunglasses. The sandals strapped around the ankles, which would keep them from getting lost if they did flip over. They also floated.

Taking just enough money to pay for the canoe rental, Robert hid his wallet under his pillow. Janet hid her purse in the bottom dresser drawer, concealing it behind her underwear.

Locking the cabin's door behind them, they walked to the bait and tackle shop. Even though it was still early, there were already several people moving about the camp. The driver of a faded blue pickup was slowly backing a trailer down the boat ramp in order to launch his bass boat for a day of fishing. Two more pickups waited in line for their turn to use the ramp. Several people were already fishing at the little wooden dock just downstream from the boat ramp, although Robert doubted if they were catching anything with so much boating activity happening nearby.

Next to the dock, three empty canoes sat waiting for use.

Entering the bait and tackle shop, they squeezed past several people lined up at the register. Ross was behind the counter, ringing up purchases and talking with the customers. Even though he was busy, he paused long enough to greet the three of them.

"Good morning, folks," he said, smiling. "I hope you slept well."

"Slept great," replied Robert. "Until a stupid mockingbird decided to sound off outside our window."

"They can be pretty noisy." Ross laughed. He waited on the last customer and then turned his attention to the Pattersons.

"Now. What can I do for you? You guys ready to do some fishing, or would you rather go canoeing?"

"I think we're going to do a little canoeing this morning," Robert answered.

Ross nodded. "You picked a good day for it. Not too hot. Not too cold. And the weatherman said it isn't going to rain either." He set a receipt book on the counter and opened it. "Okay, canoes rent for six bucks an hour, or twenty dollars for all day. Since you're staying guests, you only have to pay half price. But I still have to charge you a fifty-dollar deposit, which you'll get back when you turn in the canoe. The deposit's just in case you decide to keep paddling and not come back. It doesn't cover the cost of buying a replacement canoe, but it's better than nothing."

"Have you ever had anyone not come back?" Janet asked.

"More than once," Ross answered. "Canoes are

easy to steal. You just paddle them downstream a ways, and then have a buddy pick you up in a truck."

"I promise we'll bring it back," Robert said, pulling three twenties out of his pocket. He handed the money to Ross. "Go ahead and give us the full-day rate. We're pretty slow paddlers, so it might take us awhile to get back."

"All day it is." Ross filled out the receipt, handing a copy to Robert. "The canoes are tied up at the dock. Take any one you want. The paddles are already in them. You'll also find a wooden bin filled with life jackets next to the dock. The law says you have to have life jackets with you, but adults can usually get away with not wearing them as long as they have them in the canoe. However, your daughter will have to wear hers."

"That's not a problem."

"Good," Ross said. "Then you're all set. Have yourselves a good time."

Robert thanked Ross and started to step away from the counter.

"Er, there is one other thing," Ross said.

"What's that?"

"About a mile downstream there's an old wooden cabin along the water's edge. It's owned by a Seminole Indian named Jimmy Cypress. Folks around here sometimes call him 'Three Fingers,' because he lost part of the two smallest fingers on his left hand wrestling an alligator. He's a squatter, and somewhat of a nuisance.

"Jimmy's kind of crazy in the head; all the time talking nonsense about old legends, and evil spirits.

He used to come around here once in a while, but no one ever paid much attention to what he had to say."

"Is he dangerous?" Janet asked, worried.

Ross shook his head. "No. No. Nothing like that. I just wanted to let you know about Jimmy in case you saw him. I didn't want you to be startled. Far as I know, Jimmy is harmless. He keeps to himself most of the time, and doesn't bother people unless they go snooping around his house. Just don't stop at his place and you'll be fine."

"I'll give him a wide berth," Robert promised. Sticking the receipt in his pocket, he opened the door and followed his family outside.

The three fiberglass canoes were still tied up by the fishing dock. Krissy wanted to take the blue canoe, but the red canoes were in better shape, so they chose one of those. Robert grabbed two life vests, size large and medium, out of the bin and tossed them in the canoe. He and Janet were both excellent swimmers and probably wouldn't need to wear the vests. Besides, the bright orange vests were cumbersome and took most of the fun out of canoeing. But Krissy would need to wear her vest, so Robert fished around in the wooden bin until he found one small enough to fit her comfortably.

Slipping the vest over Krissy's head, he fastened the straps and then lowered her into the canoe. Krissy would sit in the middle of the canoe, while Robert sat in the back and Janet up front. Climbing into the canoe carefully so it wouldn't rock, he untied the anchor rope from the dock and pushed off.

Paddling out into the middle of the tiny river, they turned right, allowing the current to catch the canoe and carry it downstream. The river would now do most of the work, with Robert and Janet only needing to paddle in order to keep the canoe on course and to avoid obstacles. Since it was still early in the day, there was an abundance of wildlife along the water's edge.

Krissy squealed in delight when she spotted three turtles lined up in a row on a partially submerged log. Shortly after that they spotted a gray heron standing in shallow water, fishing for his breakfast. Overhead, a red-tailed hawk and a pair of ospreys glided through the air on their morning hunts.

"Do you think we'll see any alligators?" Krissy asked.

"Maybe," Janet replied. "But alligators are hard to see in the wild, especially in the water."

"Why's that?" Her daughter wanted to know.

"Because they only keep their eyes above the water. That way they can sneak up on their prey. Sometimes you'll see them along the bank, sunning themselves, but they usually slip back into the water when people come around."

"Alligators are easier to see at night," Robert added, "because their eyes shine in the light. You still won't see their bodies, but you'll see their eyes shine if you aim a flashlight at them."

"Neat," Krissy said, obviously impressed with her parents' knowledge of alligators. Krissy didn't know it, but her mother was more than just a little knowledgeable about wildlife and nature. Janet had been a member of the Sierra Club for years and had even written several articles about endangered wildlife for nature and environmental magazines.

The river curved slowly to the left, passing under an old stone railroad bridge. Paddling beneath the bridge, they left behind all the sights and sounds of modern civilization and became one with the natural beauty of Florida.

The section of the Wekiva River they traveled was no more than twenty feet wide, narrowing down to less than half that in many places. Robert wondered how the anglers were able to get their bass boats through such narrow passages without getting stuck, but they probably headed upstream to do their fishing.

Robert and Janet had to duck their heads in several spots to keep from banging into overhanging branches, much to the delighted giggles of their daughter. And once they had to really paddle to keep from becoming stuck on a submerged log. One thing for sure, canoeing in Florida was nothing like canoeing on the small, midwestern rivers they were used to traveling. Here you had to really work to get where you were going.

They had just rounded a bend in the river when Robert spotted a dilapidated cabin up ahead on the left. The cabin had once been painted a bright blue, but the paint had faded and peeled over the years. It was now mostly a dull brown, with only a few patches of blue remaining.

The cabin was topped with a roof of rusted tin, and there were two windows overlooking the river. He didn't see a door, so the entrance was probably located on the opposite side of the building. The cabin all but spoiled the scenic beauty of the area.

"What's that, Dad?" Krissy asked, pointing at the cabin.

"That's someone's home," Janet answered. She

turned and looked back at Robert, a frown tugging at the corners of her mouth.

"A home?" Krissy asked, not believing what her mother had told her. "Who would live in that old place?"

"A Seminole," replied Robert.

"A what?"

"A Seminole. That's the name of an Indian tribe that lives here in Florida. I believe there are two tribes in this state: the Seminoles, and the Miccosukee. I think they're related, but I'm not sure how."

"Are there a lot of Indians in Florida?" Krissy asked, fascinated by what her father was saying. She had always been interested in history, especially American history. Growing up in St. Louis, the gateway to the West, she had learned in school about the pioneers and Indians.

"I think there still are quite a few Indians living in Florida," Robert answered, "but not as many as there used to be."

"Really?" Krissy turned to look at her father.

He nodded. "There used to be Indian tribes living all over Florida: the Timucua, the Calusa, the Apalachee, to name but a few. Before the first Europeans arrived, in the sixteenth century, there were probably around one hundred thousand Indians living in what is now Florida."

"Wow, that's a lot of Indians," Krissy said.

Robert smiled. His daughter didn't know it, but he had read up on the history of Florida prior to their vacation. "When the Spaniards started settling this area, a lot of the Indian tribes were pushed off of their land. Many died from diseases that were brought here from Europe; others were captured and forced to work as slaves. When the Spaniards finally left Florida, they took with them the last few remaining Indians.

"The state was uninhabited for years, and then the Seminoles moved in. They were originally a mixture of several different southern tribes: Creeks, Yamasses, Yuchis. The name Seminole is supposed to mean 'wild people,' or 'runaway,' but I've read where some think the name actually means 'many tongues.' "

He quit speaking as they neared the cabin, for suddenly the lore of the Seminole Indians didn't seem quite so fascinating. He had always heard that Indians were supposed to be the keepers of the land, living in harmony with nature, but here was something that was a direct insult to Mother Nature. The cabin was an eyesore, marring the scenic beauty of the area.

"I'm surprised they let him get away with that," Janet said, her gaze focused on the crumbling building.

"He must have been here a long time," Robert replied.

"It doesn't matter," she argued. "They should make him move. Ross said he was a squatter, which means he doesn't have a title to the land. They should make him move, and tear that shack down."

"Maybe he's old. Maybe they're waiting for him to die, rather than risk creating a public outcry by telling him to get out. I imagine it wouldn't look good telling a Seminole Indian to get out when they were here first."

They drifted slowly by the old cabin. The windows facing the river were caked with years of grime, making it impossible to see inside. Still, Robert suddenly had the feeling that they were being watched. He didn't see anyone, but felt that their slow progress down the river was being observed by someone inside the cabin. That feeling did not subside until they were well past the building.

Leaving the cabin behind them, they again relaxed and went back to enjoying the scenery. But soon they were faced with a new problem, because the river forked into two branches. Robert put his paddle in the water and held steady, attempting to slow the canoe. He hadn't taken more than a quick glance at the map Ross had given him, so he wasn't sure which branch to take.

"Which way?" Janet asked.

"I'm not sure," he said. "I guess I should have taken a better look at the map. We could always turn around and go back."

"I don't want to go back yet," Krissy protested. "Can't we keep going? Just a little farther? Please."

"The left fork looks wider," Janet pointed out.

Ross studied both directions, trying to make a decision. The left fork did look wider, so it was probably the main path of the river. "Left it is," he said. "Always follow your heart."

They turned left, guiding the fiberglass canoe up the wider branch of water. They had only gone about half a mile, however, when they realized they had gone the wrong way. The branch of the river they had chosen to follow ended in a swampy lagoon of black water.

"It looks like we went the wrong way," Robert said, stating the obvious.

The lagoon was surrounded by ancient cypress and oak trees, many of them thick with Spanish moss and hanging vines. In the middle of the lagoon was a small island, upon which grew a massive cypress tree that must have been at least two hundred years old.

Beyond the lagoon, barely visible through the trees, was a charred wooden structure that Robert recognized as a burned out section of boardwalk. Apparently, the nature trail had once passed through the area, prior to the boardwalk being destroyed by fire.

"You want to double back and continue downstream?" he asked. "Or do you want to head back to camp?"

"Let's keep going," Krissy said, a fountain of endless energy.

Janet looked around the area, then turned to her daughter. "I think we should go back. We've had enough canoeing for one morning. Besides, I'm getting kind of hungry. Aren't you? Those Pop-Tarts we ate won't last us all day."

"Aw. . . ." Krissy protested.

"Maybe after lunch we can get a couple of fishing poles and do a little fishing from the dock," Robert suggested. "How does that sound?"

"Okay, I guess," the little girl said, giving in to her parents' suggestions. "Can I use rubber worms? I don't like the real ones."

"You sure can. Any color you like," he said, happy that his daughter wasn't too upset about turning back.

Turning the canoe around, they headed back to camp. They again passed the cabin owned by Jimmy Cypress, the dirty glass windows watching their passage like the empty eye sockets of a grinning skull. Though he could see no one, Robert again had a feeling that someone was watching them. Someone who looked upon him and his family as trespassers.

They had planned to go fishing after lunch, but Mary offered to teach Janet and Krissy how to make real Florida crab cakes. It was an offer they just couldn't refuse. Since the girls were busy in the restaurant's kitchen and he didn't feel like fishing alone, Robert decided to take a walk down the nature trail. It would be a great way to work out a few kinks in his back that he had gotten while canoeing. At the ripe old age of thirty-five, kinks and sore muscles after exercise were becoming a way of life. Janet, who was three years younger than him, didn't suffer such afflictions.

Most of the nature trail featured a wooden boardwalk elevated above the ground to keep hikers from trampling the native foliage. The boardwalk forked several times, allowing hikers to choose their own path through the forest. There were also places where you could step off the boardwalk in order to follow narrower trails, if you so desired. In places where the boardwalk came close to the Wekiva River there were gaps in the railing, and steps leading down into the water so a person could go swimming.

Walking along the boardwalk, Robert couldn't help but laugh at the tiny brown anoles that darted in front of his path. There must have been hundreds of the little lizards scurrying to get out of his way. It was almost as if they were playing a reptilian game of chance, daring each other to dart just in front of his feet. The one that came closer without being stepped on won the contest.

In addition to the brown anoles, he spotted a couple of green ones hiding in the foliage that lined the boardwalk. There was also a blue-headed skink sitting on the handrail sunning itself. It watched him with only mild curiosity as he walked by.

Robert stopped when he heard the sound of rustling coming from off to his left. Standing perfectly still, he watched as a mother raccoon and her two babies made their way through the forest. He knew that raccoons were nocturnal, so the family was probably heading back home after a night of foraging for food. The raccoons must have seen him, but they were apparently used to people and not frightened by his presence. They just continued their slow walk until they were out of sight.

He watched the raccoons until they disappeared from view and then continued on his way. He wished that Krissy had been with him, for she would have been thrilled at seeing the masked animals. But raccoons were common in Florida, and there would probably be plenty of opportunities to see more.

About a mile along the trail he came to a section of the boardwalk that was now closed to the public due to a previous wildfire. A wooden barricade, complete with a pair of warning signs, prevented hikers from continuing in that direction. Beyond the barricade the boardwalk was nothing more than a tangle of charred timber. Definitely not safe to walk on.

Not wanting to backtrack in order to follow one of the other trails, he decided to step down off the boardwalk and continue forward by walking a path parallel to the burned section. Surely the fire hadn't destroyed all of the boardwalk from there on, and he would be able to get back on the remaining section once he bypassed the burned area.

But Robert didn't reach another section of boardwalk. Instead he found himself standing in front of a backwater lagoon. A narrow stream led away from the lagoon, apparently joining up with the Wekiva River. Looking around, he realized it was the same lagoon he and his family had stumbled upon while canoeing.

"Looks like I took a wrong turn again," he said, shaking his head. He started to turn away when he spotted a strange wooden staff standing next to the water's edge. He hadn't noticed the staff on his first visit to the lagoon because it stood next to a towering cypress tree, almost invisible in the tree's shadow. Curious, he approached the object to get a better look at it.

The staff was about five and a half feet in length, and a little over an inch in diameter. It was wrapped in leather and decorated with beadwork of bright blue, yellow, and red beads. An animal skull of some kind was attached to the top of the shaft, its open jaws grinning toward the water. Robert wasn't sure what kind of animal it was; perhaps it was a fox.

Beneath the grinning skull three eagle feathers were fastened to the staff. There were also a couple of hawk feathers. In addition to the feathers, several strips of colored cloth—red, white, yellow, and black—were tied to the top of the shaft. Just below the strips of cloth hung a small leather pouch, decorated with dyed quillwork, horse hair, and what looked to be a pair of bear claws.

A lot of work had obviously gone into the making of the strange staff, and Robert wondered why its owner would just leave it at the lagoon. He looked around, but didn't see anyone. The owner had apparently stuck the staff in the ground and walked away.

"Strange," he said, stepping around to look at the staff from a different angle. There was something about the wooden object that gave him the creeps. For one thing it looked old, like something out of a museum. Then there was the grinning skull that sat on top of the shaft, conjuring up images of bizarre rituals. The skull faced the water as if it were watching for something. Watching for what?

Wanting to get a better look, he grabbed the staff and pulled it from the ground. As he picked up the staff a strange tingling shot through his hand, like he had just been shocked with a mild electrical current.

"What the hell?" He quickly let go of the staff, allowing it to fall to the ground. The beaded staff was made of wood, and he saw no electrical cords attached to it, so how could it possibly shock him? Maybe what he felt was static electricity of some kind. Maybe the wood contained unusual properties, enabling it to build up a mild charge of positive electrons.

Robert wasn't an expert of electricity, so maybe such things were possible. One thing for sure, he no longer had any desire to touch the staff. Nor was he going to stick it back in the ground. He could see it just fine where it lay.

Wanting nothing more to do with the strange staff, he moved back from the lagoon and took a seat on the ground. Resting his back against the trunk of an oak tree, he looked out over the water. The lagoon and the area surrounding it was quiet and peaceful, a place of filtered sunlight and tranquil shadows. It was a pleasant change from the hectic hustle of city life.

Taking a deep breath, he closed his eyes and relaxed. His spirit was soothed by the whispered rustling of leaves and tall grass, and the distant sound of running water. Soon he was fast asleep.

Robert awoke with a start. Someone was yelling at him, shaking him. A man stood over him. The man was dark skinned and muscular, with long black hair and piercing eyes. He was dressed in blue jeans, boots, a black T-shirt, and a bright yellow vest made of patchwork material. A Seminole vest. He was also missing the tips of the two smallest fingers on his left hand. There was little doubt that the man standing over him was Jimmy Cypress.

Robert tried to stand up, but his feet and ankles were wrapped with kudzu vines as though someone had tied him up while he slept. He tried to kick free, but he was wrapped so tightly he could barely move.

"Hold still," the Indian said, pulling a large hunting knife from the sheath on his belt. Leaning over he cut through the vines around Robert's ankles with one quick motion.

"Thank you," Robert said, getting to his feet. "I don't know how that happened." He started to offer his hand, but Jimmy Cypress only glared at him.

"What are you doing here?" The Indian made no move to put away the knife.

"I . . . I was taking a walk," Robert replied. "I got tired and sat down for a few minutes. I guess I fell asleep."

"The boardwalk is closed. You should not be here."

Robert nodded. "I know. I should have turned back

and gone the other way, but I wanted to keep going straight."

"Why did you move my staff?" Jimmy asked, angry.

"I'm sorry. I was only looking at it. I was going to put it back in the ground, but the thing gave me a shock." Robert turned toward the lagoon, seeing that the staff was again standing upright by the water's edge.

"That staff is not to be touched . . . by you or anyone else. You don't know what you have done by moving it. What dangers you may have awakened."

"It's just a staff," Robert argued, not liking the Indian's tone of voice.

"To you it is just a staff, because you are stupid. Your people are stupid. Stupid and blind."

Robert would have argued that point, but the Indian was still holding the knife. They were alone in the forest, no witnesses anywhere, so the last thing he wanted was to make him even more upset than he already was.

"This ground is unholy. Evil," Jimmy Cypress continued. "A place of great danger. Stick to your wooden sidewalk, white man. Leave this area. Now."

Afraid that physical harm might come to him at any moment, Robert turned away from the crazy Indian and hurried back in the direction from which he had come. His heart beating fast, he didn't slow his pace until he reached the boardwalk. Even then he did not stop until he was safely back at camp.

Chapter Three

Jimmy Cypress adjusted his medicine staff, turning it so the skull again looked out over the dark waters of the lagoon. The skull belonged to *coo-wah-chobee*, the "big cat," a Florida panther that Jimmy's great-grandfather had shot during his youth, back before it was against federal and state law to shoot such animals. The skull had been passed down for several generations, from father to son, a treasured heirloom that represented the clan of the Seminoles to which they belonged.

He brushed loose dirt from the skull, thankful that none of the fangs had been damaged in the fall. Jimmy was furious that the white man had moved his staff, even madder that he had allowed it to fall on the ground.

"Stupid tourist."

The staff was decorated with eagle feathers, and it was an act of desecration to let such a feather touch the ground. The eagle flew higher than any other bird, high enough to touch the home of the Great Spirit. The eagle feathers had been to the house of God and were sacred. All Indians knew this. They would never allow an eagle feather to touch the ground. If an eagle feather fell to the ground by accident during a dance, then that dancer had to stand over it, protecting it, waiting for the head dancer to pick it back up. The dancer then had to pay money to get his feather back, punishment for being careless with a sacred object.

But the white people did not consider the eagle to be sacred. To them it was just a bird of prey, the winged symbol stamped on the back of their almighty dollar. It was not the eagle that was sacred in white societies, but the money it represented. They cared nothing at all about the actual bird, other than to scream that it was endangered each and every time they saw an Indian wearing eagle feathers.

Carefully straightening the feathers on his staff, Jimmy turned to look at the forest. The white man was long gone, badly frightened by his encounter with a real, honest to God, Indian.

"Stupid white man. Stupid tourist. Come back here and I'll nail your balls to a tree."

He could tell the man was a tourist by the way he dressed: designer clothing, yuppie sandals, no suntan to speak of, a weakness about him that spoke of long hours sitting in an office chair. And only a tourist would be in that part of the forest. The local fishermen and hikers all knew Jimmy and did their best to stay clear of him. They all thought he was crazy in the head, a troublemaker, and wanted nothing to do with him.

Jimmy glanced down at the hunting knife he wore on his belt and laughed. The knife had scared the skinny white man. Scared him pretty bad. Maybe he thought a crazy Indian was about to cut him into little pieces and scalp him. The thought had crossed Jimmy's mind when he saw the staff, but he would never do anything to hurt another person. Once, long ago, in another lifetime, another world, he could have taken a life without a second thought—had even killed without feeling the least bit of remorse—but not anymore. He was now a man of peace. A man of medicine.

At fifty-five years of age, Jimmy Cypress was a different man now than he had been in his youth. When he was nineteen he had followed the warrior path, as an Army Ranger in Vietnam. In the sweltering jungles of that far-off land he had counted coup on the enemy many times, taking numerous lives with a gun, a knife, and even his bare hands. He had been wounded twice and still bore the scars, both physical and mental, of those wounds.

The second time he had been wounded was serious. He had taken two AK-47 rounds in the abdomen and nearly died. He had been sent back to a hospital in the United States, and by the time he recovered from his injuries his enlistment in the army was over. He did not bother to re-enlist.

Returning to civilian life, he had gone back to the Brighton Indian Reservation in south Florida. There he had worked on a farm, given airboat rides to hunters, and even wrestled alligators for a short time. A very short time. But he was less than happy with putting on shows for the few tourists who stopped by the reservation on their way to Lake Okeechobee or Miami. Despite being dressed in civilian clothes, he was still a warrior on the inside. He still wanted to fight.

He had been back on the reservation a little over a year when he heard about the American Indian Movement. It seemed a small band of Lakotas were trying to bring back the old ways. They were attempting to be traditional warriors, standing up against a corrupt tribal government that was backed by an even more corrupt federal government. To Jimmy, this seemed like a perfect opportunity to use the skills he knew best.

Throwing a few articles of clothing and his hunting rifle into the cab of his pickup truck, Jimmy left Florida and headed west to the Pine Ridge Indian Reservation in South Dakota. There he joined up with Leonard Peltier, Russell Means, Dennis Banks, and other AIM notables.

Jimmy Cypress's military experience was a welcome addition to the American Indian Movement. During their occupation of Wounded Knee, in 1973, he had been in charge of security, making sure the sentries were doing their job each night. He also exchanged fire with several FBI agents, but he wasn't sure if he had hit any of them.

He was only at Wounded Knee for a week, however, when something happened that changed his life forever. He had just come off guard duty and was trying to get a few hours sleep, when a vision came to him. In the vision, the spirit of his great-grandfather spoke to him, telling the young man to go back home to Florida. The spirit told Jimmy that he was needed back among his own people, needed to fight an evil far greater than the federal government.

That night Jimmy Cypress left Wounded Knee. He left his rifle and his extra clothes, even left his pickup truck, sneaking away under the cloak of darkness. Hitchhiking across the country, he arrived back in south Florida a week later. He wasn't sure why he had returned to the reservation, but he knew to follow his vision.

When he arrived back at the reservation, they were waiting for him. Actually, only one man was waiting for him: an old medicine man named Charlie Osceola. Charlie knew that Jimmy was coming home. He also knew why the young man had returned. Charlie had also had a vision. It would be his job to start Jimmy down the medicine path, teaching him the things he would need to know for a job far more important than any he had ever done before.

Jimmy turned and looked at the place where the white tourist had fallen asleep. Pieces of kudzu vine still lay scattered on the ground, pieces that Jimmy had cut away from the man's legs. The tourist didn't know how lucky he really was. Had Jimmy not come along when he did, the man probably would have been killed.

"Stupid tourist."

Most of the people who lived in the area had forgotten the story of Blackwater. They did not know of the evil that resided in the ground, waiting for a chance to be free once more. They had never heard of Mansa Du Paul, and were ignorant of the darkness that he represented.

But Jimmy was the guardian. He knew the story, and had dedicated his life to making sure the evil did not return. His was a lonely existence, living in a tiny shack that was barely fit for cockroaches and spiders. He had accepted his calling without complaint, following his original vision and the teachings of the late Charlie Osceola. He was one with the forest, and the animals in it, watching and waiting, hoping that the darkness would never again rear its ugly head.

Jimmy sighed, turning his attention toward the lagoon. The darkness was growing stronger. He could feel it. It was in the water and in the land, even in the plants and trees. Soon it would be strong enough to break free of its prison, returning again in full force. Heaven help them if it did return in full strength, for Jimmy Cypress wasn't sure he was strong enough to fight it.

Reaching into his front pocket, he removed an old leather pouch. He opened it and took out a pinch of black leaf tobacco, spreading it around the base of the staff. He whispered a few words of prayer, then closed the pouch and started down the trail toward his tiny cabin. The staff was again in place, its medicine fighting to keep the evil from spreading. Still, he would have to keep a closer watch on the area, just in case the foolish white tourist returned.

Chapter Four

Krissy was bored. She was supposed to be taking her afternoon nap, but she just couldn't sleep. If you asked her, having to take a nap was stupid. She was ten years old, not a little girl, so she didn't need a nap. And she sure as heck didn't want to take a dumb nap while she was on vacation.

She was supposed to be out doing things, not sleeping. This was her vacation, there would be plenty of time to take naps when she went back home.

The morning's canoe trip had ended far too early to satisfy her. They were supposed to go fishing after they got back from canoeing, but her mother wanted to learn how to make crab cakes. Krissy didn't really want to learn, she only said she did to make her mother happy. Truthfully, she could care less about learning how to make them. But her mother always wanted to do mother and daughter things, so Krissy had gotten roped into spending an hour or two in a hot kitchen learning how to make "authentic Florida crab cakes." She would have rather been learning how to catch crabs, or maybe taking a walk with her father.

She had asked her father to take her on the nature trail when he got back from his walk, but he had acted funny, saying that he was just too tired to go for another walk. Maybe later.

Krissy sighed. It was always "maybe later" with her parents. Maybe later we will go fishing, maybe later we will go for a walk, maybe later we will take you to Walt Disney World.

Angry, she sat up in her bed and looked around the room. "Maybe later I will take a nap, but not now."

Crossing the room, she looked out the cabin's window. Her parents were at the lounge talking with Mr. and Mrs. Sanders. Knowing how her parents both loved to talk, it would probably be hours before they came back. And if her mom and dad were drinking beer, which they sometimes did—especially on their days off—then they might not be back for a long time.

That was typical: Krissy, take a nap in a boring old cabin while we go have a good time drinking beer and talking with people we don't really know. If you get lonely, you can talk with the cockroaches. Correction, palmetto bugs. Her dad said the big ones were called palmetto bugs.

"Who cares?"

Walking back across the room, she sat down on the bed and pulled her shoes on. This was her vacation too, and she wasn't about to spend it taking naps in the middle of the afternoon. There was a strange, exciting world out there, and she was going to explore at least part of it.

Tying her shoes, she left the bedroom and went to the front door. She opened it a crack and peeked out. The camp appeared empty. No sign of her parents, or anyone else.

Checking to make sure she would not be locked out, Krissy stepped outside and closed the door behind her. Truthfully, she only planned to walk around the camp a little, maybe sit on the bench by the river and watch the fish swim by. But when she reached the beginning of the nature trail, she decided to go for a short walk in the forest.

Krissy had always liked doing things with her parents, but she also liked doing things on her own. Her father said she had an independent streak, whatever that meant.

She had only walked about fifty feet down the trail, crossing the wooden footbridge that spanned the Wekiva River, when she spotted a bright blue butterfly sitting on the wooden handrail.

"Hello, Mr. Butterfly. How are you today?"

The butterfly didn't answer her, but she knew that it wouldn't. It just sat there on the handrail, slowly opening and closing its wings, perhaps sunning itself. She stepped closer to get a better look, but her shadow fell over the butterfly, startling it into flight.

"Wait. Don't go," Krissy said, not wanting the insect to fly away. "I won't hurt you."

But the butterfly didn't listen. It flew away from her, following the boardwalk deeper into the forest. Not wanting the insect to get away, Krissy gave chase.

She hurried to keep up with it, running along the boardwalk. Suddenly, the insect turned left, flying away from the wooden walkway. Not wanting to lose the game of chase, Krissy climbed down off the boardwalk and continued after the bright blue butterfly. And when the tiny insect flew too high to be of further interest, the little girl found herself surrounded by trees.

Krissy stopped and looked around. At first she was alarmed, fearing that she might have gotten lost in the woods. But she could see a section of the boardwalk through the trees, even though the section looked old and black like it had been burned in a fire. She could also hear the whispered gurgling of water, and knew she was not far from the river. Even if she was lost, all she had to do was follow the river back to camp.

Knowing she would get into big trouble if her parents found out that she had gone off by herself, Krissy started back for the camp. She had only taken a few steps, however, when a wild rabbit darted out from under a bush. She just had to chase the rabbit, at least for a little ways. The ten-year-old forgot all about the rabbit when she stumbled upon the lagoon.

There was something terribly appealing about the lagoon. There was also something a little frightening about it. It felt old, really old, like something left over from ancient times. She could almost imagine a huge, scaly dinosaur rising up out of the dark water to stare at her, and that thought was more than a little frightening to a girl alone in the forest.

Krissy was almost certain that the lagoon she faced was the same one she and her family had stumbled upon while canoeing earlier in the day. She could even see the tiny branch of the Wekiva leading away to join up with the river's main artery. Earlier it had been nothing more than a dead end, but now the lagoon and surrounding forest was a place of dark secrets where strange creatures watched from the shadows.

The little girl looked around, suddenly fearful that something was watching her. As she looked around, she became aware of how quiet everything was. Too quiet. A spooky kind of silence, like the kind they always have in scary movies right before the monster jumps out at you.

Not that the forest itself was noisy. There had been a pleasant quietness surrounding them when they had gone canoeing that morning, broken only by the whisper of the river, the soft splashing of their paddles, and the cries of birds. That silence had been nice. There was also a calm stillness surrounding her when she had been chasing the bright blue butterfly, marred only by the sound of her footsteps.

But the silence now was far different than what she had already experienced in the forest. There was nothing soothing or serene about it. It was the silence of waiting, of holding your breath in nervous anticipation. The quietness of little kids playing hide and go seek, hoping not to be caught by the person that was "it." The silence of a big hairy spider as it slowly descends a web toward the terrified struggles of its next victim.

No. The eerie silence that surrounded the lagoon was anything but pleasant. It was a silence of something waiting, perhaps waiting for her.

Becoming increasingly nervous, Krissy started to turn away from the lagoon when she spotted something neither she nor her parents had noticed earlier while canoeing.

A narrow wooden staff stood upright by the water's edge, apparently stuck in the ground by someone who had come to the lagoon before her. The staff was wrapped in leather and covered with beadwork, decorated with feathers and strips of colored cloth. On top of the pole sat the skull of some kind of animal, its jaws open in an evil grin. The skull faced away from Krissy, looking out over the black water.

Krissy was glad the skull faced away from her. Even though it was nothing more than the bone of some long-dead animal, she had a funny feeling that it might be able to see her had it been looking her way. One thing for sure, she didn't want to get any closer to the skull-topped staff. She could see it just fine from where she stood.

Deciding that she had enough of spooky lagoons and grinning skulls, Krissy started to leave. She had just turned away from the water, when a man's voice spoke to her.

Where are you going . . . little one?

Startled, Krissy turned back around. She didn't see anyone, but someone had definitely spoken to her. "What?"

Where are you going?

The little girl looked left, then right, searching for the man whose voice she heard. But she saw no one, which meant that he was hiding somewhere: perhaps behind a tree, or bush, maybe ducked down so he would not be seen.

But why would he be hiding? A man wouldn't be hiding alone in the forest, unless he was hiding from someone. Maybe he was waiting for someone to come along, someone like Krissy.

Fear shot through Krissy as she realized just how alone she really was. Though the river was not far away, and she could still see a section of boardwalk from where she stood, she was very much alone in a forest that had suddenly grown dark and spooky. It was just her and the man.

"Where are you?" Krissy asked aloud. She wanted to know where the man was in case she had to run for help. It just wouldn't do to run toward him.

I am here, little one.

"Where?" She looked around, but saw no one.

Here. There. Everywhere.

Krissy took a step back. "You're hiding somewhere."

No. I am not hiding.

"Then why can't I see you?"

Can you see the wind, little one?

Krissy shook her head. "No."

But you know the wind is there. You can feel it. You can see the wind when it moves the trees. I am like the wind. I can be heard, but not seen.

The voice was soft and smooth, almost a whisper. Krissy suddenly realized that she didn't hear the voice with her ears, but heard it deep inside her head. The voice scared her, and she started to run, but the man she could not see again spoke to her.

Do not be afraid, little one. I will not hurt you. I am your friend. Your ssspecial friend.

"Special friend?" Krissy hesitated. Her legs still wanted to run away, but she forced herself to stand still.

That is correct. I am your ssspecial friend. A ssspecial friend for a ssspecial little girl.

Krissy was now curious. "How do you know I'm special?"

I know many things.

"Like what?"

I know the color of the butterfly that you chased, and where the rabbit is now hiding. I know that you are a brave little girl, for you have not run away. You are ssspecial. Very ssspecial. Only ssspecial people are allowed to have ssspecial friends.

Krissy was still a little afraid, but she no longer had the desire to run away. She kind of liked the idea of having a special friend to talk with. No one that she knew had such a friend.

"Will you play with me?"

Yesss. Play. Talk. Sing. We will do many things together. Many things. I will tell you the stories of the wind, and the trees, and the secrets of the dark water.

"Can we read together?" Krissy asked. "I like to read books. Can we read some books together?"

Yesss. If you like. I am your friend. We can read together.

Krissy stopped talking and frowned. "I don't know your name. How can we be friends if I don't know your name?"

My name is Mansa, said the voice.

"Mansa," Krissy repeated the name aloud. "That's a nice name. My name is Krissy."

Krisssy. Krisssy. The voice repeated her name twice, sounding like the singing of cicadas.

Krissy laughed. "Just wait until I tell my parents that I have a special friend."

The whispered hissing of her name went shrill, almost hurt her head. *No! You must not tell anyone about me.*

"Ow. You're hurting me." She grabbed her head, waiting for the voice to stop.

I am sorry, little one. I did not mean to hurt you.

Krissy lowered her hands. "Why can't I tell my parents about you?"

Our friendship must be kept a secret. A ssspecial friendship between two ssspecial friends. If you tell anyone about me I will go away and not come back. You do not want that. Do you?

"I guess not."

Good. Then you will not tell anyone about me?

I won't tell.

Promise?

"I promise."

Good. Very good.

She looked around the lagoon, but still didn't see anyone. There was only the voice, and she only heard that on the inside of her head. She wanted to tell about her new friend, but she didn't want her special friend to be mad at her. Not everyone had a special friend. No one she knew had a friend that could be heard, but not seen. That excited Krissy, made her feel that maybe she was a special little girl after all.

One thing for sure, she now had someone to talk to whenever she wanted. Let her parents hang out in the lounge if they wanted, Krissy no longer needed them to keep her company. She had something better. Something special.

Realizing that it was getting late, Krissy again promised to keep her friend a secret. She also promised to return to the lagoon as soon as possible. This made her new, special friend very happy.

Krissy made it back to the cabin with plenty of time

to spare. Lying on her bed, she waited for her nap time to be over. She still wasn't sleepy, but she was no longer bored. She now had someone to play with. A special friend that only she could hear.

Chapter Five

The next morning the Pattersons rented a small, flat-bottomed boat to do a little fishing. They also rented three rods and reels, but they had to buy their bait and hooks. In this case the bait was the nonliving kind: artificial worms in several different colors and smells. Ross Sanders had told them about several good spots on the river to catch striped bass, and they were anxious to try their luck.

Along with the rubber worms, they also purchased snacks, a small Styrofoam cooler, a bag of ice, a twelve-pack of canned ice tea, and a bottle of sunscreen.

Robert looked at the bag of supplies they had just purchased and smiled. "I guess it's a good thing we're only going fishing for the morning. Otherwise we would have to rent a bigger boat."

The boat they rented came equipped with two swivel seats, as well as a small bench where Krissy could sit without being in the way of either of her parents. It also had a small electrical trawling motor, which Ross guaranteed would not run out of juice and leave them stranded. There was a pair of wooden oars lying in the bottom of the boat, just in case Ross's guarantee failed to come true.

Robert loaded their fishing poles and supplies into the boat while his wife filled the cooler with the cans of ice tea, covering them with a layer of ice. He set the filled cooler in the middle of the boat, and then put a life vest on Krissy. Tossing two more vests on board, he helped his family into the boat and they untied from the dock.

He started the motor and steered out into the middle of the river, heading upstream to the places that Ross described as the best spots to catch the big ones. The first spot Ross suggested was underneath an old wooden bridge, but there was another boat already anchored there, so they kept going.

It was actually a good thing that they didn't stop at the first fishing spot, because shortly after passing the old wooden bridge they spotted an alligator swimming near the shore. With only its head and part of its back protruding above the water, the gator closely resembled a floating log.

Krissy was extremely excited about seeing her first alligator and nearly fell out of the boat when she changed positions to get a better look. The alligator was less than excited about seeing the three of them, disappearing beneath the surface when their boat got too close. Bidding a fond farewell to Mr. Gator, they continued in search of the perfect fishing spot.

The next place described as a good fishing spot was about a mile upstream, where the river widened and slowed its pace. Here the water was choked with a mixture of eelgrass and hydrilla, but in the middle of the green vegetation were small open patches of water where fish liked to gather.

Almost immediately Janet spotted the rainbow flash

of a freshwater bass as it moved slowly through one of the open areas. Robert slowed the boat to a crawl, spotting two more bass lurking in the shadows beneath a cypress tree.

Knowing the reeds and eelgrass could be a real nightmare to cast in, especially for an inexperienced fisherman like Krissy, he guided the boat so that it came to a stop on the edge of one of the large open areas of water. Switching off the motor, he set the anchor to keep them from drifting back downstream.

"This looks like a good place," he said, picking up one of the rod and reels. "Krissy, would you like me to put your worm on the hook?"

The little girl stood up, anxious to begin fishing. The boat rocked with her weight. "No. I want to do it."

"Okay. You can do it. Just be careful." He opened the plastic bag containing the selection of fishing lures. "What color do you want?"

"I want a red one."

Robert opened the bag of red fishing worms, handing one to his daughter. He held the pole steady while she slid the rubber worm on the hook. Once the worm was in place, he handed her the pole. "Remember how I taught you. Cast straight ahead, and then slowly reel the worm back in."

"I remember." Krissy took the pole and cast it straight ahead, plopping the worm in the center of the clearing. She had been fishing several times, so Robert knew that she could handle a fishing pole without too much trouble. She did sometimes have problems, however, when it came to taking a fish off the hook. And sometimes she got tangled up in the weeds, but that happened to the best fishermen.

Getting his daughter started, he handed a fishing pole to Janet. "Want me to put your worm on the hook?"

Janet smiled. "I think I can manage."

"You sure? I'll be glad to help."

"That's all right. Toss me a red one."

Robert tossed his wife a red worm and then got his own hook ready to cast. Within a few minutes all three of them were fishing, each being careful not to cross the other guy's line.

Even though they now lived in St. Louis, Robert and Janet had both grown up in the country. He was from the tiny town of Logan, Missouri, which had become rather famous with the discovery of an ancient Indian village, built in a series of caves and natural tunnels underneath the town. She had grown up on a farm just south of Chanute, Illinois, which was home to a large air force training facility.

Both of them had moved to St. Louis in search of work, meeting one fateful night at a quiet little tavern not far from Busch Stadium. Nine months later they were married; two years after that they were parents.

Despite being city dwellers, their country childhoods remained very dear to them. They both liked getting out of the city whenever possible, which was why they preferred fishing, hiking, and camping to taking cruises, dining in fancy restaurants, or visiting theme parks.

A couple of years ago, Robert began having thoughts that he would like to do more than just pay occasional visits to the country. He wanted to move back to rural America permanently, leaving the city behind him once and for all. He had grown weary of the hustle and bustle that came with city living. Unfortunately, there wasn't much need of an advertising executive in the country, and he just didn't have the skill, patience, or money needed to take up farming as a career.

Janet was all for moving to a small town, because the rural lifestyle was much better for raising kids than that of the big city. But she made too much money as a real estate agent in the city to throw away her career, and paycheck, on a rural trek down memory lane. So they would have to remain city dwellers, at least for the time being.

Robert had just reeled his worm back in and was about to toss it back out in deeper water when Krissy let out a sigh.

"Something wrong, pumpkin?" he asked.

She shook her head. "No. Nothing's wrong."

"You're not getting bored. Are you?" Janet asked.

"No. I'm not bored. Not yet," she answered, slowly turning her reel to bring her red worm closer to the boat.

Robert smiled. "That's good, because it takes a lot of patience to be a good fisherman."

"I know, Daddy. I was just thinking."

"Thinking, huh? What about?"

Krissy turned to look at her father, a troubled look on her face. "I can't tell you."

He could tell something serious was on his daughter's mind and that she really wanted to talk about it. "Why can't you tell me?"

"Because it's a secret."

Robert started to laugh, but coughed instead. "A secret? What kind of secret?"

"A really big secret." She stopped turning the crank on her reel, allowing her red worm to sink unnoticed to the sandy river bottom.

Janet turned to look at her daughter, suddenly interested in the conversation. "Krissy, you can share your secrets with us. You know that. We're your parents."

"Not this secret," the little girl replied.

"Why not?" Janet asked.

"Because I was told not to tell."

A look of concern came over Janet's face. Robert knew what his wife was thinking. They had both seen countless reports on the news: children sexually molested by teachers and day-care workers, being made to promise not to tell. Being convinced that their violation was a secret not to be told to anyone.

"Krissy, who told you not to tell?" Robert chose his words carefully. He knew something was bothering his daughter and that she wanted to talk about it, but Krissy was afraid of breaking her promise not to tell. He also didn't want to frighten her by showing that he was growing upset with the situation.

"My friend told me not to tell."

"Your friend?" Janet asked.

Krissy nodded. "My special friend."

"Does your special friend have a name?" Robert asked gently. "Surely you can tell us that. Their name wouldn't be a secret. Would it?"

Krissy was silent for a moment, obviously thinking things over. "I guess that wouldn't be a secret. His name is Mansa."

"Mansa what?" asked Janet.

Krissy shrugged. "I don't know. Just Mansa."

Robert ran the name quickly through his memory

but didn't come up with a match. As far as he knew, his daughter didn't have any teachers named Mansa, nor were there any boys in her class with that name.

"Is Mansa someone you know in school?" Janet asked. Apparently she too had drawn a blank on the name.

"No. I just met him."

"When did you meet him?" Robert asked.

"I met him yesterday, at . . ." Krissy turned to look at her father, perhaps aware that she had already said too much. "I met him at the cabin."

Alarm bells sounded in Robert's head. They had been with Krissy all day, except when she was taking her afternoon nap. Then she had been in the cabin by herself, while they had been at the lounge talking with Ross and Mary Sanders.

The alarm bells gave way to a sick feeling in the pit of his stomach. Had something happened to their daughter while they were out drinking beer, visiting, and having a good time? Had a man gotten into their cabin, perhaps doing something unthinkable to their little girl?

"Krissy, honey, this is serious," Janet said, fear noticeable in her voice. "I know you promised to keep a secret, but I want to know about this man Mansa. What does he look like?"

"I don't know."

"What do you mean, you don't know?" Robert jumped in, failing to hide the concern in his voice. "You said he was in our cabin yesterday, that he made you promise to keep a secret. Didn't you see him?"

"No."

"Why not? Did he put something over your eyes?"

Krissy laughed. "No, Daddy."

"Then why couldn't you see him?"

"Because he's invisible."

What his daughter said surprised him, and it was a few moments before he could find his voice. "He's invisible?"

The little girl nodded. "That's right. I can't see him, but I can hear him. That's how I know his name. He told me."

Janet looked as shocked as Robert felt. "And what did Mansa tell you?"

Krissy hesitated, then smiled. "He said I'm special, because no one else can hear him but me. He said that he is my special friend. That's why he made me promise not to tell. He said no one would believe me if I said I had a special friend. He said not to tell, but I guess it's okay to tell you. Just don't tell him I told you. Okay? I promised to keep it a secret."

"Krissy, honey," Janet said, wanting to put some logic back into the conversation. "I think maybe your new friend was nothing but a dream. I think maybe you dreamed about someone when you were taking your nap."

Krissy turned to her mother, shaking her head. "No. He's real. Honest. It wasn't a dream. I swear it."

Robert wasn't sure what to say. This was something new for the trials and tribulations of parenthood. "Pumpkin, let me see if I've got this right. You met a man named Mansa yesterday?"

She nodded.

"And he's invisible?"

Again she nodded.

"And he told you that he was your special friend, and that you were not to tell anyone about him?"

"That's what he said. Honest."

Robert rubbed his chin in thought. "And what are you and Mansa planning on doing together?"

"We're going to play, and sing, and read stories. That's what special friends do."

Janet was still looking concerned, but Robert was starting to feel somewhat relieved. At first he was afraid that his daughter had been molested by someone named Mansa, but it was now becoming apparent that his daughter had simply invented an imaginary playmate. Krissy had always wanted a brother or a sister to play with, so she had compensated by inventing someone that only she could hear. While he wasn't overjoyed about the development, he knew that such playmates were harmless. As a boy, growing up in a lonely rural environment, he too had invented playmates that only he could see.

Robert looked around the boat, as if looking for someone. "Mansa isn't here with us now. Is he?"

Krissy giggled. "No, silly. He isn't here. I'd hear him if he was."

"Good," Robert whispered. "Because I don't think we brought enough food for four people."

Krissy giggled even louder.

Janet cleared her throat, getting his attention. Her look told him that she was still less than pleased about Mansa, even if he was nothing more than an imaginary playmate. "Krissy, honey, why don't you sit over here for a while? I want to get some snacks, and talk with Daddy."

Switching places with her daughter, Janet pretended

to be selecting a snack from the bag they had brought in order to talk with Robert.

"What are you doing?" she whispered, obviously angry.

"What?"

"This isn't something to joke about."

"Relax. Krissy is probably just going through a phase. You'll see. A lot of kids have imaginary friends. I even had a few of my own. It's perfectly harmless, and it's a great way to build the imagination."

"It's not healthy," Janet argued. "What if she starts talking to this Mansa when she's in school?"

"That probably won't happen," he whispered.

"What if it does? What then?"

"Listen, you had dolls as a girl. Right?"

"Yeah, so?"

"And you spoke to them. Correct?"

She didn't answer.

"And I imagine they spoke back to you when you were playing, at least in your imagination they talked. This is the same thing, just without the dolls. Krissy will talk with her new friend Mansa when she's alone and bored, and forget all about him when she's not."

"I hope you're right," Janet said, grabbing a pack of peanut butter crackers.

"Trust me. There's absolutely nothing to worry about. Nothing at all. I promise."

Less than an hour later all thoughts of invisible playmates were forgotten when Janet caught the first fish of the day.

"Can we keep it? Can we keep it?" Krissy screamed as Janet brought the fish into the boat.

"Keep it?" Janet asked, surprised. "Why do you want to keep it?"

"I want to eat it," Krissy answered.

Janet and Robert were both big believers in the catch and release program and rarely kept any fish that they caught. But Krissy seemed to have her heart set on having fresh bass for dinner, so they decided to keep the fish.

Thirty minutes later their daughter was even more excited when she caught a two-pound bass of her own. It was the first real fish she had ever caught, and she nearly fell overboard in her excitement. Janet caught another fish shortly after that, and Robert also caught one, bringing their total number to four. Knowing they couldn't eat more than four fish, they decided to call it a day and head back to camp.

On the way back, Krissy babbled about fish and fishing. Not once did she mention her new invisible friend, so maybe she had already forgotten about her imaginary playmate. Maybe not.

Chapter Six

It was a little before twelve noon when they arrived back at the fish camp. Bringing the fishing boat to a slow stop alongside the dock, Robert tied up the boat while Janet and Krissy gathered up the fishing poles, lures, snacks, and supplies. The Styrofoam cooler was now considerably heavier with the addition of the four bass. There was also a funny smell to it that would probably never wash out.

Lifting everything out of the boat, Robert went into the bait and tackle shop to turn in the fishing poles and get his deposit back on the boat. While he was gone, Janet and Krissy stood guard over the other supplies. Actually, Janet watched the snacks and lures, while her daughter kept a careful watch on the four fish, paying extra attention to the one she caught. The little girl was still tickled pink over landing her very first bass and just couldn't resist the urge to open the cooler to look at her trophy.

A few minutes later Robert returned from the bait and tackle shop. In his hands he carried a Polaroid camera and a sheathed fishing knife. "Ross said that Mary would be more than happy to cook our fish, but we have to clean them ourselves."

"That explains the knife," Janet said. "But what is the camera for?"

Robert smiled. "I told him that Krissy caught her very first bass, and he said that such a moment needed to be saved for all eternity. He also suggested having the fish mounted, but you won't believe what a taxidermist charges to stuff a fish. Besides, you can't eat it if it's mounted on the wall. And you do want to eat your fish, don't you, darling?"

Krissy nodded. "With French fries."

"That's what I thought," Robert said. "So we'll have to get by with just a snapshot. Go ahead and lift your fish out of the cooler, sweetheart, and I'll take your picture."

Krissy did as instructed, holding the fish up high while her father took her picture. She insisted that he take two, just in case the first one didn't come out. Putting the fish back in the cooler, she waited excitedly for the Polaroid to develop.

"There. That's a good picture," Robert said, handing both photos to his daughter.

"It sure is," Janet added.

"My fish is really big. Isn't it, Daddy?"

"Real big," answered Robert.

"Bigger than the fish you caught."

Janet laughed, and Robert cleared his throat. "Yes it is, you little show-off."

Krissy giggled. "I'm a better fisherman than Daddy."

"That's enough of that," Robert said, faking an angry tone of voice. He handed the camera to his daughter. "You take the camera back to Mr. Sanders, and your mommy and I will start cleaning these fish.

Once they're clean, we'll take them over to the restaurant and have Mary cook them up for lunch. With French fries and hushpuppies. How does that sound?"

"It sounds good," Krissy said. "I'm hungry."

Janet sniffed loud enough to be heard. "You might want to clean up a little too, Krissy. You smell like bass. That's because you've been touching that fish of yours ever since you caught it."

She dug into the front pocket of her shorts, pulling out the key to the cabin. "Here. Take the key with you. That way you don't have to come back. Drop off the camera, then go get cleaned up. And change your clothes. Think you can do all that by yourself?"

Krissy nodded. "I can do it."

"By the time you get cleaned up we should be finished here, so just come on over to the restaurant."

"Okay, Mommy."

Krissy left the fish cleaning to her parents, and returned the camera to Ross Sanders. Mr. Sanders congratulated her on the fish she caught, taking a great interest in the photos. He even asked her if he could put one of them up on the wall, adding it to the collection of photos taken of other people with their fish. Krissy agreed, delighted to have her image added to the collection.

Leaving the bait and tackle shop, she crossed the campgrounds to the cabin they had rented. It took her a few minutes fumbling with the key to get the door open. Entering the cabin, she closed and locked the door behind her.

Krissy washed her face and hands in the bathroom sink. She then took off her old clothes, leaving them on the floor, and dressed in a clean shirt and shorts.

Once dressed, she ran a comb through her tangled blonde hair and brushed her teeth.

She thought about going back to watch her parents clean the fish, but there was someone else she wanted to talk to. She wanted to tell Mansa about the fish she caught, because you always shared things with special friends. She would bring along the remaining photograph to show him, and maybe one of her story books. Mansa said they could read together, so maybe he would want to read a little from her book. Just a page or two. Krissy knew she couldn't be gone long, because her parents might get mad, but it wouldn't hurt to read a page or two. That wouldn't take too long.

Grabbing her green backpack from under her bed, she placed the photo and book inside the bag and then hurried across the room. With backpack in one hand and the cabin key in the other, she stepped outside, making sure to lock the front door behind her. Running to the back side of the campgrounds, she followed the nature trail to the lagoon.

The lagoon was just as spooky now as it was the day before. It was a place of strained silence in an otherwise peaceful forest. The water was just as dark as when Krissy previously saw it, the strange wooden staff still standing by the water's edge.

Krissy stepped into the open and stopped, listening carefully. A few moments passed, but no voice spoke to her.

"Are you here?" she asked, her voice almost a whisper. There was a stirring in the branches above her and in the grass at her feet. It was as though the wind blew, but Krissy felt no wind.

Krissssy, you have come back. The voice of her special friend was soothing. It touched her mind with the liquid fluidness of warm, running water.

"Of course I came back, silly." Krissy laughed. "I said I would be back, didn't I?"

I thought you would not return.

"Not return? Why? We're friends. Right?"

Ssspecial friends.

"I caught a fish this morning. A bass. A really big one. I brought a picture of my fish. Want to see it?" She removed her backpack and took out the picture, holding it out for her friend to see. As she held up the picture, Krissy suddenly realized that she didn't know which way to turn so her friend could see the photograph.

"Where are you? Can you see my picture?"

I can see it.

"Good. It's a big fish. Right?" A frown tugged at the little girl's mouth. She looked around, but saw only the lagoon and the forest. "Why can't I see you? I want to see what you look like."

That is not possible.

"Why not? We're special friends. Right? Then, why can't I see you?"

You will see me, little one. But not now.

"When?"

Soon. Very soon.

"I won't be here very long. We're only here on vacation. Will I get to see you before we leave?"

Yesss. . . .

"Good." Krissy's spirit brightened a little bit.

I have a gift for you, little one.

"A gift? For me?"

Yesss. A ssspecial gift for a ssspecial little girl.

A troubled thought crossed Krissy's mind. "How can you give me a gift if I don't know where you are?"

Like me, the gift is hidden. You must look for it. I will tell you where to find it.

"Like a treasure hunt," she said, excited.

Yesss, like a treasure hunt. A very ssspecial treasure.

The voice told her that the gift was hidden on the little island in the middle of the lagoon and that she would have to wade through the dark water to get to it. At first Krissy was afraid, but her special friend assured her that the water was not deep and that she would be safe.

"Are you sure?" Krissy asked, standing at the water's edge.

Yesss. . . .

What about snakes and alligators?

They will not bother you, little one. I will protect you.

"Are you sure?"

Yesss. . . .

Krissy didn't like the idea of wading through the lagoon, not knowing how deep the water was or what might be hiding in it. But her special friend said that it was safe and that he would protect her. Not wanting to upset her invisible friend and still wanting the gift, Krissy decided to do as she was told. Removing her shoes and socks, she slowly stepped into the black water.

A tremor of fear passed through her body as her bare feet sank into the mud. She knew there must be snakes beneath the water. Just had to be snakes. Hundreds of them. Maybe even thousands. She wanted to jump back out of the water, but she felt compelled to continue. It was almost as if she were being gently pushed by a pair of invisible hands.

The level of the water rose higher as she slowly waded across the lagoon. Up to her knees, past her thighs, and finally up to her waist. She thought about swimming, but didn't like that idea any better than she did wading through the water. She was afraid to swim, afraid her splashing might attract the attention of unwanted alligators. Big alligators with long, sharp teeth. Hungry alligators that might consider a ten-year-old girl to be the perfect afternoon snack.

She finally reached the island, where there grew an ancient cypress tree. Grabbing on to an exposed root, Krissy pulled herself out of the water. "Okay, I'm here. I made it. Where's my gift?"

Look around, little one. . . .

Krissy looked around, but didn't see a present of any kind. "Where? I don't see anything."

Beneath your feet, Krisssy. See the roots that grow into the water? There. Between the roots.

Krissy looked down, but still didn't see anything.

"Where? There's nothing here."

Dig.

"What?"

You have to dig for your gift.

Krissy was beginning to like the treasure hunt less and less. What kind of gift did you have to dig for? A thought popped into her head, causing her to smile. Maybe this was a real treasure hunt, and what she had to dig for was real buried treasure. Her father had told her that pirates used to live in Florida, so maybe her special friend was telling her where treasure was buried: gold coins, silver, jewelry. That would be a nice gift. A very nice gift.

Following the instructions of a voice only she could hear, Krissy dug in the soft earth between the roots of the cypress tree. She only dug a few inches before discovering something, but what she found did not glint of gold or silver. Instead it looked like a flat stick, about six inches in length, yellowed with age.

She put the yellowed object aside and dug deeper. A few minutes later she found a similar object, and then another. Krissy stopped digging after she found a fourth object.

"Where's my gift?" she asked, a little angry. "You said I would find it here."

You have found your gift, little one.

Krissy picked up one of the objects and brushed it off, realizing what it was. "This? This is my gift? This is just an old bone. What kind of gift is that?"

A ssspecial gift, little one. The bones are magical, and will bring you good luck. But you must keep them safe, and you must not let anyone see them.

Krissy turned over the bone to examine it. "Magical? Are you sure?"

Yesss. . . . Magical. Ssspecial. They have lots of power. But it is a gift for you only. No one else must know about them.

"Then they're a secret," Krissy said.

Yesss, a sssecret. Your sssecret. Our sssecret. You must tell no one, or the magic will go away.

Krissy remembered she had been given a similar secret the day before, but she had told her parents about her new, special friend. But this time she would keep her secret. "I won't tell anyone."

Good. Very good. . . .

Gathering up the magical bones, Krissy waded back across the lagoon. She wasn't as scared this time as she was before, for she knew her special friend was watching over her. She also had the magical bones to protect her and bring her luck, magical objects like those in the children's fantasy stories her mother read to her at bedtime. No one she knew had anything that was really magical. Not even her parents.

Climbing out of the water, she tried to clean her feet off on the grass but failed. Even a handful of leaves didn't get all the mud out from between her toes. Giving up in frustration, she pulled her white socks back on over her still-muddy feet and then slipped on her shoes.

Once dressed she wiped off the magical bones and carefully placed them in her backpack. She asked her special friend if he wanted to read a story with her. When he didn't answer, she knew that he was gone. Placing the book on the ground as a gift for her new friend, she slowly walked back to camp. Had she looked back, she would have seen the pages of the book turn slowly though no wind blew.

Chapter Seven

Mary Sanders had loved to travel in her younger days. As the wife of a career navy man, she had practically traveled all over the world. She had lived in Spain for four years, and Greece, Italy, and Japan for two years each. Her home was adorned with memories of the places she had traveled and the people she had met: tapestries and glass clowns from Venice, a matador's cape from the *Rastro* in Madrid, alabaster statues from Athens, even a real samurai sword from Japan that Ross had smuggled out of the country.

Now that Ross was retired from the military, and now that they owned a business together, she no longer got to travel. The world now came to her, in the form of vacationing customers from all over the United States. Even from Europe. They came to Mary with hopes of finding a quiet little getaway they could call their own, bringing with them stories and customs of other places.

If it weren't for the customers, Mary might have grown bored with life along the lazy Wekiva River. The river no longer brought joy to her heart as it once had. After all, you could only look at the same river for so long. After nearly twenty years, the raccoons, gators, and eagles all looked the same. Even the fishermen and canoeists had the same look to them.

Still, she loved her customers, each and every one of them, and did all that she could to make them happy. So when Robert and Janet Patterson came knocking at her restaurant's back door, wanting to cook up a mess of fish they had caught, Mary was more than happy to oblige them.

Grabbing a couple of extra white aprons from the closet, she led the couple into the kitchen and gave them a stove to cook their fish on. She could have cooked the fish herself, but she knew that people often liked to do their own cooking when it came to fresh-caught fish. The Pattersons were no exception. Soon they were both laughing like happy school children as they filleted and battered their prize bass. Mary couldn't help but laugh too, especially when Janet applied some of the batter to the end of her husband's nose.

Leaving the young couple to their cooking, Mary decided to step out back to have a quick cigarette. She usually didn't get a chance to smoke during the daytime, what with preparing the lunch menu, cleaning up the mess, and then getting ready for the dinnertime crowd. But the lunch crowd had already left, and most of the cleaning was done, so she had an hour or so before she had to start worrying about dinner.

Grabbing a cigarette and her lighter, she went out the back door and walked around to the side of the building. She didn't like to smoke a cigarette anywhere near the back door, afraid the smoke might drift into the kitchen. Food and the smell of cigarette smoke didn't go good together, especially to those who were nonsmokers. Mary also made sure to wash her hands with soap and water after having a cigarette. She even kept a bottle of mouthwash in the kitchen's tiny bathroom, which she used after each and every time she lighted up.

Walking around the side of the building, Mary came upon Krissy Patterson. The little girl stood with her back to Mary, a green backpack sitting on the ground beside her. She had unrolled the garden hose that normally hung from a bracket on the side of the building and was using the water to clean something that she held in her left hand.

Mary couldn't see what the girl was cleaning, but found it bad manners to use someone's hose without first asking permission. Not that it was a serious crime or anything. They had a deep well, so water was free. Still, she could have asked first.

"What have you got there, darling?" Mary asked, stepping closer. She tried to get a better look at the object Krissy was cleaning, but the little girl quickly hid it in her backpack.

"Nothing," Krissy answered. She turned around to look at Mary, but didn't smile. In fact she looked nervous, as if she had just been caught doing something she shouldn't.

"Nothing?" Mary asked, suspicious. "It sure looks like you've been doing an awful lot of work for nothing."

"It's nothing," Krissy repeated.

Mary put on a smile. She wanted to know what was in the backpack, but she didn't want to frighten the girl. Krissy might only have been cleaning a shiny rock, a pebble she found while walking along the nature trail or canoeing. Kids were all the time collecting stuff: rocks, shells, leaves. One of their former tenants had a son who collected bugs, of all things. He kept jars filled with all kinds of nasty creepy-crawlers: palmetto bugs, caterpillars, worms, spiders.

"If you show me what you've got, I'll help you clean it," Mary offered, using her nicest voice.

"That's okay," Krissy said, making no attempt to reach back into her bag. "It doesn't need cleaning."

The smile slipped off of Mary's face. Whatever Krissy Patterson had in her green backpack, she definitely didn't want Mary to see it. While rocks, shells, and bugs were of no importance, there were other things a child could gather that would definitely be cause for alarm.

Birds of prey, and even songbirds, were protected in the state of Florida, and there were stiff penalties for collecting their feathers. If Krissy had an eagle feather or two in her possession she could get into serious trouble, despite the fact that eagles nested all along the Wekiva River and their feathers were easy to find. Only Native Americans were legally allowed to possess eagle feathers, and they had better have several forms of identification to prove their heritage.

Many species of turtles were also protected in Florida. If Krissy had a baby gopher turtle in that backpack of hers she could get into big trouble with the fish and game people. Baby turtles were cute, but when they were protected by the state you had better leave them alone.

There was another possibility: maybe Krissy had something in her backpack that she had stolen. Maybe she had swiped something from one of the other cabins or from someone's vehicle. It would not be the first time something had been stolen from a cabin. Nor would it be the last.

A lot of tourists who came to the fish camp on vacation felt safe. Sometimes too safe. They often left their wallets, watches, and other valuables lying out in plain sight while they enjoyed a day of fishing or canoeing. Sometimes they didn't even bother to lock their doors. Of course, a locked door wouldn't be much of a deterrent to a determined thief. The screened windows of the cabins were locked with a simple hook, easily opened with a knife or flat-bladed screwdriver.

Maybe she had taken something from the bait and tackle shop. There were all kinds of items in there that might attract a child's interest, items that would be easy to steal when Ross wasn't looking.

Heaven knows, Ross was a good man, but he sometimes spent too much time talking with the customers, and not enough time keeping an eye on the store. It wouldn't be hard to pocket an item or two while he wasn't looking. Shoot, it wouldn't be hard to sneak off with something when he was looking.

"Krissy, are you hiding something in your backpack?" Mary asked, now determined to see what the little girl was cleaning.

The little girl shook her head.

"Krissy, I don't think you're telling me the truth. I think maybe you ought to open up your backpack and show me what you have."

"No," Krissy said, clutching her backpack even tighter.

"And why not?"

"Because it's a present."

"A what?"

"A present."

"A present from whom?" Mary asked.

"A present from my secret friend."

Mary forced a smile, not entirely believing what she was being told. "I like presents. Why don't you show me yours?"

Krissy shook her head. "I can't show you."

"Why not?"

"Because it's a secret, that's why."

Still suspicious, Mary said, "I think you should show me your present. I won't tell anyone what I saw."

Again Krissy shook her head. "No."

"Why not?"

"Because you're not my mother, so I don't have to show you anything."

The woman was taken back by Krissy's tone of voice. She was definitely hiding something in that green backpack of hers, something she didn't want Mary to see.

Mary took a step forward, causing the little girl to take a step back. She was about to demand that Krissy show her what was in the backpack, but she was interrupted when her dog, Patch, came romping around the side of the building.

The black Labrador loved children and was probably looking for a playmate, but when he got close to Krissy he stopped suddenly and started to growl. The growl started deep in his throat and grew louder. He looked directly at the girl and bared his teeth, the hair along the ridge of his back standing straight up.

Krissy turned to look at the dog, her eyes going

wide with fear. She had petted the dog on several occasions, had even played with him, and was obviously frightened by his sudden threatening posture.

Mary looked from Krissy to her dog, momentarily forgetting about the little girl's backpack and what it might contain. Patch loved children. He was something of a big baby himself. She didn't remember him ever growling at a child, yet here he was, growling, looking like he was about to attack.

A fearful thought flashed through Mary's mind. If her dog bit the girl there would be big, big trouble. The police would be called, and maybe even the newspapers. There would be doctor bills, newspaper articles, police reports, and maybe even a lawsuit. It would hurt their business in more ways than one.

"Patch, what are you doing? Stop that!" Mary yelled at her dog, but to no avail. Not only did he not stop growling, he didn't even look her way when she yelled. That had never happened before. All it usually took was a firm word to make Patch drop his head and cower in fear.

"Patch, you quit that. I mean it."

The black Labrador ignored her. His growling grew louder, more threatening. But instead of advancing toward the little girl, he started to slowly back up.

"You stupid dog. What in the Sam hell is wrong with you?"

Still growling, Patch continued slowly backing up until he disappeared from view around the side of the building. And then, once he was safely out of sight, he began to howl. It wasn't a fun-loving, I-want-to-sing, kind of howl. On the contrary, it was an I'm-scared-shitless, dying-in-pain, heaven-help-me, howl.

A long, drawn-out howl that sent shivers racing down Mary's back.

"What on earth is wrong with that dog?" Mary said, no longer interested in Krissy or the secret present in her backpack. Patch's howls grew louder, longer, sounding like the poor dog was dying in agony.

"Ross, tell that stupid dog of yours to be quiet!" She yelled at her husband but knew that he would not hear her inside the bait and tackle shop. But surely he could hear Patch howling. He was probably waiting for her to quiet the dog.

"If you want something done, then you have to do it yourself." Tossing her unlit cigarette on the ground, she hurried in pursuit of her howling pet. She found Patch standing in the middle of the parking lot, howling his fool head off. The dog was oblivious to everything around him and seemed not to care about the noise he was making.

"Patch, damnit, stop that!" she yelled at the dog, but it had no effect. Head back, eyes closed, he continued to howl at the top of his voice.

"What has gotten into you?" She hurried to the howling dog and gave him a good swat on the back of his head. The dog quit howling and looked at her with his one good eye, as if to inquire what he had done wrong.

"What's the matter with you, boy?" Mary asked. "Have you lost your mind?"

As if to answer, Patch lowered his head and began to shake. Not just a little tremble, like the ones he made when he was glad to see someone. He began to shake in great, side-rattling tremors of fear. Maybe it was because she had hit him; maybe it was because she had yelled at him. Whatever the reason, Patch began to shake in fear from the tip of his tail to the tip of his nose. It had to be fear, for as he shook, the dog relieved himself, right there in the middle of the parking lot. Patch never peed when people were watching unless something scared him. Scared him real bad.

Mary looked down at the dog, not knowing what to think. "Patch, old boy, whatever is wrong with you?"

The dog looked up at her but did not stop shaking. If anything, his tremors grew more violent.

"Are you sick, boy? Is that it? Are you sick? Maybe something bit you? Maybe you got stung by a bee again? Did a bee get you, baby? Show Momma where it hurts." She reached down and gently petted the dog, slipping her fingers beneath his leather collar.

"Maybe you smelled something that you didn't like. Is that it? Did you smell something bad? Real bad? A skunk maybe?" Mary sniffed the air but didn't detect anything. If Patch had smelled a scent that scared him, then it was an odor that only he could detect.

Holding the dog by the collar, she slowly led him back to the bait and tackle shop. There was a chain fastened near the front door of the shop that they sometimes hooked Patch to when they didn't want him to run around, or when he had gotten into trouble for something. Patch didn't mind being chained near the door, for that allowed him to watch the customers coming and going.

Fastening the chain to the dog's collar, Mary patted him on the head. His howling had stopped, and his tremors were starting to slack off. Whatever had upset him, it was passing.

Giving Patch a final pat and a few soft words, she went inside the bait and tackle shop to talk with her husband. Ross had heard the dog howling and wanted to know what was the problem. She said that she didn't know, but he was quiet now.

Leaving the bait and tackle shop, Mary slowly walked back to her restaurant. Krissy was no longer using the garden hose and had hung it back up on the side of the building. Mary smiled and shook her head. Most kids would have just left the hose out, leaving it for her to put away.

Maybe she had gotten upset for nothing earlier. Krissy seemed like a good kid and probably didn't have anything of value in her backpack. It was probably just a shiny rock or a shell she had collected while out canoeing. Valuable treasures to a child, but of no interest to anyone else.

One thing for sure, it had definitely been a strange day, and the day was only half over.

Mary smiled. "I could really use a cigarette."

Chapter Eight

Krissy had been nervous at lunch, having to eat in the restaurant of the lady who had gotten mad at her. Sitting down at one of the tables with her parents, she had avoided eye contact with Mary Ross, pretending to be interested in one of the stuffed fish hanging on the wall. And when they had been served the bass they had caught, she had looked down as if carefully placing her napkin on her lap.

She expected Mary to say something to her, because she had been really mad at Krissy. Mary Ross had wanted to know what Krissy was hiding in her backpack, what she had been cleaning with the garden hose, and had been upset when Krissy refused to tell her. But she couldn't show Mary what she was cleaning, because it was a secret. Her special friend would be mad if she showed anyone. He had said the bones were a special gift, magical, and she was not supposed to show them to anyone.

She had already broken one secret by telling her parents about her special friend, and she was not going to break another. Krissy did not want her special friend to be mad at her, didn't want to be called a tattletale, so she was being careful about not showing the bones to anyone. Mrs. Ross did not know about the secret, and Krissy couldn't tell her, so she had gotten mad earlier in the day. But maybe Mary Ross wasn't mad anymore, because she didn't say anything to Krissy or her parents. Still, lunch had been very uncomfortable. Dinner was even worse.

Krissy told her parents she wanted to go to McDonald's for dinner, but her parents wouldn't hear of it. They didn't want to eat burgers and French fries, not when the fish camp's tiny restaurant served excellent food at a reasonable cost. Besides, the closest Mickey D's was miles away.

It wasn't that she really wanted to eat burgers and fries, or even Chicken McNuggets, Krissy just didn't want to eat at the restaurant again. She was scared of Mary Ross, afraid the woman might say something to her parents about what had happened earlier in the day. Her parents would also want to know what Krissy was hiding in the backpack and why she had been rude to an adult. Krissy would be in real trouble for being rude; they might even make her stay in the cabin as punishment. She couldn't have that. If she had to stay in the cabin, she wouldn't be able to visit her special friend again.

So it was with a heavy heart that Krissy accompanied her parents back to the restaurant for dinner. The tiny restaurant was crowded, with only a couple of the tables still empty. There was a waitress on duty to greet customers, a young woman with short red hair. That was a good thing. If the restaurant was busy, then Mrs. Ross had to stay in the kitchen cooking. She wouldn't have time to come out to see who was eating in her restaurant, wouldn't know that Krissy and her family were back again.

Seeing that the restaurant was busy, Krissy's spirit actually picked up. Not having to worry about Mary Ross looking at her was a relief, and she actually looked forward to eating dinner.

The waitress brought them glasses of ice water, with slices of lemon in them, then took their drink orders. She returned a few minutes later with the drinks and asked what they would like for dinner. Robert and Janet both chose the stuffed pork chops, while Krissy again ordered chicken fingers.

"Anything else?" the waitress asked, jotting down the order on the tiny pad of paper she carried.

"Nope. That should do it," Robert replied, handing her his menu.

The waitress started to turn away, but Janet stopped her. "Is Mary in the back?"

"Yes, ma'am," nodded the waitress.

"Please tell her thank you for lunch today. It was very nice of her to let us use her kitchen. The fish we caught were a real treat."

The waitress smiled. "I'll tell her."

"And if she's not too busy later, we would love to thank her personally," Robert said.

"I'll give her the message." The waitress smiled again and walked away.

Krissy's heart sank. Moments ago she had been happy that Mary Ross was nowhere to be seen, now her father was asking the woman to come out of the kitchen. Why couldn't he have been quiet instead? Why did he have to be so friendly?

The food came, and Mary Ross still had not come

out of the kitchen. Maybe she was too busy to come out. Perhaps she didn't want to come out to talk with Robert and Janet. Maybe she wouldn't be able to come out before they finished their meal. With these thoughts in mind, Krissy starting eating her chicken fingers, hoping to be finished and gone before Mary had a chance to come out of the kitchen.

Krissy was on her last strip of chicken when Mary Ross came out of the kitchen and approached their table, causing her appetite to suddenly die.

"Good evening, folks," Mary said, stopping in front of their table. "How is everything tonight?"

"Excellent," Robert replied. "Everything's great."

"The stuffed pork chops are wonderful," added Janet.

Mary smiled and nodded. "How are the chicken fingers, Krissy? Good, I hope."

A piece of chicken stuck in Krissy's throat. She swallowed hard, nearly choking. "They're good."

"Glad to hear it." Mary nodded. "I wouldn't want any unhappy customers. By the way, thank you for hanging the garden hose back up."

Krissy shifted in her seat, uncomfortable. "You're welcome."

Mary Ross looked at her for a moment longer, then turned her attention to Krissy's parents. Krissy expected the woman to say something else, perhaps tell her parents about what happened earlier in the day, but she didn't say anything about it. Instead, she chatted politely with Robert and Janet and then excused herself so she could go back into the kitchen.

Krissy picked up her last chicken strip. Her appetite had returned, having endured another meal without

Mrs. Ross saying anything to her parents. And Krissy hadn't said anything either, not one word about the bones she had hidden in her room at the cabin. Her special friend would be proud.

That night, after dinner, Krissy went into her room and locked the door. The four bones she had found were hidden in the bottom drawer of the dresser, carefully wrapped up in one of her T-shirts. Opening the drawer, she took out the shirt and carried it to her bed.

She set the shirt on the center of her bed and carefully opened it to reveal the treasure she had found earlier in the day. Not found. She hadn't found the bones. Not really. She had been given them. They were a gift from her special friend. A magical gift.

Krissy frowned. Her special friend had said the bones were magical, but they didn't look very magical. They just looked like old yellowed bones and nothing more. Pieces of a dead animal, like something a dog might dig up.

None of the bones were very big; the largest was only about six inches long and about an inch wide. She picked that bone up and looked at it, holding it up to the light for a better view. It looked like a rib bone, like the kind her dad left on his plate after eating at Jack's Bar-Be-Que.

The other three bones didn't look like any bones Krissy had ever seen before. They looked like big knuckles. She thought they might be back bones, but she wasn't sure. Science and biology were not her best subjects in school. She thought back bones had a different name, but she couldn't remember it.

"Vertebras," she said, suddenly remembering the word. That was the word. That's what they called back bones. Three of the four bones that lay on the bed before her were vertebras. Back bones. The other was a rib bone of some kind.

"They don't look magical," she said, setting down the rib bone and picking up one of the vertebras. She held the bone in her left hand and wrapped her fingers around it. The vertebra didn't feel warm; it didn't vibrate in her hand, or tingle.

"I wish I had a strawberry milk shake," Krissy said aloud, closing her eyes. "A thick strawberry milk shake, with whipped cream and a cherry on top." She opened her eyes and looked around, but there was no strawberry milk shake to be seen. In her storybooks, if you made a wish with a magical object, those wishes always came true. But maybe the bones were a different kind of magic.

"Big deal," she said, turning the vertebra over in the palm of her hand. What good were magical bones if you couldn't use them to wish for things you wanted? Some gift. "These aren't special."

But they are special, little one. Very ssspecial.

The voice startled her, nearly causing her to jump up off the bed.

"You're here? In my room?" She looked around. "Where? I don't see you."

Yes. I'm here, Krissy. The bones are ssspecial. As long as you have them I can visit you.

"But where are you? I can't see you."

I am here. There. Everywhere.

Krissy pouted. "No one can be everywhere."

I can.

The little girl still wasn't convinced. "I want to see you."

Very well, the voice said. *You can see me. Look to the window, little one. What do you see?*

Excited, Krissy turned to look at the window. But there was nothing to be seen. "I don't see anything."

Look closer, Krisssy. I am there.

She stood up and crossed the room, stopping in front of the window. "I still don't see anything. It's too dark outside."

There. You do see me. I am the darkness that touches the glass of your window. I am the night that waits in the forest, beyond the campfires of men.

She was disappointed. "All I see is the night. I don't see you. You said that I would get to see you, but you lied."

I did not lie, little one.

"Then when will I get to see you?"

Soon. Very soon. But first you have to help me.

"Help you do what?"

I need you to find more bones, only then will you be able to see me. Only when all the bones are gathered will I be able to be seen.

"Why do you need my help?"

Because you are the only one who can hear me, little one. That is because you are ssspecial. You are a special little girl. That is why I am your special friend. A special friend for a ssspecial little girl.

Krissy thought it over, then asked, "How many bones do I have to find?"

There are many left to be found. But you can do it. You are ssspecial.

Krissy shook her head. "I can't. My parents will be

mad if I sneak off without telling them. I have to ask their permission."

Noooooo. . . . hissed the voice. *You must tell no one. This is our secret.*

"I can't go," Krissy said, still shaking her head. "I'll get into trouble."

Do not disappoint me, little one. Do not be like the others.

"Others?"

Yessss. Others. Boys and girls your age. I asked for their help and they refused me. Refused to help their ssspecial friend.

The voice she heard inside her head had changed. It was no longer warm and fluid. Instead it was as cold as ice, and as sharp as the blade of a knife. It entered her head and grated across her mind, sending shivers down her back.

Krissy swallowed hard, suddenly afraid. "What happened to the others?"

Bad things. Terrible things. Things you do not want to think about. They made me mad and bad things happened to them. You do not want bad things to happen to you. You do not want to make me mad. Do you?

The little girl shook her head, wishing the voice would go away and leave her alone. She was suddenly thinking that maybe having a special friend was not so nice after all.

Good. Then you will help me?

Krissy nodded.

Good. Very good. I will guide you, Krissy. I will show you where to find the rest of the bones. But you must tell no one about what you have found. You must not let anyone follow you. It must be a secret. A ssspecial secret between ssspecial friends. Once you find the rest of the bones I will let you see me. Would you like that, Krissy?

"I guess so," Krissy muttered.

Good. We can play then, little one. Play games if you like. We can sing, and you can read me one of your stories.

"Which story?" Krissy asked, suddenly interested.

Any story you like, the voice replied. *But do not fail me, little one. Bad things happen to those who fail. Look to the window, Krissy, and see what will happen if you fail.*

Krissy lifted her head and looked at the window that was only inches from her face. As she looked out the window, a large brown palmetto bug crawled across the glass. Another palmetto bug followed. And then another.

Krissy stepped back as palmetto bugs started scurrying across the window. Not just one or two bugs, but dozens of them. Maybe even hundreds. Thousands. In a matter of only a few seconds the window's glass surface was completely covered with the oversized cockroaches.

As Krissy stared in horror at the bugs, the voice inside her head again spoke. *Look what I can do, little one. See the power that I have. Do not fail me, Krisssy. Do not disobey. For if you fail me, I will open your window and let the bugs in.*

The voice in her head slowly faded, leaving behind an icy numbness that caused the skin at her temples to pull tight. As the voice left, the palmetto bugs disappeared back into the darkness surrounding the cabin. The window was again empty, and a very frightened little girl found herself staring into the night.

"I won't disappoint you," Krissy said, her voice small with fear. "I promise I won't."

Chapter Nine

Krissy slept little that night, and when she did sleep her dreams were filled with visions of cockroaches, millions of them, crawling over the windows of her room, scurrying over her bed and over her body. Twice she awoke from her dreams to swat at imaginary bugs, and each time her eyes were drawn to the window. Beyond the glass was the night, and somewhere in that darkness was her special friend, Mansa. A friend she could not see, who spoke only in her head, and who would summon cockroaches if she did not do what he asked.

But Krissy was afraid, worried that she would get into trouble with her parents if she sneaked off to the lagoon to look for more bones. It was her vacation, and she didn't want to spend it sitting inside the cabin. And if her parents got really mad, they might not take her to Walt Disney World.

On the other hand, she didn't want to upset her special friend either. None of her friends back home had special friends, so that made Mansa's friendship even more important. Krissy wanted to be a good friend. She didn't want her special friend mad at her. She had seen what he could do if he got mad, and that had scared her. Scared her really bad.

The sun came early that morning, filtering softly through the branches of the trees that surrounded the rented cabin. But the sun's light did little to warm Krissy's heart. She felt cold on the inside, alone, frightened of getting into trouble with her parents, but more afraid of making her new friend mad at her. So, as the blackness of the night began to be pushed back by the first light of morning, Krissy climbed out of her bed and quickly dressed.

Tiptoeing quietly across the room, she opened the door and looked out into the cabin's tiny sitting room. The room was empty, which meant her parents were not awake yet. That was good. They were probably sleeping late this morning, especially since they had not made any plans to go fishing or canoeing. This was their vacation too, so maybe they just wanted to take it easy today.

Gently closing the door and locking it, she grabbed her backpack from under the bed and placed the four magical bones inside it. She then crossed the room to the window. There were no palmetto bugs on the glass this morning, no insects of any kind. The voice she heard was also silent, at least for the moment.

Krissy unlocked the window and slowly slid it open. The window squeaked slightly, but not loud enough to be heard by her parents. Her mother and father were both sound sleepers, especially if they had been drinking the night before. She unhooked the screen and pushed it outward, allowing it to fall to the ground.

She climbed out the window and lowered herself to the ground. Once outside, she closed the window and set the screen back in place. The window now looked exactly as it had only moments before, so no one would be suspicious that something was amiss. Not that anything was wrong. Not really. Krissy was just going to do a favor for a friend. She just wasn't telling her parents.

From the cabin, she made her way through the camp to the back side of the bait and tackle shop. Krissy had seen several shovels leaning against the back wall of the shop the day before. They were probably used by local fishermen to dig worms. She didn't think anyone would get mad if she borrowed one of the shovels. At least she hoped they wouldn't get mad.

There were still two shovels leaning against the wall. There was also a folding army-shovel that was small and lightweight. Since Krissy was also small and lightweight, she chose the folding army-shovel to take with her into the woods.

With shovel in hand, she hurried across the footbridge that crossed the Wekiva River at the beginning of the nature trail. It was still early, so there weren't very many people up and about. She only saw two men, and they were busy putting a cooler and supplies into a flat-bottomed fishing boat. Neither of them noticed her as she crossed the bridge and disappeared into the forest.

She hurried along the elevated boardwalk that led deeper into the forest, paying little attention to the nature that surrounded her. Ordinarily, Krissy would have slowed her pace to check out the birds and animals that were so active in the morning, but she just didn't have time to admire the wildlife. She needed to help her special friend and still get back to the cabin before she was missed. She didn't have much time, so she couldn't afford to do any sightseeing.

Reaching the part of the nature trail that was scarred by fire, she climbed down off the boardwalk and continued onward. The grass and foliage were still wet with morning dew, so Krissy was completely soaked by the time she reached the lagoon.

Emerging from the forest, she stopped to look at the lagoon. A layer of gray mist covered the water, making the pool look even spookier than it had the first time she saw it. The staff with the skull mounted on it still stood by the water's edge, but it now leaned slightly to the right and appeared in danger of falling over. Perhaps the wind had blown it off balance, or maybe the ground was just too soft to support its weight.

Krissy didn't care about the staff and wasn't worried if it fell over or not. Turning away from the beaded staff, she let her gaze wander over the tree line that surrounded the lagoon, looking for her friend. But Mansa was no where to be seen. He remained nothing more than a voice, someone that could be heard but not seen.

"Are you here?" Krissy asked aloud. She waited for an answer, but all was silent. She wondered if her special friend was even around and knew she would be mad if he wasn't. Maybe he was still sleeping. She had gone to a lot of trouble sneaking out of the cabin, so he had better be waiting for her.

"Mansa, are you here?" she asked louder, worried that she had made a trip for nothing.

Suddenly there was a feeling of movement behind her. She couldn't see anything, but it felt as if someone had just stepped past her. She turned and looked, but there was no one there. Only the wind that whispered through the treetops, stirring the leaves and grasses at her feet. A cold wind that spoke of ancient ice fields and deep dark places. A wind that brought a shiver to the little girl, making her arms break out into goose bumps. With the wind came the voice of someone who claimed to be a special friend.

Krisssy, my dear, dear child. You have come to help me. You did not disappoint me like the others. Good. Very good.

Something moved by her feet, touched her ankle and caused her to jump back. She thought it was a snake, but she looked down and saw that it was just a vine. Krissy could have sworn that the vine reached out and touched her, but it must have been just her imagination.

"I told you I would come," she said, hoping to catch a glimpse of her friend. But there was no one to be seen. He remained as invisible as the wind. "Where are you?"

I am here.

"Where? I still can't see you. You said that I would be able to see you."

Soon you shall see me, little one. But not now.

"When?"

Later. But first you must help me, the voice whispered in her ear. *You must find more magical gifts.*

"More bones?" Krissy asked.

Yesss . . . more bones. They are magic. Strong magic. Strong enough to bring me back into your world.

"Then can I see you?" Krissy wanted to know.

Yesss. . . .

"Then can we play together?"

Yesss. . . .

"And read stories?"

Yesss . . . anything you like.

"Good." Krissy smiled. "But we won't play hide-and-seek. That wouldn't be fair, because you can hide anywhere and I still couldn't see you.

"I brought a shovel, in case we have to dig, but I can't be gone long. My parents will be mad if they know I sneaked out."

Not long. Not this time.

"Okay." She set the shovel down and took a seat on the ground, taking off her socks and shoes. Standing back up, she picked up the shovel and started walking slowly toward the lagoon. "Are the other bones in the same place?"

Yesss . . . the same place.

Guided by the voice inside her head, Krissy waded across the lagoon to the little island in its center. There, among the twisted roots of an ancient cypress tree, she dug in the soft mud looking for more bones. Magical items that would allow the little girl to see her special friend.

She found the first bone right away, and then another shortly after that. They both looked to be rib bones, but she couldn't really be sure. Bones were bones as far as Krissy was concerned; they all looked pretty much the same. She wondered what kind of bones they were, but only for a moment. It didn't really matter what kind of bones they were. The important thing was that she was making her special friend very happy.

Good. Very good, the voice whispered deep inside

of her head, pleased with her results. *Now look over there. To your left. Beneath the water. Not far from the shore. Not deep. Dig in the mud with your hands. Yessss. . . .*

Krissy waded a few feet from the shore and reached beneath the water, sticking her hands in the soft mud. At first she didn't feel anything, but guided by the voice of her special friend she soon found a bone bigger than all the others. Slipping her fingers beneath the bone, she tugged and tugged until it came loose.

Very good, little one.

She lifted the bone above the water and looked at it. The bone was long and round, with a knob on each end of it. It looked like a leg bone of some kind, but again she couldn't be sure.

Carrying the leg bone back to the island, she set it on the pile of bones she had already collected. It wasn't a large pile, but there were too many bones to fit into her tiny backpack.

Krissy was suddenly worried. Mansa had told her the bones were magical and she needed to keep them a secret, but there were too many bones to hide in her backpack, probably too many to hide in her dresser. Her parents would find them, and then she would be in trouble. They would be mad at her for having the bones, and Mansa would be mad that she had revealed the secret.

"I can't take these with me," Krissy said, looking around. "There are too many of them. I won't be able to hide them. My parents will find them."

You do not have to take them with you, Krisssy. We will hide them here, hide them where they will be safe from animals and people. No one will find them. No one will be able to scatter them again.

"You're not mad?"

No. Not mad. You have worked hard. We have enough bones for now. Enough magic for what I need.

"Then I'll be able to see you?" asked Krissy.

Yesss . . .

"Oh, goodie!"

Mansa instructed her to carry the bones across the lagoon, to hide them in the hollowed log of a fallen oak tree. Carefully placing the bones inside the tree, she opened her backpack and added the four bones she had found the previous day.

There were twenty-two bones all together. Some were fairly large, others were smaller than her little finger. Carefully placing all the bones inside the hollow log, Krissy covered them with handfuls of dried leaves and grasses to keep them hidden from sight.

"There. All done," Krissy said, pleased with her effort. "Now can I see you?"

Not now, but soon. Tonight, when the moon is full. Tonight you will be able to see me, little one. Tonight, when the moon is high in the sky, I will show myself. But I will only show myself to you. Come alone, and tell no one that you're coming.

"I won't tell anyone."

Good. Come back here tonight and I will show you magic, things you have only dreamed of. Strange things. Wonderful things. Now go, before you are missed.

Krissy smiled and nodded. Grabbing her shovel and backpack, she hurried off through the forest to the camp. It was still early, so she felt safe that her parents were still sleeping. Maybe she would go back to bed too, but she knew that she wouldn't be able to sleep. Krissy was far too excited, for soon she would be able to see her special friend. She had only to wait for the night.

Patch, the dog, liked many things. He liked sleeping in the shade of an oak tree on a hot, lazy summer afternoon. He liked sitting by the restaurant's front door, begging for handouts from the customers. He even liked barking at the fish that the fishermen caught, all shiny and rough, flipping around on the ground like smelly play toys. The fish were funny, and Patch enjoyed barking at them.

Patch also liked the little girl named Krissy. The girl played with him, and scratched him behind the ears, in the place that always itched and was impossible to reach. She also gave him food, tiny morsels of meat and fish that she carried out of the restaurant concealed in a white paper napkin. The food was good, but there never seemed to be enough of it. Just a bite or two, quickly swallowed, and then it was gone. Gone in one bite and then nothing more than a memory, a tiny taste left on the tip of his tongue. Just a memory. Never enough.

Sometimes Krissy gave him candy. Sticky sweet candy that stuck to his teeth and fur. Strawberry candy. Licorice. Even the forbidden taste of chocolate. Jelly beans were his favorite, and he would do tricks to get them: sit pretty, roll over, even play dead. The tricks always worked. Silly tricks that made people laugh at him, made them give him candy.

Patch liked Krissy, but he did not like the bad smell that now clung to her. Bad smell that belonged to the bad thing in the forest, the thing that lived in the water. Bad thing that could not be seen, only smelled. The thing beneath the water that waited, and watched. Bad smell. Bad thing. Dangerous.

Krissy was not bad. She was good. She gave him candy, called him "good doggie," and scratched the place that always itched. She was a very nice little girl, but the bad smell was now on her. The others couldn't smell it, but Patch could. It was there, clinging to her skin, the smell of the bad thing in the forest. The smell of evil, and death.

He liked Krissy, but he did not like the bad thing. Nor did he want her to get hurt; therefore, he decided to follow the little girl into the forest to protect her. He didn't follow too close. No. Not close. She didn't even see him as he followed her along the boardwalk, staying back so he could see but not be seen, keeping to the shadows that still lingered beneath the trees.

Patch wanted to scare away the bad thing, scare it from the girl so she would be safe, but he didn't know if the bad thing could be scared. How could you scare something you could smell but not see? The bad thing was old, very old; it had been around a long time. Long before Patch. It would not be easy to scare something that had been around for a long time, something that could be smelled and not seen.

Patch hung back as he followed the little girl along the nature trail, taking care not to be seen. In his younger days he had been a good hunter, so he knew how to move quietly through the forest. He knew how to sneak up on rabbits and squirrels, so he had no problem sneaking behind a little girl, especially a little girl that never looked behind her as she hurried along the trail.

Patch didn't want the little girl to get hurt, so he decided to go into the forest to scare away the bad thing. Scare away the bad thing and the girl would be safe.

As he neared the lagoon the forest grew quiet. All the birds and squirrels had left this part of the forest a long time ago. Patch liked to chase squirrels, but there weren't any to chase. The bad thing had scared the squirrels away. Maybe they would come back when the bad thing went away. But Patch was afraid that the bad thing was not going to leave. The little girl was helping the bad thing, making it stronger. Patch bared his teeth as he thought of the thing with the bad smell. He wanted to bite it, but he couldn't see it. Can't bite something you cannot see.

The dog slowed his pace as Krissy reached the section of boardwalk that had been burned by fire. He hoped the girl would turn around and go back to camp, but she climbed down off the boardwalk and continued onward. Patch felt a shiver of fear pass through his body. The land beyond the burned area belonged to the bad thing. It was his home, a place of strange silence where roots moved and the trees danced at night.

Being careful where he stepped, Patch climbed down off the boardwalk and continued to follow the little girl. Already he could smell the lagoon, the odor of its brackish water carried on the morning wind. He was still about a hundred yards from the lagoon when he spotted a dead toad not too far from the trail. Curious, he left the trail to investigate.

The toad was stiff and old and had the smell of the bad thing on it. Bad smell. A very bad smell. The dog raised his head and looked around, a nervous growl forming in the back of his throat. The toad smelled of the bad thing, so did the ground it lay upon. So did the trees, and the bushes, and the air.

Everything smelled of the bad thing. The smell was strong, overpowering, much stronger than ever before. The bad thing's smell should be only at the lagoon, but now it seemed to be everywhere. The bad thing was growing larger, stronger. The little girl was helping it get stronger, helping it to reach out into the forest.

Patch looked for Krissy, but the little girl could no longer be seen. She had walked up the trail that led to the lagoon. He started to race after her, no longer concerned with following her unseen. The bad thing was stronger now, dangerous, and he had to get the girl back to the safety of camp, even if he had to drag her back. She didn't know the bad thing the way he did, did not understand the danger she was in. But Patch knew the bad thing; he understood the danger.

He started to race after the girl, but he had only taken a few steps when the ground around him started to ripple. Patch stopped dead in his tracks as he saw the ground moving. He tried to back up, tried to turn around and run away, but he wasn't fast enough. He might have been faster when he was younger, but not now.

The ground beneath the dog's feet continued to roll and ripple, as if some great snake moved below its surface. Suddenly a cloud of dirt exploded into the air as a tree root shot out of the ground. Patch tried to jump out of the way, but the root grabbed him by the front leg and held tight.

Patch growled and snarled as he fought to get free from the root's grasp. He twisted his body and bit at the root, but his teeth had little effect on it.

A second root shot out of the ground and encircled the dog's chest and stomach. Patch was in a frenzy now, fighting to get free, but the roots tightened around him like a pair of boa constrictors. They were nothing more than the roots of a nearby oak tree, but these roots were alive and moved. And they were very deadly.

There was a sharp pop as the dog's spine was snapped in two. Patch would have howled in pain, but his chest was being crushed and he could not draw a breath to cry out. He couldn't even whimper. More pops sounded as the tiny bones in his neck were crushed, his neck being squeezed so tight that his eye bulged out of his head.

Patch the one-eyed dog gave a final sigh and slumped to the ground, his body going limp. He had failed to protect the little girl from the bad thing, had failed to protect himself. As he slowly died, his last thoughts were of chasing squirrels, barking at silvery fish, and the sweet taste of jelly beans.

Chapter Ten

Jimmy Cypress didn't own a television, or a radio. He had no need for such things. His entertainment was provided by the wildlife that lived in the forest surrounding his tiny, one-room cabin. The squirrels and birds, even the alligators, were his entertainment, providing hours of simple pleasures with their rituals and antics. On those days when the animals weren't up to performing, he would pass the time reading one of the many books that he borrowed from the public library.

He enjoyed nonfiction books mostly, texts on history, philosophy, or social studies. He had traveled around the world many times through the books he read, marveling at the cultures of other countries. In opposition to what the army had tried to teach him, he had learned that people in foreign lands weren't much different than those he encountered closer to home. A man was a man, with the same dreams, hopes, and desires of all men.

Most men wanted nothing more than to be left alone by others, lead a simple life, and be able to provide for their wives and families. They did not want to be involved in politics, did not desire to be filthy rich, and had absolutely no craving to go to war against someone else. People in other countries were not the enemy. They were just different, that's all, and that difference made them all the more interesting.

Along with the nonfiction books, he also had a passion for the works of dead poets. There was something about a well-written poem that brought great happiness to his heart. Like a song without music, a good poem would stick in his mind all day; he carried it with him as he made his daily treks through the forest.

His favorite poems were sonnets about sunsets, mountains, and endless oceans dotted with undiscovered island paradises. Or poems about love. Verses written by a man that spoke of a woman's flawless beauty: long flowing hair the color of ripened wheat, eyes as blue as a deep spring pool, and a smile that hinted at whispered secrets on a warm summer's night.

Jimmy had written such poems when he was in love, mailing them off to a woman on the opposite side of the world. He had spoken of his devotion to her, how he would lay the mountains at her feet and string the stars on a silvery chain for her to wear around her neck. But the love he spoke of had not been true love after all, for the woman he desired had not waited for him to return home from the war. She had given her heart to another, a rich young man who never served his country, while Jimmy had slept cold and alone in the trenches atop a nameless mountain in Vietnam.

He never fell in love again after that, and never, ever wrote another poem. The wound in his heart hurt far more than any he had ever received in combat. But that didn't stop him from reading poetry. He still enjoyed the verse of others, but he could no longer write of love himself.

It was almost sundown, so Jimmy Cypress decided to put away his borrowed books and take a walk through the forest. Most of the hikers and fishermen would have already gone home, so he would not be disturbed. He always laughed at how quickly the whites left the forest when darkness approached, but sunset was the best time for being in the woods. It was the quietest part of the day, a time when a man could be alone with his thoughts. It was a time when the animals of the day surrendered their hunting grounds to their brothers of the night. A time when a crack between two very different worlds opened and the spirits came through.

He was a firm believer in spirits, both good and evil, which was one of the reasons he had started down the medicine path. He had been summoned from South Dakota by a spirit. Had he not been a believer, he might have dismissed what he saw as nothing more than a dream brought on by bad food, or a hallucination left over from all the marijuana he had smoked in Southeast Asia.

Pulling the cabin door shut behind him, he started through the forest on a path rarely used by anyone but him. The path connected to the wilderness trail at a place where the boardwalk had been burned by fire.

No one knew that it was Jimmy who had set fire to the boardwalk. He had burned it in an effort to keep people away from the lagoon. They did not know about the evil that lurked within the black waters, but he did. Jimmy burned the boardwalk shortly after a small girl had been lost in the forest. Lost and never found.

Though he had no way of knowing for sure, Jimmy suspected the girl's body, or what was left of it, could be found at the bottom of the lagoon. Those suspicions he kept to himself, however, for fear of being blamed for the girl's disappearance.

Crossing the wilderness trail just south of the burned section, he turned and made his way toward the lagoon. He wanted to make sure that his staff was still in place, especially after his run-in with the white tourist. The man had moved the staff once, and he might do so again. Maybe he was looking for a genuine souvenir to take back home from Florida. If Jimmy found that his staff had been moved again, he would give the tourist a souvenir he would never forget: a swift kick in the ass from a pissed-off Seminole. Now, wouldn't that be something to tell the folks back home?

He had just turned toward the lagoon when he spotted the dead dog lying a few feet off the trail. Jimmy recognized the dog, for it was the one-eyed Labrador that belonged to the owners of the fish camp.

"Damn," he said, stopping to look at the dog. "How did this happen?"

Jimmy had made friends with the dog years ago, and would often give him scraps of food when he came around the cabin. The dog was the friendly type, more lovable than fierce, and Jimmy wondered what had killed him.

Kneeling down beside the dog, he ran his hand over the lifeless body. At first he suspected the dog had died of sickness, or snakebite, or maybe a hunter had accidentally shot him, but a quick examination revealed that the dog's neck had been broken and his spine crushed. A piece of root was lodged in the dog's mouth, yet no roots grew across that section of trail.

"Damn. Damn. Damn."

Jimmy knew from what he saw that the evil was growing stronger. He had seen such things before. Rabbits found dead in the forest for no apparent reason. Birds crushed by vines that seemed to have a life of their own. But never a dog before. Never an animal so large. And never a person.

But it was only the other day that he had found the white tourist sleeping by the lagoon, kudzu vines wrapped tightly around his legs. Jimmy wondered what would have happened had he not come along when he did. Would the vines have climbed the man's legs to encircle his neck? Had the evil that infested the lagoon, and the forest surrounding it—the evil that was Mansa Du Paul—grown strong enough to take a man's life? Was the spirit of the voodoo sorcerer returning to this land in force, seeking its revenge on any and all that crossed its path?

The land was haunted, cursed, but up until now Jimmy had been able to keep the evil in check. For over twenty years he had lived in the forest where the slave village of Blackwater once stood, a Seminole medicine man standing guard against the evil trapped at the bottom of the lagoon.

During those twenty years he had fought the evil many times, and each time he had won. But Jimmy Cypress was growing older, while the evil of Mansa Du Paul was eternal. The Indian knew in his heart that he would soon have to battle that evil again, all signs pointed to it, but this time he wasn't sure who would win.

Saying a silent prayer for the Labrador named Patch, he picked up the dog's lifeless body and slowly carried it away to be buried.

Chapter Eleven

A full moon rose slowly above the treetops, casting a silvery glow over the forest and river. The moon's glow did little, however, to lighten the feeling of dread that had settled deep in the heart of Jimmy Cypress. The guardian could feel the evil of Mansa Du Paul growing stronger, could almost see the blackness rising out of the lagoon.

The lifeless dog he had found earlier in the evening was proof that the evil was gaining strength. The dog had been strangled, its bones broken and crushed, apparently by roots that moved under their own power. The evil was in the lagoon, in the ground, and even in the roots.

Yes, the blackness was growing stronger, but there was nothing he could do about it. Not yet anyway. He could only wait, and pray.

The wind rustled the fronds of the palm tree just outside Krissy's bedroom window. The fronds made a dry, whispering sound as they moved in the breeze, bringing to mind images of skeletons and dried bones.

She lay on her bed, facing the window, staring out at the moonlit night. Somewhere in the darkness waited her special friend, Mansa. He was part of the darkness, invisible as the wind that stirred the palm tree.

Krissy turned to look at the travel alarm clock sitting on the floor beside her bed. It was 8:25 P.M. Back home she would have been watching television with her parents, or reading a book, maybe even coloring. But she had no desire to do such things here. Not now. Not when there were more important things to be done, more important things to be seen. Tonight she was going to see her special friend. Tonight she was finally going to put a face with the voice she heard.

Krissy frowned. What if Mansa was ugly? What if he was fat and dumpy looking, like the man that dipped ice cream at the Baskin-Robbins near her house? What if Mansa looked like that man? Would she be disappointed if her special friend was not tall and handsome, like the kings and knights in her storybooks? Would she turn away if he didn't have long flowing hair and shiny armor, or if he didn't ride a tall white horse like the heroes in the fantasy stories she read? What if he looked more like the Cat in the Hat than a knight?

Krissy almost giggled, imagining Mansa to be the Cat in the Hat. Or maybe he would appear before her and offer green eggs and ham, like Sam I Am. Krissy laughed aloud, thinking of what she might say if someone suddenly offered her green eggs and ham. Would she eat them in a box? Would she eat them with a fox?

The sound of footsteps approaching her door silenced her laughter. Her heart began to pound as the doorknob turned and the door opened.

"What's this? Ready for bed so soon?" Janet Patterson opened the door and stepped into the room, surprised to find her daughter dressed and ready for bed. For once there was no contest of wit to stall for a few extra minutes, no pleas to stay up a little longer, no arguments about brushing teeth or washing dirty hands. She wondered if Krissy was coming down with something, the flu perhaps, but her forehead felt cool to the touch.

"Aren't you feeling good?" Janet asked, stepping back from the bed.

"I'm feeling okay." Krissy smiled, reassuring her mother that she wasn't sick. "I'm just a little tired. That's all. And I don't want to be sleepy for the fishing trip tomorrow. Daddy said he was going to catch the biggest fish, but I'm going to beat him. My fish will be the biggest. Just you wait and see."

Janet smiled, relieved that her daughter's desire to go to bed early was because of fishing, and not the results of a virus. Tucking Krissy into bed, Janet gave her a kiss on the cheek and left the room, closing the door behind her.

Krissy listened to her mother's footsteps as they faded away, and then sat up in bed. She didn't dare lie down, afraid of falling asleep. Her special friend had promised that tonight she would get to see him.

She waited for over three hours, sitting there on her bed and forcing herself to stay awake. Adding, subtracting, doing multiplication tables in her head, spelling all the words she could think of to spell, anything she could do to keep from falling asleep. Not that she was sleepy. Not really. She was much too excited to sleep.

She was also a little afraid, scared of what would happen to her if her parents caught her sneaking out. Scared too of the darkness and what might wait for her in the night. The forest was filled with animals, snakes, and creepy bugs. But she was willing to conquer her fears and face such dangers in order to see her special friend.

She waited until it was almost midnight, certain that her parents would be asleep, before taking off her pajamas and slipping into a pair of blue jeans, a sweatshirt, and sneakers. Opening her window slowly, Krissy pushed out the screen and climbed out of the bedroom.

A full moon hung bright in the sky, but the night still seemed awfully dark to the ten-year-old. Shadows appeared to reach out for her, threatening to grab her with skeleton fingers. Circling the cabin, she hurried toward the nature trail.

The fish camp was dark and quiet and appeared deserted, except for a couple of vehicles parked in the parking lot. Two pickup trucks were also parked in front of the lounge. She could hear country music coming from the Blackwater Lounge, carried faintly upon the night wind like ghostly melodies.

Krissy paused to listen to the music, a chill suddenly dancing down her spine. She was completely alone, away from her parents, the two people who could protect her from any and all dangers. She was nothing but a little girl who was about to enter a very big forest by herself, a forest that might be infested with dangerous animals and snakes. Maybe even ghosts.

She looked around, nervous. She didn't know if she believed in ghosts or not. Ghosts were fun to think about in the daytime, but not at night. She loved to watch Scooby Doo and his friends hunt for ghosts in old haunted houses on the cartoon show, but the show came on in the afternoon, so there wasn't anything scary about it. And she liked to draw ghosts in school for Halloween. Once she had even dressed up as a ghost for a masquerade party.

That was all fun. Ghostly fun. Nothing spooky about it. But now, as she stood there listening to the haunted sound of country music drifting out of the lounge, she couldn't help thinking about ghosts. Real ghosts. And if ever there was a place to find real ghosts, then it was the forest she was about to enter.

The clumps of Spanish moss that hung from the oak trees shone a pale gray in the moonlight, looking like unearthly spirits as they moved gently in the breeze. She knew it was nothing but Spanish moss, and the worst thing she had to fear was a bad case of red bugs should she happen to handle it, but it still looked rather spooky in the darkness.

Convincing herself that there was absolutely nothing to be afraid of, Krissy put on her bravest face and turned away from the lounge. Reaching the bridge that crossed the Wekiva River, she looked behind her to make sure no one was following, then crossed the bridge and started down the nature trail.

Luckily, the moon was bright enough for her to see where she was going. The boardwalk glowed a pale silver in the moonlight, as did many of the trees surrounding it. Her footfalls echoed off the wooden boards as she hurried along the boardwalk, blending in with the nocturnal sounds of crickets and tree frogs.

She reached the section of boardwalk that was burned and closed to the public. Climbing down off the boardwalk, she continued onward following the narrow path that wound between trees and brush. As she hurried along, footfalls now muffled by layers of dead vegetation on the forest floor, she noticed movement around her. Vines slithered over the ground like snakes, touching her ankles as she passed, caressing her legs. At first she thought it was just her imagination, but the closer she got to the lagoon the more the forest seemed to be alive. Alive and reaching out to touch her as she passed.

In places where palmetto bushes grew thick, the sharp leaves of the foliage seemed to move out of the way to allow safe passage, quickly closing in behind her once she passed.

She finally reached the lagoon. Emerging from the forest, she stood mesmerized by the brightness of the moon's glow off of the water. It wasn't just the lagoon that seemed to glow: the ground, the trees, even the smallest of bushes all seemed to shine with a radiance that hurt her eyes to look upon.

"Are you here?" Krissy asked, looking around.

There was a rustling in the branches above her, a sudden gust of wind in a place where the wind rarely visited. The crickets and frogs grew quiet. The sudden silence startled Krissy, made her afraid. She heard the voice of her special friend, but it was no longer warm and soft. It was icy cold. The voice caused the skin at her temples to pull tight.

I am here, Krisssy. In the water. Come closer. Closer.

Krissy didn't move. She was suddenly afraid, terrified to get any closer to the strange glowing lagoon. The spell of excitement that had been cast over her earlier was gone now. All that remained was a nervous feeling that something very bad was about to happen.

The voice lured her closer to the water's edge. *You do want to see me, don't you?*

Krissy nodded.

Then come closer. Closer. . . .

If Krissy had been a little older, she might have questioned her present situation, might have realized the danger she was in. But she was only a child. Innocent. The evil one knew this. That was why he chose her.

In the center of the lagoon, the calmness of the water was suddenly broken by a patch of bubbles rising to the surface. Tiny bubbles of oxygen once trapped in the black mud at the bottom of the lagoon and now released as something pulled itself out of that mud. More bubbles appeared; the surface of the water began to ripple and roll. A stench of decay traveled across the lagoon. The wind blew stronger. Branches of trees began to sway.

"I can't see you," Krissy said.

That is because I am still on the other side.

"Other side?"

The spirit world. The place all people go when they die.

"Are you dead?" Krissy asked, a little frightened.

No. I am only a visitor to this world. But someone has played a trick on me. They have taken my body, scattered my bones so I cannot cross back to the land of the living. That is why I need your help, Krisssy. I need you to help me cross back over. I need your body.

The ground under her feet began to tremble, as though a million bugs crawled beneath its surface. Terrified, Krissy stepped back and turned to run. She had just turned when the ground seemed to explode as something broke free of the earth.

Krissy screamed and staggered back as a gnarled tree root, black and twisted with disease, shot out of the ground and wrapped itself around her left leg. She tried to free herself, but the root climbed higher and encircled her waist.

She screamed again as a kudzu vine, thin and leafy, climbed up her back and wrapped around her neck. She tried to call for help, but the vine filled her mouth with its scratchy leaves. Krissy coughed and struggled to draw a breath.

Another vine grabbed her. And another. They dragged her toward the lagoon. Krissy tried to resist, fighting to stay on her feet, but slipped and fell, sliding down the bank. As she was pulled into the water, the voice of her special friend again entered her head.

I promised you would see me, Krisssy. I did not lie. Behold, you have your wish.

The surface of the lagoon rolled and boiled. Krissy watched in horror as something slowly rose out of the water in front of her. It was a towering, manlike creature made from the black mud and muck that lined the bottom of the lagoon. In the face of this foul abomination glowed two red eyes . . . eyes that watched with interest as the kudzu vine slowly choked the girl into unconsciousness. As blackness descended over Krissy something entered her body and seized her thoughts. Something evil and unclean with a voice that was smooth as honey.

Chapter Twelve

The surface of the lagoon was again calm as the little girl pulled herself out of the water. Gone were the ripples and bubbles so visible only moments before. Gone too was the creature of mud which had arisen from beneath the water. Even the wind had died down to nothing more than a gentle breeze. Everything was calm and eerily quiet.

The girl got to her knees and shook her head, as if she was trying to shake the water from her ears. She took several deep breaths, forcing air deep inside oxygen-starved lungs.

She leaned back and looked around. Her eyes, once a soft brown, now had a strange bluish-green glow to them that had never existed before, a nocturnal shine similar to the eyes of the predators who hunted the forest at night.

The diseased root that had encircled her waist was gone, as was the scratchy kudzu vine that had grabbed her around the throat. She placed the fingertips of her right hand to her throat and pressed gently. The delicate skin beneath her fingers was already starting to darken with bruising.

She opened her mouth and tried to speak, but only

a hissing of air escaped her lips. She tried again and was successful.

Throwing her head back, the little girl looked up at the night sky and laughed. But the laugh that came from her was not the high-pitched giggle of a child. On the contrary, the voice was that of a man . . . a man who had been dead for over one hundred and fifty years.

Mansa Du Paul pushed himself off of his knees and stood up. He had done it. His spirit had crossed back over into the land of the living. His power was still strong, perhaps stronger than it had ever been before. He was a *Loa* now, a spirit from the other side that could return to earth and inhabit the bodies of the living. He was death itself, and he had returned.

He looked down, studying the body of the girl where his spirit now resided. He would have preferred taking over the body of someone bigger, but Krissy's body would have to do. The little girl was healthy, and what strength she had lacked his spirit would now provide.

She was also innocent and had offered little resistance to him. Krissy had fought back with her body, but not with her mind. She had not tried to block his spirit with her mind, had not resisted his invasion of her flesh. And because she had not resisted him mentally, Krissy Patterson still lived. The bodies of the other children he had tried to take over, those who had resisted, now lay rotting at the bottom of the lagoon, buried deep in the mud.

Krissy Patterson was now his host, and he would ride her like a wild horse. She would do his bidding, gathering the scattered bones of his former self from the black waters of the lagoon.

The little girl had already found some of his bones, twenty-two in all, mostly those that had washed up on the island over the years. The rest of his bones lay beneath the water, buried in layers of soft mud and decayed vegetation. Those bones would not be a problem to find, now that he had a physical form to serve him.

Once all of his bones had been gathered together, he would conduct a voodoo ceremony to get his old body back. Then he would be at full power once again. A blood sacrifice would be needed for the ceremony, but that was no problem. Once he had gathered the bones and invoked the ceremony, he would use the blood of the girl for that sacrifice. All of her blood. Then he would drink her soul and feed on her delicate flesh. It had been a long time since he last tasted the sweet flesh of a child. Much too long.

Mansa stood still, focusing his attention inward. It only took a moment to find Krissy's spirit, which still resided inside her body with him. He had not killed the girl, had not set her spirit free. Instead, he had pushed her spiritual being into a tiny corner where it could not interfere with his plans. Her spirit was now just a tiny flame flickering in the darkness, a flame he could extinguish anytime he felt like it. From that tiny flame a voice could be heard, a small, frightened voice of a child crying out in the darkness . . . crying out for help.

Mansa laughed and wet his lips, allowing his tongue to savor the taste of flesh that was now his. "I did not lie, little one. I did not lie. I told you that you would see me tonight, and here I am. Pity that we look exactly alike, you and me. But do not fret, little one. Do not scream. We will be spending much time together.

"And we will play many games, painful games that will make your spirit dance and hop about. Games that will take your soul to the brink of madness and beyond. I will show you what it is to be a slave, what it feels like to have the flesh stripped from your back, forced to grovel at the feet of others."

He reached down and touched himself between the legs, feeling soft flesh through tiny fingertips that were now his. "Maybe I will show you other games too, little one. Big people games. Games your mother and father never showed you. Games of the flesh. Maybe I will destroy this pretty little body of yours, tear and stretch your delicate little flesh until the blood flows like tiny rivers.

"Maybe I will do to you what the white slavers did to my mother. I will make you scream like they made her scream, teach you pain and humiliation, as I commit a thousand unforgiving sins upon your flesh. I will make you old, little one. And I will make you wise . . . wise in the ways of the flesh. When I am done playing, I will give your body back to you. I will allow your soul to return from the darkness so you may quiver in the pain of a thousand agonies as I slowly roast you over an open fire and feed upon your pretty little body, one piece at a time."

Mansa raised his fingertips to his nose and sniffed, smelling the faint odor of urine. The little girl had wet herself, probably when the kudzu vine choked her into unconsciousness. He smiled. "Naughty little girl. No more drinks for you.

"Yes, little one. We are going to play so many games together. Just you wait and see. But first we have work to do, for I do not plan to stay in your body forever. No. Not forever. Just for a little while."

Turning, he looked out over the lagoon. Somewhere beneath the dark waters were the remaining bones of his former self. Once he found the rest of his bones, and he knew he would, he would be able to bring to life his old body. A body that was tall and ebony and very strong. Once his body and soul were reunited, he would have his revenge on any and all that crossed his path. And there would be no one strong enough to stop him. No one.

Chapter Thirteen

It was a little after 1:00 A.M. when Janet Robertson awoke from a strange dream. She started to roll over and go back to sleep, but decided to check on her daughter. Krissy had gone to bed early, which wasn't at all like her, and Janet wanted to make sure she wasn't coming down with something.

Slipping out of bed, she crossed the room and opened the door. All of the lights were out in the sitting room, but there was enough moonlight streaming in through the window for her to navigate without tripping over something. The door to Krissy's bedroom was closed, but it wasn't locked. Opening the door slowly, Janet entered the room and approached the bed.

She was about to lay a hand on Krissy's forehead when she realized there was no child in the bed to touch. She looked around the room and spotted the open window.

"Krissy?" She hurried to the window. The screen had been removed and was now lying on the ground outside the cabin. Janet looked down at the screen, a sick feeling settling in the pit of her stomach.

"Krissy?" she called again, looking out the window

at the surrounding forest. A full moon hung bright in the sky, giving illumination to the area. Still, there was no sign of the girl.

Turning away from the window, Janet hurried out of the bedroom. She checked the bathroom, found it empty, then crossed the sitting room to the front door. She opened the door and ran outside, hurrying around to the side of the cabin where Krissy's bedroom was located. There was no sign of her daughter, or any clues to her whereabouts.

Janet was starting to panic now, her heart racing. She told herself to be calm, but nothing could stop the fear that was quickly coming over her. Her daughter was missing, the bedroom window open and the screen pushed out. That meant Krissy, for some unknown reason, had opened the window and sneaked out while they were sleeping. Or it could mean . . .

She stopped dead in her tracks, her eyes going wide. Or it could mean that someone had opened the window from the outside, entering the bedroom while Krissy was sleeping. That would mean someone, some fiend, had sneaked into the bedroom and taken their daughter.

"Dear God, no . . ." she whispered, terrified beyond words by the thought. Kidnapped. Her beautiful daughter had been kidnapped. "It can't be."

Why not? Why couldn't it be? Kidnappings happened all the time in America. Sex fiends and murderers snatched kids every day, many of them never getting caught. When they did get caught, they rarely spent much time behind bars for their crimes. Smoke a joint and you would get twenty years in prison. Kidnap and molest a little kid and you would get a slap on the hand and therapy.

And wasn't Florida a state full of weirdoes? Didn't all the nuts roll downhill to the sunshine state? Florida was just as bad as California: full of murderers, rapists, kidnappers, and fugitives on the run. She watched *America's Most Wanted*, and it seemed that half of the criminals the police were looking for had last been seen in Florida.

Just because they were on vacation didn't mean there weren't dangerous people around. Tourists were often the victims of crime in Florida, but few people knew that fact because it was rarely published. That would be bad for business.

What about the place they were staying? The fish camp looked peaceful enough, nestled away among the cypress and oak trees. But there was no security. None at all. Anybody could pull off the road into the camp, drive right up to one of the cabins. The boat ramp was also open to the general public, as was the restaurant, bait and tackle shop, and the lounge.

She turned in the direction of the lounge. This part of Florida was rural. Redneck. What kind of good old boys did the lounge cater to? Construction workers? Farmers? White trash? Members of the Ku Klux Klan? The kind of people who lived to get drunk and fight? The kind who carried rifles in their pickups, and pistols in their pants? The kind of perverts who could only get laid through force, and would think nothing of having their way with an innocent ten-year-old girl?

Had one of the bar's customers, or one of the local fishermen, seen Krissy earlier in the day and decided she might be just the thing for a little fun and games?

Had someone watched the Pattersons walk to their cabin this afternoon and then sneaked back at night to snatch a sleeping girl from her bed? When had they done it? Ten minutes ago? An hour? Two?

Had Krissy disappeared two hours ago? Had she been abducted? If so, she could be halfway to Miami by now. Miami. The gateway to Cuba and South America. That's where stolen cars ended up, in Miami, loaded on board ships for a slow trip to South America and places unknown. Was it also where missing kids ended up? Did they get sold into slavery and shipped off to some Spanish-speaking country? A little blonde girl might fetch a high price to a white slaver, especially a little girl as cute as Krissy.

Janet shook her head. "No. No. No. Don't think such thoughts. She has not been kidnapped. She's here, somewhere. You'll find her."

Pressing her fist against her stomach to push back the fear that was knotting her guts, Janet ran back inside the cabin. Racing into the bedroom, she grabbed Robert by the shoulder.

"Robert, wake up. Wake up." It only took two shakes to wake him. He opened his eyes and looked at her.

"What is it? What's wrong?" he asked, sitting up in bed.

"Krissy's gone," Janet replied, forcing the words out, barely able to speak.

He threw back the covers and jumped out of bed. "What do you mean, Krissy's gone? Gone where?"

"I don't know. Her window is open, and she's missing. I looked around outside, but I can't find her."

"She's not in the bathroom?"

"No. I already checked."

He hurried across the bedroom, still half asleep and staggering. Janet followed her husband out of the bedroom and into Krissy's room. Robert flipped on the light, and they both stared toward the open window.

Robert crossed the room and stuck his head out of the window. "Krissy!" There was no answer.

Turning, he went back into their bedroom. He slipped on his pants and shoes and then grabbed a pair of flashlights and headed for the front door. Slipping on her yellow robe and a pair of flip-flops, Janet hurried after her husband.

Knowing that every minute was critical, that Krissy could be lost, hurt, or something far worse, the Pattersons hurried outside to look for their daughter.

Robert circled around to the side of the cabin, as Janet had, to look at the open window leading to Krissy's bedroom. He shone the flashlights at the ground, but didn't see any footprints. The grass and vegetation grew thick beneath the window, so there probably weren't any prints to be seen. No prints, which meant no clues as to whether Krissy had climbed out of the room by herself, or if she had been taken by someone.

Circling the cabin once more, Janet and Robert hurried through the camp calling their daughter's name. They called loud enough that their voices echoed through the fish camp, causing lights to come on in some of the other cabins.

"Krissy!" Robert called, stopping to look around him. "Krissy, where are you?"

"Krissy!" Janet yelled, stopping beside her husband.

A light came on in the cabin closest to them. A door opened, and Mary Sanders stepped out onto the tiny porch. She wore a brown robe, which she held tight at her neck. "What's wrong? What's the matter?"

"Our daughter is missing," Janet answered, turning to face the woman.

"Missing?"

Janet nodded. "I went to check on her, and she's not in her bedroom. The window was open, and the screen's pushed out. We looked around the cabin, but she's not there."

"Oh dear," Mary said, her eyes growing wide. "Oh dear." She turned to look behind her and yelled. "Ross, get dressed and get out here. We have an emergency."

Mary stepped back inside for a moment. When she returned, she was carrying a six-celled flashlight. Stepping off of her front porch, she walked quickly to where Janet and Robert were standing. Switching on the flashlight, she put her arm around Janet's shoulders and gave her a hug. "Don't worry. Everything is going to be all right. We'll find your daughter."

"But where could she have gone?" Janet asked. "And why sneak out at night?"

Mary gave her a reassuring smile. "You know how kids are, all the time full of mischief and excitement. Maybe she saw a possum and wanted to follow it. Or an armadillo. Those things can be quite fascinating to a kid. Maybe she went down to look at the alligators."

"Alligators? You have alligators here?"

Mary shook her head. "We don't really own any, but there are a few that swim up in this area at night looking for food. We don't feed them, but some of the fishermen throw fish scraps into the river and that draws them."

Janet was starting to get a little uncomfortable with what Mary was telling her. She knew Mary was only trying to make her feel better, but thinking that Krissy might be down at the river watching the alligators frightened her. What if her daughter fell into the river? Would an alligator be able to tell the difference between fish parts and a little girl? Would it even care? *Hello, pretty one. I see you. Chomp. Chomp.*

They only had to wait a couple of minutes before Ross joined them. He was fully dressed and carried a Coleman lantern and a flashlight. Two men also walked up to the group. They were fishermen staying in one of the rented cabins. Ross handed them his spare flashlight while Mary quickly explained what was going on.

"Have you searched the whole camp?" Ross asked, looking around.

Robert shook his head. "No. Not yet. We were doing that when Mary came out."

Ross nodded. "Okay, then let's start searching. We'll save time if we split up and search." He pointed at the two fishermen. "You guys look around the cabins, and the woods behind them. The little girl's name is Krissy. Give us a shout if you find anything. And make sure you don't scare her. She may have gotten herself turned around, and might be lost."

"You've got it," said one of the men. They turned and headed off to search around the cabins.

"Lost?" Janet asked. "Do you think she's lost?"

Ross shook his head. "No. Not really. It's harder to get lost around here than you think. The river separates the camp from the rest of the forest, and the road separates it from the woods on the other side. If she didn't cross the bridge, or the road, she'll still be around here somewhere.

"We had better split up too," he said. "Mary, you and Janet search the area around the restaurant and other buildings, and along the river on that side of the camp. Robert and I will cross over the bridge and search along the river on the other side. We'll also search the nature trail."

Janet watched her husband and Ross start in the direction of the footbridge before following Mary toward the restaurant/lounge, and bait and tackle shop. They looked around all of the buildings, even looked around the few vehicles parked in the parking lot, but didn't find anything.

They had just searched behind the bait and tackle shop when Mary turned and shone the flashlight at the wooden doghouse sitting beside the building. "That's odd. Patch is also missing."

"Your dog's gone?" Janet asked.

Mary nodded. "That's not like him. He doesn't go out much at night, not since he lost his eye to that raccoon. He lost all of his wanderlust after the fight. He's usually in his doghouse at night or sleeping on the front porch of our cabin. With all of this noise, I'm surprised we haven't seen him. He's the nosy sort, always comes around when he hears people."

"Maybe he's with Krissy," Janet suggested, hoping the dog was with her daughter to protect her. "She's a dog lover, and she liked Patch an awful lot."

"Maybe." Mary frowned, remembering how Patch had acted toward the little girl the other day. How he had growled at her, then backed away as if he were scared of her. He had acted funny, and Mary was suddenly worried that Patch might have something to do with Krissy's disappearance. Come to think of it, she had not seen the dog all day. He was even absent at supper time, and Patch rarely missed a meal. The dog food she had put in his bowl earlier was still untouched.

Mary turned away from the doghouse, the frown still upon her face. "I think we should search along the river."

They reached the river, searching around the boat ramp and canoe racks. Following the river south, they walked along its bank as far as possible before a thick growth of foliage stopped their progress. It was a bright night, a full moon hanging in the sky, so the river shone like a milky jewel. The full moon made it easier for them to search, illuminating areas that would have otherwise been dark.

Not finding Krissy on the south side of the camp, they turned around and started walking in the opposite direction. Again, they followed the river as far as possible before being turned back by a thick growth of cypress trees that grew along the water's edge.

Janet was almost relieved that they had not found Krissy anywhere near the river. Though her daughter was still missing, Janet had been terrified that she would find her as part of an alligator's dinner. Not only had she not found Krissy, she had not seen any alligators.

They had just made it back to the boat ramp when they spotted Ross and Robert coming across the footbridge from the nature trail. "Did you have any luck?" Robert called.

"No," Janet answered, concerned that Krissy was not with her father. "How about you?"

"No. Nothing," he answered, approaching his wife. "We followed the trail all the way back to where the boardwalk is burned. I didn't see much point in going any farther, because Krissy would have never gone that far."

Janet felt tears sting her eyes. She didn't want to cry, but she couldn't help it. The love of her life was missing, and they couldn't find her. Krissy had to be somewhere, safe, but they just didn't know where. Maybe the other men would find her. Maybe she had sneaked out to watch a baby raccoon, or something like that, and she was right behind the camp.

Janet's hopes that the other men would find her daughter were quickly dashed, however, when she spotted the two men walking their way. They were by themselves. No little girl was with them. No Krissy.

"You find anything?" Ross called, already knowing the answer.

One of the men shook his head. "No. Nothing. We looked all over, but didn't see anything."

"Saw a raccoon, and two deer, but I guess that doesn't help much," said the other man. He was trying at levity in an attempt to lighten the mood, but his humor failed miserably.

"Patch is also missing," Janet said, remembering the empty doghouse. "Maybe they're together."

"Patch is missing?" Ross asked.

Mary nodded. "His doghouse is empty, and he hasn't touched his food."

Ross rubbed his chin in thought. "Not like Patch to go off at night. Maybe he followed the girl."

"Maybe," Mary repeated.

Robert looked around at the others, then said, "Look, we're not getting anywhere here. My daughter is still missing. I appreciate your help, but I think we need professional searchers out here. I think it's time to call the police."

Ross nodded. "I think you're right. We can call the Palmetto County Sheriff's Department. They've got a helicopter that can search this area a lot better than we can, and a lot faster." He reached into his pants pocket and pulled out a set of keys. "There's a phone in the bait and tackle shop. We can call from there."

Robert followed Ross, leaving the others to remain standing near the river. And though Janet was surrounded by other people, she suddenly felt alone and very frightened. She turned to face the river and the forest beyond. Somewhere in the darkness was her daughter.

Krissy, where are you?

Chapter Fourteen

Chaos descended upon Blackwater Fish Camp as two patrol cars from the Palmetto County Sheriff's Department arrived in response to the emergency call placed by the Pattersons. They pulled into the parking lot with lights flashing, the brilliant blues bouncing off the surrounding buildings and trees.

Robert stood in front of the bait and tackle shop, his arm around his wife's shoulders. Mary stood with them, but Ross and the two fishermen had gone back into the forest to continue searching for Krissy. Two more men, anglers visiting from out of town, had gone with them, having been awakened from a sound sleep by all the shouting.

From where he stood, Robert could hear the men calling his daughter's name and suspected they were making their way down the nature trail. He wanted to join the search, but he knew that his wife needed his support. He also needed to be available to answer any questions the sheriff's department might have to ask.

The two patrol cars pulled to a stop not more than ten feet from where they stood, their lights still flashing, and three men climbed out. Anxious to find their daughter, Robert and Janet approached the officers as soon as they got out of their vehicles.

"Good evening officers," Robert said. "I'm Robert Patterson. This is my wife, Janet. We made the nine-one-one call. Our daughter is missing. Her name is Krissy. She's ten."

One of the three men stepped forward and nodded. "I'm Sergeant Chris Andrews." He opened a note-book and jotted down their names. "How long has your daughter been missing?"

"I'm not sure," Janet answered. "I tucked her into bed around eight-thirty. She doesn't usually go to bed that early, but she said she was tired. And when I went to check on her she was gone."

"What time was that?" Sergeant Andrews asked.

"It was a little after one."

The sergeant glanced at his watch. "You didn't call right away?"

"No, sir," Robert answered. "We didn't want to call until we looked around first. We found her bedroom window open, and the screen pushed out, and thought maybe she might have sneaked out."

"Does your daughter have a habit of sneaking out?"

"No. Never," Janet said. "Nothing like this has ever happened before."

The sergeant jotted down what she said. "Mrs. Patterson, what was your daughter wearing the last time you saw her?"

"She was wearing her pajamas."

"Do you know if she's still wearing them, or did she change clothes?"

Janet paused for a moment. "I'm not sure. I never thought to look."

"If she changed clothes, then she probably wasn't abducted," Sergeant Andrews said. "It's doubtful that a kidnapper would risk being caught by letting your daughter change clothes, knowing her parents were in the next room. I want to look around your cabin. We'll also check to see if any of Krissy's clothes are missing."

Grabbing a flashlight from his vehicle, the sergeant called the sheriff's office to report his findings. He also instructed the two men with him to begin searching the forest immediately behind the cabins. He had just given instructions to the two deputies when a fire truck and a paramedic unit pulled into the parking lot.

Though there was no fire, the emergency vehicles had been dispatched in case paramedics were needed on the scene. A missing child was taken seriously, especially in such a rural area. Even though the weather was warm, there was still a danger of exposure or injury. With a river in the area, drowning was also a serious consideration.

No sooner had the two emergency vehicles pulled into the parking lot, than a white van also showed up. Painted on the side of the van were the words CHANNEL 6 NEWS.

"A news crew?" Robert said out loud. "We didn't call the media."

Sergeant Andrews turned to look at him. "Most of the news vans have police scanners. They probably heard the report and followed the fire truck out here. Must be a slow night for the media." He smiled. "I'll keep them away from you. Heck, I'll give them a flashlight and make them help search. Don't worry, we'll find your daughter."

The sergeant left the Pattersons to speak to the firemen who had just arrived. He also took time to speak to the reporter and cameraman who had climbed out of the news van. The reporter, a young woman, looked toward the Pattersons and frowned, apparently unhappy that she was being told to stay away. Robert wanted to smile and wave, but didn't, knowing that such actions would be considered an invitation to the press.

The firemen and paramedics listened to what the sergeant had to say. Leaving one man behind to monitor the radio, they grabbed flashlights and started toward the forest. They obviously thought joining in the search was a better use of their time than standing around and waiting for someone else to find Krissy. Perhaps some of the men were fathers; maybe they even had children Krissy's age.

The reporter and cameraman didn't offer to join in the search. Instead, they stood by their vehicle and watched everyone else. Perhaps they were worried that they might be in the wrong section of forest when the girl was found. Better to stay where they were so they could keep an eye on the comings and goings of the search crew, hoping to catch a tearful reunion between missing child and worried parents.

Robert frowned when he saw the cameraman remove his video camera from the van and aim it at the reporter. The woman reporter grabbed a microphone and stepped into the spotlight of the camera, taking a moment to straighten her clothes and fluff her hair. She was apparently about to do a live broadcast from the scene of the search.

Robert wondered if what he saw around him was

normal procedures, because everyone appeared to be jumping the gun. Police, firemen, paramedics, and a television crew for a girl who had only been missing a few hours. What if Krissy was only sleeping somewhere? What if she had been chasing a raccoon and would reappear any moment? Not much of a story in that. He was happy to have so much help so quickly, but he wondered if they did this for every missing child.

Finished speaking with the emergency crews, Sergeant Andrews walked back over to where Robert and Janet stood. "The firemen are going to join in on the search, so it won't be long before we find your daughter. The sheriff's department is also sending a helicopter out this way to help search.

"In the meantime, I would like to take a look at your daughter's bedroom."

Robert and Janet led the sergeant back to their cabin, showing him Krissy's bedroom. Sergeant Andrews examined the open window, then turned to look at the room. The covers on Krissy's bed were made, as if she had not gone to bed.

Approaching the bed, the sergeant asked, "Mrs. Patterson, you said that you tucked your daughter into bed earlier this evening?"

"Yes, sir. Around eight o'clock."

"So, I'm assuming she was under the covers?"

"That's right."

"Does your daughter make her own bed in the morning?"

"Sometimes she does, but not always. I usually have to help her."

"Well, it looks like she tried to make her own bed

this time." He pulled back the covers. Krissy's pajamas were beneath the blankets.

"Those are Krissy's," Robert said.

Sergeant Andrews nodded. "It looks like she changed clothes, and made her bed, before leaving. That probably rules out an abduction."

Janet breathed a sigh of relief. "Thank God. But why would she sneak out? She's never done anything like this before."

The sergeant turned to look at her. "You said your daughter went to bed early, around eight o'clock, and that was not her normal bedtime?"

Janet shook her head. "No. We usually let her stay up until nine. Later on weekends, holidays, and during the summer. This is our vacation, so she could have stayed up to midnight if she wanted. She went to bed early tonight because she didn't want to be tired for the fishing trip tomorrow."

"Outside of going to bed early, was she acting odd in any way?"

"How so?" Janet asked.

The sergeant rubbed his chin. "Was she sad, or depressed, or upset?"

"No. She was just tired," answered Robert.

"There is one thing," Janet glanced quickly at her husband. "The other day Krissy told us that she had made a new friend: an invisible friend named Mansa."

Robert cleared his throat. "What my wife is trying to say is that Krissy now has herself a make-believe playmate. It's worth mentioning, because it's not at all like our daughter to have such a friend. Truthfully, I think it's just a phase she's going through, but you did ask if there was anything odd. And having an invisible friend named Mansa is definitely odd."

The sergeant nodded and wrote the name down in his notebook. "Invisible playmate named Mansa. Got it."

Sergeant Andrews looked around the room. "Okay. Listen. There's not much else I can do in here. Not now anyway. I'm going to go back outside and help look for your daughter."

"We would like to help too," Robert said. "I mean, if that's okay."

The sergeant smiled. "Of course it's okay. If it was my little girl, I would be out looking too. No way anyone could stop me."

Walking back across the fish camp, Robert saw that another patrol car had arrived on the scene. "I'm glad to see everyone's taking this seriously."

Sergeant Andrews turned to him as they walked. "Missing children are taken very seriously around here."

"Why is that?" Robert asked, suddenly suspecting the sergeant wasn't telling him everything.

The sergeant stopped walking. "Because we lost a couple of kids in these woods over the years."

Janet stopped dead in her tracks. "What?"

Sergeant Andrews looked at them a moment before speaking. "I didn't want to mention this, because I didn't want you any more upset than you already are, but a couple of kids have gotten lost in this forest and were never found."

"Lost?" Janet asked. "Are you sure?"

The sergeant nodded. "Yes, ma'am. They wandered off at night, and we never found them. Not that we didn't look. We turned these woods upside down, but never found anything. Not a trace."

"No wonder Ross told us not to let Krissy wander around in the woods by herself," Robert said. "How many children were never found?"

"Three that I know of: two boys and a girl."

"Were they local children, or tourists?"

"The two boys were locals. They were on an overnight canoe trip and disappeared. We found the canoe, but not the boys."

"And the third?" Janet asked.

"The little girl was a tourist. She was staying in one of the cabins with her parents."

"Like Krissy. . . ."

"Yes, ma'am. Like your daughter." Sergeant Andrews nodded. "Now, do you see why I didn't want to say anything?"

"How long ago did this happen?" Robert asked.

"The boys disappeared about fifteen years ago. The little girl about seven. I wasn't living in this area when the two boys disappeared, but I helped search for the girl."

He nodded toward the rescue vehicles. "Some of these guys also helped look for the little girl, and they weren't too happy about not finding her. It really got to them. That's why so many are showing up now to help search. I can promise you that they will look behind every rock and tree to find your daughter. And they will find her."

He switched on his flashlight. "So, let's say we give them a hand looking."

* * *

Robert and Janet chose a section of the forest to look for Krissy that wasn't already being searched. They walked north of the camp until they were far enough away that they could barely hear the shouts of the men.

He wondered if all the shouting was actually a good thing. Krissy could hear the men if she was anywhere close, but could they hear her? What if she had stepped in a hole and sprained her ankle and was now lying hurt somewhere? Would they be able to hear her if she cried out for help? With this thought in mind, Robert and Janet would call out their daughter's name, and then stand quietly for a minute or two listening for a reply.

They walked perhaps a mile north of the camp before turning east toward the river. Just to the south of them a helicopter circled low over the tree tops, sweeping a spotlight slowly back and forth. The helicopter had flown over them a few minutes earlier, the spotlight bathing them and the surrounding trees in its white brilliance. Robert thought it might turn back to take another look at them, but it never did. Obviously the pilot could tell the difference between two grown adults and a little girl.

Reaching the river, they reluctantly turned back toward the camp. They both wanted to keep going in the opposite direction, but knew that it would be foolish to do so by themselves. The forest was far too large for two people to search it effectively. Better to rejoin the others and search as a group, because then there would be less chance of walking past Krissy without seeing her.

Besides, the batteries in Robert's flashlight were

growing weak. The flashlight's beam was already a dull yellow and fading fast. The moon was also lower in the sky, making it harder to see without a secondary light source. Better to head back now than risk becoming lost themselves.

The moon had disappeared behind the treetops, so the Wekiva no longer looked like a shining jewel. On the contrary, the river now looked like an ebony serpent, twisting its way through a prehistoric forest of palmettos and saw grass. It was a serpent, a deadly predator that came to life at night, waiting, watching, hoping for the foolish to venture too close, carrying its victims down to the darkness, never to be seen again. Three children had disappeared in these woods, perhaps swallowed by the river that drew people to the area. Had Krissy also been swallowed by the serpent? Had she drowned?

Robert shook his head. No. No. No. She couldn't have drowned. Krissy was a good swimmer, he and Janet had made sure of that. They had put her in a swimming program at the YMCA when she was only six. Their little girl was a natural in the water. She would not have drowned in a river as small, or as slow moving, as the Wekiva. More of a spring than a real river. Just a trickle compared to the mighty Mississippi River that flowed past St. Louis.

He blinked and again looked at the Wekiva River. Though it was still ebony in the darkness, it no longer looked like a serpent to him. Nor did it appear sinister or deadly. It looked like a small river, and nothing more, its whispering waters the lifeblood of timid forest dwellers.

Their daughter had not drowned in the river. That

was out of the question. At least such a thing was impossible to imagine, and he would not even allow himself to think about it. Never focus on the negative. Think instead only on the positive. Their daughter was lost in the forest. While her being lost was bad enough, they still had a lot to be hopeful about.

For one thing the weather was warm, so there was little chance of Krissy suffering from hypothermia. A child could easily spend a night alone in such conditions without any adverse physical effects. Krissy could probably spend several nights in the forest without any problems, not that he was hoping for that to happen. Even one night worrying about his daughter alone in the woods would be far too many.

Also, Krissy had not been gone long, so she couldn't have gotten very far away. It was only a matter of time before the searchers found her. Finally, she had changed clothes before leaving the cabin, which meant she had left on her own free will and had not been abducted.

Unless she had been forced to change clothes.

The thought popped into his head, startling him. What if his little girl had been abducted? What if someone had sneaked into her bedroom, placed a hand over her mouth to keep her from screaming, then ordered her to get dressed without making any noise? Someone could have threatened her with a knife, telling Krissy that if she made any noise he would hurt her and maybe kill her parents. She would have obeyed then, wouldn't have made a sound as she got out of her pajamas and into her clothes.

Maybe she had made noise. Maybe she had whimpered, or cried softly, as she struggled to get free from her attacker. Janet was a sound sleeper, so it would have taken a loud noise to wake her. A whimper or a cry would have gone unnoticed. And he'd had several beers before going to bed, so he was dead to the world.

Robert cursed himself under his breath. Why had he drank those beers? He was normally a light sleeper, except when he had been drinking. He might have heard Krissy otherwise. Even if she had been extra quiet, he might have heard the window being slid up and gone to investigate. But he had heard nothing, his hearing and senses dulled by alcohol. If his daughter had been abducted, then his actions might be partially to blame.

They arrived back at the fish camp to find a large, muscular black man standing on the porch of their tiny cabin, waiting for them. He was dressed in black slacks, matching dress shoes, a red sports shirt, and a pair of gold, wire-rimmed glasses. On his belt was a holstered revolver and a badge.

"Mr. and Mrs. Patterson?"

Robert nodded. "I'm Robert Patterson. This is my wife, Janet."

The man nodded. "I'm Captain Williams. I'll be in charge of finding your daughter. I know you've already spoken with Sergeant Andrews, but I would like to ask you a few more questions."

Opening the front door, they invited the captain inside. Captain Williams entered the cabin and closed the door behind him. He was a large man, and the room seemed to shrink in his presence. Despite his powerful physique, there was a gentleness to his eyes and the set of his mouth that made Robert like him immediately. Here was a man you did not want to cross, for he could easily take on even the toughest opponent; yet here too was a father, a man who lived for quiet Sundays with his family.

Robert and Janet sat down in the two oversized chairs while the captain grabbed one of the folding chairs, placing it so he could sit directly in front of them. Opening the small notebook he carried, the captain proceeded with his questions.

"Mr. and Mrs. Patterson, do you know of any reason why your daughter might have sneaked out of her room?" Captain Williams chose his words carefully and kept soft the tone of his voice, knowing that the people seated before him were already traumatized by the disappearance of their daughter.

"No. No reason," Robert answered, shaking his head. "And we're not sure that she sneaked out."

"Meaning?"

"Meaning she might have been abducted," Robert said, stating what he thought was the obvious.

"That's a possibility, but it's not very likely," Captain Williams answered, glancing toward Krissy's bedroom. "I've already been in your daughter's bedroom. The two of you were gone, and the front door was unlocked, so I came in and looked around. Hope you don't mind. There's no sign of a struggle, and neither of you heard anything. Also, the window and screen both lock from the inside, and cannot be unlocked from outside. Someone on the inside had to unlock it: either one of you, or your daughter."

"We didn't unlock it," Janet said. "And I don't think Krissy unlocked it either. She didn't like sleeping with the window open because she was scared of bugs getting in."

"Apparently she must have unlocked it," the captain said. "Maybe she wanted some fresh air. The owner of the fish camp said the jasmine was blooming, so maybe your daughter wanted to smell the flowers. Maybe she heard an owl and opened the window so she could hear it better.

"That still doesn't explain why she disappeared," Captain Williams continued. "But I have a feeling she left her bedroom of her own free will."

"And how do you come to that conclusion?" Robert asked.

"For one thing she changed clothes before she left, hiding them under the blankets on her bed. Not too many kids would do something like that if they were being dragged from their room. The ground foliage outside the bedroom is also basically undisturbed, the way it would be if only a small child stepped on it. A man's weight would have flattened it."

Captain Williams paused for a moment to jot down a few notes. "How would you describe your relationship with your daughter?"

"What kind of question is that?" Robert wanted to know.

"A standard question. Nothing more. The more information you can provide, the quicker we can find your daughter."

"We have a good relationship with Krissy," Janet answered.

"Was she upset about something today? Angry perhaps?"

"No. She was fine," Robert replied. "She said she was a little tired, so she went to bed early."

"I see." Captain Williams nodded. "Don't you think it's odd for a kid her age to go to bed early, especially on vacation?"

"Not at all," Janet jumped in. "Krissy wanted to get some sleep so she wouldn't be tired on the fishing trip. She wanted to catch more fish than her father."

The captain turned to look at Robert. "Is it important that your daughter catches more fish than you? What happens if she doesn't?"

Robert felt his face flush with anger. He didn't like the captain's questions, nor did he like what the man was suggesting. "Nothing happens if she doesn't catch more fish than me. Nothing at all. We fish strictly for fun. Krissy likes to catch more fish, so I'll call her the champ."

"And what do you call her when she loses the contest?"

"Look. Enough," Robert said, feeling his temper rise. "None of your questions are relevant to our daughter's disappearance."

"On the contrary, they are all relevant," argued the captain. "We have to figure out why your daughter is missing. We have to know if she was abducted, or if she simply ran away. If she did run away, then it would be helpful to know why. Was she upset over something that was said? Was she mad? Does she have a happy home life? As painful as it is to hear these questions, I can assure you that it's very important for me to ask them."

Captain Williams looked out the window, then turned his attention back to them. "That should be enough information for now, but I may stop back by to talk with you later in the day. The search has been postponed for now."

"Postponed? Why?" Janet asked, shocked.

"The moon is setting, so it's much too dark to continue. Too dangerous. We want to look for your daughter, but we can't risk any of our men getting hurt in the process. We'll start the search in a few more hours, once it gets light out."

"What about the helicopter?" Robert asked. "It has a spotlight."

The captain nodded. "It has a spotlight, but the pilot can only do so much. He's already gone back to refuel, and grab a few hours sleep. He'll be back bright and early in the morning.

"We're also going to bring in a team of bloodhounds. We'll bring the dogs through the cabin, let them get your daughter's scent off her clothing—something that she's worn that hasn't been washed. Bloodhounds are amazing animals. If your little girl is anywhere around here, they'll find her."

Captain Williams cleared his throat and lowered his voice. "I don't want to upset you, but if we don't find your daughter we may have to drag the river."

"Dear God," Janet said.

"This doesn't mean that we think your daughter has drowned. Dragging the river is strictly routine. The Wekiva River isn't very deep, but there are certain areas that warrant investigation."

Robert nodded. "I understand."

The captain stood up and shook hands. "I'll stop back by in the afternoon, but hopefully by then we will have already found your daughter."

Captain Williams left the cabin, closing the door behind them. Robert considered getting up to lock the door, but he just didn't have the strength to stand. He thought about what had been said to him, feeling a sick sensation in his stomach.

They were going to drag the river for Krissy's body.

Chapter Fifteen

Daylight seemed to come unusually late that morning, as if the night was refusing to release its hold on the land. When the sun finally did rise above the treetops to the east, it brought little warmth to the forest along the Wekiva River. At least it seemed that way to Sergeant Chris Andrews.

At the end of his shift, the sergeant had gone home to grab a few hours sleep, but he had returned to the Blackwater Fish Camp to help search for the Patterson's little girl. Not that he had to return. It was his day off. He could have stayed home with his wife and kids, might even have spent the day doing a little shopping, or helping out around the house. If he was lucky, he would have been allowed to sleep late without being awakened by the sound of the neighbor's barking dogs.

But he had not wanted to stay home and sleep. Nor would he feel right spending the day with his family, not with a child lost in the same forest that had swallowed up several other children. Several of his fellow officers felt the same way, for they too had given up their day off to help out in the search.

Sergeant Andrews parked his Ford Explorer alongside a row of patrol cars and emergency vehicles. The truck he drove was unmarked, his personal vehicle, but there was another Ford Explorer sitting in the lot that was adorned with blue lights and a big gold star decal on each of its white doors. Behind that vehicle was a trailer carrying a small, flat-bottomed boat. Two deputies stood beside the boat, sorting the ropes and grappling hooks that might be used to drag the river for Krissy Patterson's body.

The sergeant felt a lump form inside of his throat as he spotted the hooks. His youngest son, Billy, was only eight, two years younger than the missing girl. What if it was Billy they were looking for? Would he be strong enough to watch as the deputies dragged the river with those damn hooks, hoping to snag the bloated, swollen body of an all too small child?

Feeling an uneasiness settle in his stomach, he turned away from the deputies with the grappling hooks and spotted Robert and Janet Patterson standing in front of the bait and tackle shop. He waved as he climbed out of his truck, but they did not wave back. Either they didn't recognize him, or they were both too tired, or too dazed, to wave. Probably the latter, for the two of them looked like hell.

Though they were wearing different clothes from the last time he saw them, it was obvious the Pattersons had not gotten any sleep. There were dark circles under Janet's eyes that showed clearly, even from a distance. Her eyes were also puffy, probably from a combination of no sleep and too many tears. Dark circles were also visible under Robert's eyes, and he was sporting a noticeable stubble of beard. They would both look dreadful if their daughter was found and the news crews filmed the happy reunion, but personal appearances were the least of their troubles.

Grabbing his hat off the seat, Sergeant Andrews closed the truck door and locked it. Though it was his day off, he had chosen to wear his uniform. There would be searchers from several agencies in the area, plus volunteers, and he did not want to be mistaken for a civilian while tramping through the woods. Cops didn't always take too well to outsiders in emergency situations, and wearing the uniform would keep him from having to show his badge, or do any explaining, to those he didn't know. The holster and utility belt he wore with his uniform was also more comfortable than the shoulder holster he wore when off duty.

Checking in with the day supervisor, Sergeant Andrews was assigned a section of the forest to search. The search they were conducting that morning would be slower paced, and more thorough, than the one which had taken place in the predawn hours. They would leave no stone unturned, looking for clues that might tell them why Krissy Patterson had disappeared. The sergeant had been assigned a stretch of land along the Wekiva River, opposite the river from the fish camp.

Walking over the narrow wooden bridge that spanned the river, he turned right and started his search downstream. As he walked along, he paid particular attention to the soft earth close to the water's edge, looking for the tiny footprints of a child. So far he saw none. He also searched the river itself for a piece of clothing, a shoe, anything that might indicate that the little girl had drowned. Images of a pale, lifeless hand sticking out of the water kept coming to mind, and he truly hoped that he would not see such a sight for real. The last thing in the world he wanted was to find a dead child.

A pair of doves suddenly took flight before him, startling the sergeant. He stopped, watching as the birds flew across the river and headed south. As he watched the birds, his attention was drawn by something that looked out of place in the forest. Up ahead, the sunlight was reflecting off an object nestled among the trees along the water's edge. It took him a moment to realize that what he was seeing was sunlight bouncing off the glass windows of a tiny wooden cabin.

Sergeant Andrews squinted his eyes, studying the strange building that stood close to the river's edge. It was more of a shack than a cabin: a tiny, dilapidated, tin-roofed structure that appeared to be made of plywood and scrap lumber. The cabin had once been painted blue, but most of the paint had flaked and faded, leaving behind a mostly brown building.

He wondered what the cabin was used for. It didn't look like a boathouse. Perhaps it was used to store tools or equipment. Surely, it couldn't be a dwelling of any kind, because it looked far too run-down to be inhabited. He also wondered if it had already been searched. That was doubtful. The shack was so dark in color that it had probably been invisible last night, even with a full moon. He had better take a look inside, just to be on the safe side.

As he slowly approached the cabin, a strange feeling came over Sergeant Andrews. It felt as if he was being watched. Twice he stopped and looked behind him, but didn't see anyone. Was he being watched by someone inside the cabin? The windows he had seen earlier faced the river and could not be seen from where he stood. But that didn't mean he wasn't being watched.

Having spent several years working for the Palmetto County Sheriff's Department, Sergeant Andrews knew it was always better to be cautious when facing unknown situations. He also knew to trust his instincts; therefore, as the feeling of being watched increased, he casually reached down and unsnapped the safety strap on his gun holster. In that holster he carried a Glock model 23, a 40-caliber semiautomatic with a thirteen-round clip. For extra stopping power, the handgun was loaded with hollow points.

The sergeant slowed his pace as he neared the cabin. He could no longer see the dirty glass windows, but he could see the entrance. A narrow path through the forest led up to a wooden door that faced away from the river. The path was well worn, suggesting that it had been used often, and in recent times. The door was closed, but Sergeant Andrews didn't see a lock of any kind.

The feeling of being watched still hung over him, so he didn't want to directly approach the cabin's door. Instead he circled around to the side, staying out of sight of both window and doorway. Of course, the cabin was in bad shape, so there were probably hundreds of cracks in the wood. If someone was inside the cabin, watching him, they wouldn't need a window, or a doorway.

He was only about twenty feet from the cabin when he spotted a small, rectangular mound of earth piled a few feet from the base of an oak tree. Alarm bells sounded in Sergeant Andrews's head, because he had just stumbled upon what looked to be a freshly dug grave.

"Oh, Jesus," the sergeant said, stopping dead in his tracks. The grave was small, measuring no more than four and a half feet by two and a half feet. Much too small to be the grave of an adult, but it was the perfect size for a child.

Sergeant Andrews knew he might be looking at a crime scene, so it was time to call in the experts. Keeping an eye on the cabin, he thumbed the microphone on his radio and called his supervisor. After waiting for the day-shift supervisor to respond, he said, "Lieutenant, this is Sergeant Andrews. Sir, I think I may have found something."

"What do you have?" asked the lieutenant.

"I'm here on the edge of the river, about a mile south of the fish camp, on the opposite side of the water. I've come across a small wooden cabin, and what looks to be a freshly dug grave."

"Roger, Andrews," responded the lieutenant. "I'll get some men down there to you. In the meantime, I want you to secure the area the best you can. Have you looked inside the cabin?"

"No sir. Not yet."

There was a pause. "You might want to hold off until help arrives. It's your call. Just be careful."

"Ten four," said the sergeant. "Out."

He released the microphone and turned his attention back to the grave. He didn't have any barrier tape with him, so there was really nothing he could do to secure the scene for the investigators, other than to make sure that no one walked through the area. It would take a little while for the others to reach him; in the meantime, he was going to see what else he could find.

The sergeant turned his attention back to the cabin. He probably should wait for backup, but he would look like a fool if it turned out he was afraid to check an empty shack by himself. And if it turned out the little girl was sleeping inside, then he would look like an even bigger fool for guarding the shack and not being the one to actually find her. Someone else would grab all the credit out from under him, leaving him standing stupid on the sidelines.

"Screw that," the sergeant said, wiping a hand across his face. He looked back down at the grave. What if the little girl wasn't sleeping peacefully in the cabin? What if she was sleeping a more permanent sleep? If the grave did contain her body, then it meant that she had been murdered. Perhaps raped, tortured, and murdered. The cabin might truly be a crime scene.

He swallowed hard as a hideous image came to mind. He saw the interior of the cabin as it must have looked last night, silvery moonlight filtering in through cracks in the walls. A blonde-haired little girl lay naked atop a wooden bench, tied and gagged. Her eyes were wide and filled with fright; her terrified screams muffled by the gag she wore. On the walls around her hung rusted tools—pliers, hammers, saws—that were being used as implements of torture. . . .

He shook his head, forcing the image from his mind's eye. He didn't want to think about what might have happened to Krissy Patterson, dared not imagine that the grave he stood over belonged to her. He had no proof that she was dead, and was not about to think such thoughts if he didn't have to. He had to think positive, had to act positive, and not let the darkness of his thoughts turn his stomach and stop him from doing his job.

Again he turned his attention to the tiny cabin. He should wait for the others, but he had to know if what he imagined could possibly be true. He had to look inside, otherwise the dreadful images would again float up from the darkness of his imagination.

He pulled his pistol and approached the cabin from the side, quickly slipping around to the front of the building. He now stood to the right of a faded, red, wooden door. There wasn't a padlock. There was only a brass knob, the metal tarnished with age.

Sergeant Andrews stepped forward and tried the knob with his left hand. The door was locked. A chill shot through him. The door was locked, but there wasn't a keyhole. That meant the door was locked from the inside.

There's someone inside the shack.

The sergeant had to make a quick decision: either wait for backup to arrive, knock on the door to see if he got an answer, or kick it open. Knowing that procedures had to be followed, even at a time like this, he struck the door twice with the palm of his left hand and called out, "Sheriff's department. Open up."

There was no response to his knock. Not wanting to wait for the others, he kicked the door just below the knob. The wood cracked and splintered, but the door did not open. He was about to kick it again, when the door was flung open by somebody on the inside.

"Look what you did to my door!" A dark skinned man stood in the doorway. He was thin and muscular, his long black hair falling loosely over his shoulders. The man looked to be Indian, or maybe Mexican. "What the hell's wrong with you? Are you crazy?"

Sergeant Andrews was taken by surprise, and it took him a few moments to recover. Realizing he was still aiming a loaded weapon at an unarmed man, he quickly lowered his pistol. "Sheriff's department. I knocked."

"You knocked?" said the man, angry. "How many times? Once? And when I didn't answer you thought it was okay to kick my door down?"

"I didn't know anyone lived here. I thought it was a storage shed."

The Indian frowned. "If that's true, then why did you knock?" He looked down at his door. "You broke my lock. Who's going to pay for this?"

Recovering from the sudden surprise, Sergeant Andrews reholstered his gun but left the thumb strap off. "Do you live here?"

"I said this was my door. Didn't I? You do the math."

The sergeant tried to look past the Indian to see what was inside, but the man blocked his view. "I thought this land belonged to the state."

"Check your history books, this land belonged to my people long before it belonged to the state. I'm Seminole. We're the only tribe that never surrendered to the government. Technically, we're still at war with you." The Indian grinned. "What are you doing out here anyway? Did you get lost?"

"No. I'm not lost," Sergeant Andrews answered,

feeling his face flush with anger. "I'm looking for a missing girl: ten years old, blonde hair. Have you seen her?"

The Indian rubbed his chin in thought. "Ten years old? Blonde hair? White girl?" He lowered his hand and grinned. "Nope. I haven't seen her."

"Well, then Mr. . . ."

"Cypress. Jimmy Cypress."

"Mr. Cypress. You wouldn't mind if I came inside and looked around. Would you?"

"Do you have a warrant?"

"Not exactly," Sergeant Andrews answered, very much not liking the Indian.

Jimmy's grin widened. "Then you're not exactly coming inside. Not unless you've got yourself a warrant."

"I can go get one," threatened the sergeant.

"Good. Go get one. I'll wait here."

"No problem. But when I come back with a search warrant, I'll probably have to tear this place apart. I may have to even tear it down. After all, we're still at war. Right?"

Jimmy's grin faded. He opened the door. "Go ahead. Look around. See for yourself. I'm not hiding a little girl in here."

Sergeant Andrews stepped past the Indian and entered the cabin, astonished at how different the inside was from the outside. On the outside the building was in serious need of paint and repair and looked like it was falling down, but the inside was neat and well maintained, damn-near spotless.

The cabin only had one room, which housed a sofa, a folding card table and chair, and a wood-burning stove. There was no refrigerator or electrical appliances; no sink, bathroom fixtures, or anything to indicate that the cabin was equipped with running water. An old manual typewriter and several candles sat atop the folding card table; two more candles were sitting on an old orange crate in front of the sofa that served as a coffee table.

What looked like new paneling covered the walls, with a set of purple lace curtains hanging over the windows. The two windows offered a spectacular view of the Wekiva River as it flowed slowly past the cabin.

On both sides of the windows were homemade bookcases holding hundreds of books. The sergeant glanced at some of the titles, surprised to find dozens of books on religion, philosophy, and American history. A book on the Civil War lay open on the orange crate. Beside it was a pair of reading glasses.

Apparently, Jimmy Cypress was well-read, and maybe not quite the bum Sergeant Andrews first thought him to be. Perhaps he was only poor, a member of the ever-growing army of the unemployed. Maybe he was just a hermit, hiding out in the woods to escape society.

One thing for sure, the missing little girl was not in the cabin. Nor was there any indication that she had ever been there. But what about the grave outside the cabin? Was it a grave, or was it something else?

The sergeant turned away from the bookcase. The Indian still stood in the doorway, watching him. If he had done something wrong, then he was very cool about it. There was no fear in his eyes, nothing to indicate that he was nervous about the law being in his home.

"Are you satisfied, officer?" Jimmy Cypress asked, a half smile on his face. "Or would you like to stay awhile, maybe move in? I could bake cookies."

Sergeant Andrews was not amused with the Indian's sarcasm. "I'll be satisfied when you tell me what you have buried beside your cabin."

Jimmy's smile faded. "Buried?"

"I saw a grave. It looks fresh."

"And you think I dug it?"

"It's next to your cabin, that would make you the most likely person to dig it."

Jimmy smiled again. "I'm a heavy sleeper. Maybe someone else dug it."

Sergeant Andrews knew the Indian was lying to him, perhaps trying to hide something. He also had a feeling that Jimmy was about to take off running, so he slowly moved closer to him. From outside the cabin came the sound of voices, which meant the other officers were already descending on the area. There was no place now for Jimmy Cypress to run if he tried to get away.

Jimmy Cypress turned his head and looked outside, seeing the other deputies arriving on the scene. "Backup? For little old me? Do you really think you need to call in the cavalry for one unarmed Indian?"

The sergeant started to reply when he spotted something lying on the folding card table. It was another book, but it seemed strangely out of place with the rest of the collection. It was a children's book, a Dr. Seuss story entitled *Green Eggs and Ham.*

Curious, Sergeant Andrews reached down and opened the book. On the inside cover, printed neatly in the careful handwriting of a child, was Krissy Patterson's name and address.

Jimmy Cypress turned back around and saw the children's book in the sergeant's hands. His eyes went wide. Sergeant Andrews pulled his pistol from his holster, pointing it at the Seminole. "I think you have some explaining to do. Where did you get this book?"

"I found it in the woods."

The sergeant didn't believe that, not for one minute. Keeping his gun aimed at Jimmy Cypress, he set the book back on the card table and thumbed his microphone. "This is Sergeant Andrews. I'm inside the cabin. I have a possible suspect here with me. I need backup."

No sooner had he made the request for backup, than two more deputies appeared in the doorway behind Jimmy Cypress. "What have you got, Chris?" asked one of the deputies.

"I've got a book here that belongs to the missing girl, and what looks to be a grave outside. Put the cuffs on this guy, because he just became a suspect."

"What am I suspected of doing?" Jimmy Cypress asked.

"Kidnapping. Maybe murder."

The two deputies handcuffed Jimmy and took him outside, reading him his rights. While they were doing that Sergeant Andrews took a closer look around the inside of the cabin, searching for more clues. Other than the book, he found nothing to indicate that the missing girl was ever inside the cabin. A few minutes later the day-shift supervisor appeared on the scene.

A team of investigators spent hours searching through the cabin of Jimmy Cypress. Several other officers dug up the grave beside the cabin. It was a grave all right, but it did not contain the body of a little girl. Instead the grave contained the body of a black Labrador, still wearing the eye patch that had given the dog his name.

The lieutenant looked at the dog for a moment, then shook his head. "I think I know that dog. The owners of the fish camp said their dog was missing. They said he wore a black eye patch because he only had one eye. There can't be that many one-eyed dogs around here. This must be him. From the funny way his head is laying, I would say his neck is broken. Looks like we have ourselves a dog murderer."

"What about the little girl, and the book I found?" asked Sergeant Andrews.

The lieutenant was about to answer him, when his cell phone rang. He answered the call, listening carefully to what was being said to him. Hanging up, he turned back to Sergeant Andrews.

"It looks like you get the prize, sergeant. One of the deputies just spoke to the Pattersons. It seems Robert Patterson was threatened the other day by an Indian fitting Jimmy Cypress's description. The Indian warned Robert to stay out of the forest, otherwise something bad was going to happen to him.

"A murdered dog, a book belonging to a missing girl, a death threat against the little girl's father. It looks like we have ourselves a possible suspect. Good job, sergeant."

"Thank you, sir," Sergeant Andrews responded, smiling.

The lieutenant patted the sergeant on the arm, then started walking toward Jimmy Cypress and the deputies who guarded him. "All right, boys, let's take him in. Our friend here has a lot of questions he needs to answer, and I'd rather he answer them back at the station."

Chapter Sixteen

Jimmy Cypress was taken to the Palmetto County Sheriff's Office, in the nearby town of Abina. The sheriff's office was a two-story, gray, concrete-block building that sat on the corner of Main Street and Elm Avenue, directly across from several law offices and a gun shop. Palm trees and bushes had been planted in front of the building to enhance its appearance, but it was still a depressing looking structure. The row of barred windows on the second floor only added to the gloomy atmosphere.

The Indian had ridden in silence from his home to the sheriff's office, despite the talkative nature of the two deputies in the front seat of the patrol car. They had tried to engage him in conversation, but Jimmy had remained silent, knowing that anything he said, even in casual conversation, could be used against him at a later date.

Not that he had anything to hide. Jimmy was completely innocent when it came to the disappearance of the little girl they were looking for. He had not even known that a child was missing until the police showed up knocking at his front door. Correction, they had showed up kicking, nearly breaking down the wooden door of his cabin. It was obvious the police thought him guilty of a crime; finding a book in his home that belonged to the girl had not helped the situation. Now they had a reason to consider him a suspect.

He had tried to tell the police that he had found the book in the forest, but they would not listen to him. No surprise there. Jimmy was a poor Indian, so, in the eyes of the law, he just had to be guilty of a crime. Innocent until proven guilty was a rule that applied only to the rich. Everyone else was automatically guilty until proven otherwise.

Jimmy was not too worried about being blamed for the little girl's disappearance, because he knew they could not convict him in a court of law until they had sufficient proof. Finding a book in his home did not make him a kidnapper, despite what the arresting officers might think. Sooner or later they would have to let him go. But he was worried that a child had disappeared. Had the girl wandered off, had she actually been kidnapped by someone, or had she become a victim of the evil that dwelled in a patch of forest along the Wekiva River?

Krissy Patterson was not the first child to vanish in that forest. Two boys and a girl had also disappeared. The authorities had looked for those kids for weeks, finally giving up in frustration. They never did find out what happened to them, but Jimmy suspected their bodies could be found in the lagoon, buried beneath sediment and black mud. He could never tell anyone what he believed, not without becoming a murder suspect.

The little girl they were now looking for might also be dead, her body buried in the lagoon. She too might be a victim to the evil of Mansa Du Paul. But somehow he felt that Krissy Patterson was still alive. In the past couple of days he had felt the darkness growing, spreading slowly outward from the lagoon. The feeling had puzzled him, but now he understood what he felt. The spirit of Mansa Du Paul was attempting to reenter the world of the living, and he was using the girl to help him. He had not killed her, and probably would not until he was done using her. But time was running out for Krissy Patterson.

The patrol car pulled into a parking space behind the sheriff's office, the two deputies in the front getting out and unlocking Jimmy's door. Ushering him out of the car, they led him into the building by way of a back entrance. Once inside, he was taken down a narrow hallway to a room that was apparently used for questioning suspects.

A wooden table sat in the middle of the room. Two wooden chairs sat on opposite sides of the table, facing each other. The only other item of interest inside the room was the large mirror that covered most of one wall. It was obviously a two way mirror, allowing officers in the next room to watch, and perhaps record, the question and answer session.

Entering the room, Jimmy was instructed to have a seat on one of the chairs. The two deputies then left, closing the door behind them. Jimmy sat in the chair and stared at the mirror. He could see only his own reflection, but knew that someone was probably in the next room watching him. Having been arrested before, during his militant days, he knew that police officers liked to size up their suspects before questioning them. He also knew that they liked to make people wait.

Their theory was that the guilty would grow increasingly nervous the longer they waited. Jimmy was not guilty of anything, so he was not particularly nervous. To pass the time, he sat and made funny faces at the mirror.

His faces must have proved annoying to those on the other side of the mirror, for it wasn't long before the door opened and two plainclothes officers entered the room. The first officer to enter was a large black man, looking more like a professional football player than a cop. He was followed by a thin, bald, white man only half his size. The black man sat down at the table opposite Jimmy, while his partner stood in the corner of the room.

"Mr. Cypress, my name is Captain Williams," said the black man, "and this is Officer Mills. Do you know why you have been brought here today?"

Jimmy smiled. "You think I've committed a crime. Or maybe you just like having your deputies handcuff people."

Captain Williams frowned. He nodded toward the other officer, who stepped forward and removed the handcuffs from Jimmy's wrists. "Better?"

Jimmy rubbed his wrists and nodded. "Much."

"We've brought you here to ask you a few questions," Captain Williams continued.

"Am I under arrest?" Jimmy asked.

"Not yet. Not if you cooperate with us."

"And if I don't cooperate?"

The captain gave Jimmy a harsh look. "Then I can make things very unpleasant for you."

"Sounds like a threat."

"Not a threat. A promise." Captain Williams

reached into his shirt pocket and pulled out a small card. "I would like to ask you a few questions, but before I do I have to read you your rights."

The captain read Jimmy his rights, saying that he had the right to remain silent, and that anything he said could be used in a court of law. He also had the right to have an attorney present, and if he couldn't afford an attorney one would be appointed for him. Captain Williams asked Jimmy if he wanted an attorney to be present, but the Indian just shook his head.

Putting the card back into his pocket, Captain Williams shifted his weight in the chair. "Mr. Cypress, a book was found at your home today. The book belongs to a little girl that disappeared last night. Her name and address were on the inside cover of the book. I would like you to explain why you had that book inside your home."

"I found it."

"You found the book?"

Jimmy nodded. "That's right. I found it."

"I see. And where exactly did you find the book?"

"I found it in the forest."

"Where in the forest?"

"I don't remember," Jimmy lied. He had found the book by the lagoon, but didn't want to say so. With the evil of Mansa Du Paul growing stronger every day, the last thing he wanted was a bunch of idiot cops hanging out around the lagoon.

Captain Williams frowned. "You don't remember where you found the book?"

"That's what I said," Jimmy replied.

"Mr. Cypress, I find that hard to believe."

Jimmy smiled. "I don't care what you believe. I don't remember."

Captain Williams leaned forward in his chair, placing his hands on the table. "You found a copy of *Green Eggs and Ham* in the woods, and you expect me to believe that you don't remember where you found it?"

"That's right."

"And why is that?"

"I find a lot of things in the woods. Don't always remember where I find them."

"You found the book, and you didn't think to call the authorities?"

"Why should I have done that?"

"Because the book belongs to a missing child. Her name is on the inside cover."

"I didn't know there was a kid missing," Jimmy replied. "Not until your deputy told me about it."

"You didn't know about Krissy Patterson? Why's that?"

"No one told me."

"The story has been on the news."

"I don't own a television. Or a radio."

"There's been a search going on. Don't tell me you didn't know about that."

"I live in a tourist area. I see people in the woods all the time. I don't pay attention to what they're doing."

"That's not what Robert Patterson said."

"Who?"

"The little girl's father. He said you threatened him, warned him to stay out of the forest or something bad would happen to him."

"I don't remember that."

"You never threatened Robert Patterson?"

"I didn't say that. I said I don't remember threatening him."

Captain Williams looked at him for a few moments, then asked, "Do you make a habit of threatening tourists?"

"Only when they need to be threatened," Jimmy answered.

"And Robert Patterson needed to be threatened?"

"I don't know. I don't remember. Maybe I didn't even do it."

"And what did you mean by something bad was going to happen to him?"

"Am I under arrest?" Jimmy asked, changing the subject. He knew the captain would not believe him about the evil that resided in the lagoon, and the land surrounding it, or that he had scared off Robert Patterson for his own safety.

"No. You're not under arrest. Not yet," Captain Williams answered.

"Then I want to go home."

"You can go home when we're finished here," said the captain.

Jimmy smiled. "We are finished. If I'm under arrest, then you lock me up. If I'm not under arrest, then you had better release me. One thing for sure, I'm not answering any more of your stupid questions—not without my lawyer. And my lawyer happens to be a Seminole, from the reservation. He's also a tribal chairman. I'm sure he won't be too happy to hear that a tribal member is being held without being charged. He might even alert the federal authorities, and the media."

Captain Williams glared at the Indian for a moment, then stood up. "Okay, if that's the way you want it."

Jimmy's smile widened. "That's the way I want it."

The two officers started to leave the room, but Captain Williams stopped in the doorway and turned back to Jimmy Cypress. "You can sit there and clam up if you want to, but I know you're lying. I will get the truth out of you sooner or later. And let me tell you this: if I find out that you had anything to do with the disappearance of Krissy Patterson, anything at all, I'll nail your Seminole ass to a tree. That's a promise."

With those parting words, Captain Williams and his partner left the room, leaving Jimmy sitting alone at the table. But the Indian wasn't worried about the captain's threat, for he had more important things to worry about. A little girl's life might be in danger, and there was nothing he could do to help her if they locked him up. Nothing at all.

Lowering his head, Jimmy whispered a short prayer under his breath. He prayed to the Creator, and the spirits that guided him, asking for help with his current situation. He asked that they aid him in getting released, because he could not help anyone if he was sitting behind bars. He asked that they watch over Krissy Patterson, keeping her safe from the evil of Mansa Du Paul—an evil Jimmy could not have told the officers about, because they never would have believed him. Finally, he asked, just for spite, that the spirits give Captain Williams a real bad headache.

Finished with his prayer, Jimmy Cypress raised his head and went back to making funny faces at the mirror.

Part II

Chapter Seventeen

Two days had passed since Krissy disappeared: two long, frustrating, and even painful, days. Robert and Janet Patterson were trying their best to keep their composures and stay positive, but it wasn't easy. Not easy at all. Along with the additional patrol cars from the sheriff's department, more reporters had arrived at the fish camp. Krissy's disappearance was now the lead story on several local news channels.

Channel 2 had been joined by news crews from Channel 6, and Channel 9. They were all jockeying for the best position, trying to be the ones with the exclusive pictures when Krissy was finally reunited with her family, or when her lifeless body was carried out of the woods or dragged from the river. It was doubtful if any of them cared how the search would turn out, as long as they got their stories.

Robert and Janet wanted to help with the search, but every time they stepped out of their cabin half a dozen microphones where shoved into their faces. At first they tried to be polite, hoping the press coverage might actually help to find their daughter. If she had wandered off, then someone might recognize her from the news reports and call the authorities. And if Krissy had been abducted, then having her picture shown on the evening news might make it harder for the kidnapper to sneak her out of the area.

They had tried to be helpful by answering the reporter's questions, for Krissy's sake. But as time passed, the news crews became anxious for something new to report about, so they made up new questions: painful questions that hinted at Robert and Janet's inability as parents, and allegations that portrayed Krissy as a troubled and disturbed child.

"Mr. Patterson, is it true you were seen drinking in the bar the night your little girl disappeared?" asked the young woman from Channel 6, a wry, all-knowing, grin twisting the corners of her mouth.

"I had a few beers that night. That's all. Why? Is that a crime?"

"No, sir." Her grin widened. "It's not a crime."

"Mrs. Patterson, is it true that you didn't call the police right away when your daughter was discovered missing?" asked the man from Channel 2.

Janet frowned. "We looked around first. We thought she might have sneaked off somewhere."

Seeing the opening, the reporter moved in like a shark. "Oh? Does your daughter have a habit of sneaking out at night?"

"No. She doesn't."

"But you didn't seem concerned when she sneaked out this time."

"I didn't say that," Janet argued.

"But you didn't call the police right away."

"I said we went looking for her first. She wasn't in her bedroom, so we didn't know what to think and wanted to look around before we called the police."

The reporter refused to back off. "But by looking around yourself you may have wasted valuable time. If your daughter was abducted then you should have immediately called the police."

"We don't know that Krissy was abducted," Robert said, wading into the argument.

"The police seem to suspect she was abducted."

"Which police?" Robert said, his face growing warm with anger. "As far as I know there are no clues to my daughter's whereabouts."

"What about the book that was found yesterday? I've heard it had your daughter's name and address in it."

Robert and Janet looked at each other. They had been told by the sheriff's department that no information about the case would be given to the press, but apparently someone had been talking. The book the reporter was referring to was a copy of *Green Eggs and Ham* by Dr. Seuss. The book had belonged to Krissy, and her name and address were on the inside cover. It had been found at the home of Jimmy Cypress, who was now a possible suspect in the disappearance of their daughter.

Along with the book, a fresh grave had also been discovered beside the cabin belonging to the Seminole. Luckily, the grave had not contained the body of a little girl. Instead, it had contained the remains of Patch, the dog, who had also been missing. The dog had been murdered, his neck and several of his ribs broken.

After finding the book and the grave, the police had taken Jimmy Cypress into custody for questioning. They had also made a thorough search of his cabin and the surrounding forest, but found no other clues to aid in the investigation. If the Indian had kidnapped Krissy, then he had her hidden away somewhere. Or he had buried her.

Robert swallowed hard, remembering the threat the Indian had made toward him. Jimmy Cypress had been mad about his staff being moved, threatening that something bad would happen if Robert ever returned to the area. Had that bad thing happened to Krissy? Had she wandered into the forest and been attacked by a crazy Seminole Indian?

Why in the hell did they even let that Indian stay around there in the first place? The land along the Wekiva River belonged to the state of Florida. Jimmy Cypress had built his cabin illegally on state property. The authorities should have torn it down years ago. It wasn't right that they let him stay for the simple reason that he had been living there a long time. What kind of logic was that? One thing for sure, if that son of a bitch had anything to do with Krissy's disappearance, or if he had so much as harmed a single hair on her head, Robert would do everything within his power to send Jimmy Cypress on a one way trip to the happy hunting ground. He would also sue the shit out of the state of Florida.

Robert turned his attention back to the reporter. "Yes, they did find a book that belonged to my daughter, and they are questioning a possible suspect in my daughter's disappearance. That's all we know. Anything else you will have to ask the police about."

"But—"

He didn't give the reporter a chance to ask another question. "Now. If you don't mind, my wife and I would like to have a little peace and quiet. This has been very hard on the both of us, and we're just not up to answering any more questions."

Taking Janet's hand, he turned his back on the reporters, ignoring the questions that were shouted at them. He opened the door and led his wife back into their tiny cabin, closing and locking the door behind them. He had just locked the door when Janet burst into tears.

"Those bastards! How can they ask such questions?"

He turned to his wife, offering her a hug of support. Janet, who was usually the strong one, buried her face in his chest and sobbed. He held her tighter, stroking the back of her head with his hand. "It's their job. Reporters get paid to uncover dirt on people, to get the scoop that no one else can. A missing little girl isn't much of a story without a scandal to go along with it."

Janet sniffed, but did not raise her head to look at him. "Did you see their expressions? They're like wolves, and we're fresh meat."

"I saw. And you're right, they are wolves," Robert agreed. "I never had much use for the press, even less now. But in their own twisted way, they are trying to help. Krissy's photo has been on all the local channels. It's only a matter of time before they find her."

She lifted her head and looked at him. "Do you really think so?"

Robert looked at his wife, feeling a love so deep it hurt. He also felt pain, because when he looked at Janet he also saw his daughter. They had the same color hair, the same brown eyes, even the same cute nose. It was all he could do to keep from crying himself. "Yes. I really think so. They will find her. I know it. They'll find her safe and sound, curled up and sleeping somewhere, and then we can put this whole ugly mess behind us."

She looked at him, unblinking, studying his face to see if he was lying. After a moment she lowered her eyes and nodded. "I think so too. She's not dead. I know it. I can feel her, like she's a part of me. If she was dead I wouldn't have that feeling. God, I wish someone would hurry up and find her."

"They will," he said, reassuring. "They will."

"But they're taking so long, and everything seems to be going wrong. I thought the bloodhounds would find her—that's what they told us—but the dogs weren't any help."

The sheriff's department had brought in a team of bloodhounds early yesterday. Two deputies had brought three dogs into the cabin, with the intention of walking them through Krissy's bedroom. They wanted the bloodhounds to pick up the little girl's scent from her bed, and from some of her dirty clothing, but the dogs had started barking and howling uncontrollably as soon as they entered the bedroom. One of them had even relieved himself, right there in the middle of the floor.

The deputies had tried to quiet the dogs, but the bloodhounds had refused to settle down and had to be taken back outside. They tried twice more to bring the dogs into the cabin, but each time the results were disastrous. Thinking there must be something in the bedroom that the dogs didn't like, one of the deputies had carried some of Krissy's old clothing outside for the bloodhounds to sniff, but the dogs wouldn't get near the articles of clothing. The deputies had finally given up, putting the hounds in the back of a pickup and driving away.

Robert shrugged. "I don't know what was wrong with those dogs. Ross said they must have picked up the scent of a skunk. Maybe Krissy picked up a little skunk scent somewhere, perhaps got a little bit on her clothes. Not enough for us to notice, but enough to drive the bloodhounds crazy. Their noses are more sensitive than ours."

A knock sounded at the door, startling them. Robert frowned. "If that's another reporter, I swear I'm going to punch him in the nose."

He let go of Janet and walked over to the door, opening it. Captain Williams stood in the doorway.

"Sorry to disturb you," said the captain, "but I thought I would stop by and give you an update."

"Please, come in," Janet said, quickly wiping the tears from her eyes.

The captain glanced behind him at the reporters milling around in front of the cabin and then entered and closed the door. "I wanted to stop by and check on the two of you, and give you an update on what's been happening. I'm afraid there really isn't much to tell you at the moment."

"What about the Indian?" Janet asked.

"We took Jimmy Cypress in for questioning, but we didn't learn much. He said that he found your daughter's book in the forest and brought it home. He didn't know who the book belonged to, but he didn't want to see it get ruined. The man is something of a book collector, well-read, and couldn't stand the sight of seeing a book just lying out in the woods."

"Do you believe him?" asked Robert.

"Truthfully, we're not sure. Mr. Cypress is obviously a reader, but your daughter's book seems strangely out of place to the other books he has in his house. We've done a background check and he doesn't have any living relatives, nor, from what we know, does he have any friends. He's kind of a hermit, so we doubt if he was saving the book to give to anyone."

Robert didn't believe the story that Jimmy had given the sheriff's department. "You said that you've done a background check? Does he have a criminal record?"

"No. Not really. At least not on the local level."

"What do you mean?"

"He's never been arrested for any kind of crime, but the FBI was keeping a file on him back in the seventies."

"FBI?"

Captain Williams nodded. "It seems Jimmy Cypress used to belong to a militant group known as the American Indian Movement. You may remember hearing about them. They took over the town of Wounded Knee, South Dakota, back in 1973. They also took over a federal building in Washington, D.C. Jimmy joined AIM shortly after returning from Vietnam, so the FBI was keeping a file on him."

"Do you think he might have kidnapped our daughter for political reasons?" Janet asked.

"Again, we're not sure. It's possible, but not likely. As far as we know, AIM has never been involved in crimes against civilians. They consider themselves to be warriors, attempting to bring back the 'good old days.' And like I said, Mr. Cypress has no criminal record that we know of."

"What about illegally living on state property?" Robert asked.

"There is that," agreed the captain. "Jimmy's a squatter, but he's been around here for so long the authorities have looked the other way. I'm not sure if they'll continue doing that now, especially after all of this."

"What about the threat he made to me?" Robert asked. "Surely, you guys don't think he's harmless?"

"We asked him about that, but Mr. Cypress claims he never threatened you."

"Bullshit," Robert said.

Captain Williams shrugged. "I didn't believe him, but that's the story he gave. We tried to question him further about the threat, but he clammed up and wouldn't say anymore."

"What about a polygraph?" Janet asked.

"We asked him to take one, but he refused on religious beliefs."

"Religious beliefs?" Robert asked. "What religious beliefs? If he refuses to take a polygraph then he's obviously lying, or he has something to hide."

"That's what we're thinking," agreed Captain Williams. "But we can't force Mr. Cypress to take a polygraph if he doesn't want to, especially not now. He hasn't been charged with anything yet. And if we force him to take a polygraph now, it might jeopardize the case if we do find him guilty of something."

"Hasn't been charged?" Robert was shocked. "But

what about Krissy's book? What about the dog? Isn't that enough to charge him with something?"

"We can't prove he killed the dog. Even if we did, that would have nothing to do with your daughter. And we can't prove he kidnapped your daughter just because he had one of her books inside his house."

"So, that means you're going to let him out?"

The captain nodded. "I'm afraid so. We can only hold him so long without charges."

"Then he's going to get off scot-free?" Robert asked.

"Not necessarily," said the captain. "We may have to release him for now, but I guarantee we will be watching his every move very closely. If he did have anything to do with your daughter's disappearance, then it will only be a matter of time before he makes a mistake and we find out where she is."

"A matter of time?" Janet asked, tears forming in her eyes. "How much time?"

The captain looked at her and was obviously moved by her tears. "Soon, ma'am. We're going to get your daughter back very soon."

Captain Williams turned to face Robert. "I know this is hard for both of you, but I promise we're doing everything we can. We have every available man out here searching these woods. We've also gone over the river, from here all the way to the St. John's. Your daughter's body was not found, so it's a safe bet that she did not drown."

Janet let out a sigh of relief. "Thank God."

"My feelings exactly." The captain smiled. "I'm sorry I don't have more to tell you. I wish I did. If we find out anything, I'll make sure that you are notified immediately."

Robert shook the officer's hand. "Thank you."

Captain Williams nodded and started for the door, stopping halfway across the room. "Oh, I almost forgot. Sergeant Andrews told me about your daughter's invisible playmate, so I've been asking the locals if anyone knows a man by that name—just in case he isn't quite so invisible after all."

"And?" Robert asked.

"None of the people I spoke with know anyone named Mansa, so it probably is just an imaginary friend. Still, it's better to be safe than sorry, so I'll keep asking. But I really don't think it's a clue."

The captain opened the door and stepped out into the bright light of the day. Robert watched him go and then turned back to his wife. All they could do was wait and hope for the best. At least no body was found when the deputies dragged the river. But where was Krissy?

Chapter Eighteen

The sun had set, and night had come once again to the forest surrounding the Blackwater Fish Camp. The police had called off the search for the day, going home to their wives and families. Even the news crews had packed up and left, hurrying off to cover the story of a much more exciting bank robbery in Apopka.

The darkness that covered the forest made searching for the girl nearly impossible. Yet, had the deputies and firemen known where to look, they might have discovered Krissy, for she was not far from the fish camp. Not far at all. She was hiding beneath dense foliage, waiting for the others to leave the area so she could continue looking for things hidden beneath the black waters of the lagoon.

Mansa Du Paul, who's spirit now resided in the girl named Krissy, waited for the moon to rise high in the night sky before crawling out from under a clustering of palmetto bushes. For hours he had lain beneath the bushes, watching as dozens of men searched for the missing child. Twice someone had passed within inches of his hiding place, but they had not seen him. Mansa had become like a chameleon, blending in with the shadows and colors of the foliage. When one of the officers had paused to look his way, he had called upon the *Loas* to distract the man, causing him to look elsewhere. The officer thought it was a brightly colored bird that had taken flight, causing him to look away, but it was much more than that. A spirit had come to do the bidding of the voodoo sorcerer, appearing in the form of a bird.

Now that night had fallen, Mansa felt reasonably safe that he would not be seen by anyone. Even if he was seen, he could quickly vanish into the darkness. Still, he moved cautiously, quietly, always on the lookout for intruders.

He had not known the little girl would be missed by so many people. In his previous lifetime there never would have been such a fuss made about a missing child. Life was hard back then, and bad things happened to those who were careless. Only a few people would have searched, and not for very long. Even the Seminoles, who valued their children above all else, would not have made such a fuss over the loss of one child.

Perhaps Krissy was special. Maybe she was the daughter of a rich man. Why else would so many people spend so much time looking for her? But they would never find her. Mansa was quite sure of that. While he used her body to do his bidding, he would make certain that he was not seen by anyone. Once he was finished with the girl, he would eat her flesh, leaving only the bones to be found.

Mansa Du Paul licked his lips, tasting the sweet saltiness of the child's flesh. It had been a long time since he last ate a little girl. Much too long. He was looking forward to the feast.

In the meantime, he had much work to do. He had to retrieve the rest of the bones that made up the physical body of his former self. Those bones lay scattered at the bottom of the lagoon, buried beneath nearly two centuries of mud and rotten vegetation. They would be difficult to find, but not impossible, because all the bones were buried in the same area.

Mansa knew that the missing bones were still in the lagoon because he could feel each and every one of them. His bones seemed to possess a magical life of their own, calling to him from the darkness and causing his spirit to itch. The remaining bones were all there, waiting to be found and reassembled. After all the bones were gathered, he would add a few necessary items, then he would bring to life his previous physical form.

The girl that was now Mansa smiled, a twisted smile that was all but grotesque on her tiny face. Once he was back in his own body he would rebuild the empire that had been stolen from him. He would make others his slaves, forcing them to do his bidding. Those he could not make his slaves he would destroy, slowly, painfully, one small inch at a time. He would destroy their physical bodies and feed on their souls, adding to the powers he already possessed.

But he had to hurry, for he was running out of time. He could only remain in the girl's body so long before the fiery strength of his spirit consumed her. Mansa's spirit was like a tiny sun, burning up Krissy's body from the inside. He only had a few days before her body would fail him and die.

Hurrying through the forest, he reached the lagoon. Here his spirit was still in touch with the earth, maintaining some control over the plants and vines. Standing at the water's edge, he allowed his spirit to reach out and feel the darkness around him. He instantly became aware of the tiny forest creatures which hid in the night, watching him in fear. They knew his evil was no longer trapped at the bottom of the lagoon. They recognized the darkness of his spirit and feared him more than they feared the predators that stalked the forest.

But Mansa was no threat to the timid animals of the night, for he had other things to occupy his mind. Facing the lagoon, he focused his attention beneath the black water and searched for a part of him that was still missing. He could feel the various bones of his being beneath the water, but he could not see them.

Had anyone been watching, they would have seen a little blonde-haired girl standing at the water's edge, her arms reaching out toward the lagoon, palms up. They would have seen the strange light in her eyes and the even stranger green glow that suddenly encased her fingertips. The glow floated in luminous tendrils from her fingertips to the surface of the lagoon and then dipped beneath the water in search of objects unseen.

"Come to me, my little brothers," Mansa said, focusing all of his energy on the task at hand. "Come back to where you belong."

The tendrils of green glow grew brighter as they spread out over the lagoon, like heat lightning on an August night. It was a glow like nothing ever seen before; ancient magic brought to life in a new world. The girl swayed with exertion, nearly stumbled and fell. In the treetops surrounding the lagoon, birds left their roosts and took to flight, their terrified cries shattering the quiet of the night.

"Come to me, little ones. Come." Mansa called upon powers he had never used, called upon spirits he had faithfully served in his former life. Black spirits. Evil spirits. Demons of the night. *Baccas.* He called upon them to do his bidding, to lend him their powers so he might accomplish the impossible.

A cold wind sprang up from the west, from the direction of darkness and death. The wind caused the bushes to rustle and the trees to dance, sending ripples across the water. A strange cloud blew in front of the moon, and an owl cried out. On the opposite side of the lagoon, the trunk of a cypress tree began to glow from within, as dark powers came to the voodoo sorcerer's aid.

"Come." Mansa gave his powers a final push, snatching the objects he sought from the mud and muck that had covered them for over a hundred years. The psychic push was too much for the tiny body his spirit now rode, causing blood to flow from the little girl's nose.

Mansa ignored the bleeding. Instead he watched as a dozen bones rose to the surface of the lagoon. He dared not lose his concentration now, for if he did the bones would sink again and be lost to him. Straining at the body that now encased it, Mansa's spirit reached out to the bones and guided them safely to the shore. More blood flowed from the girl's nose, heavy and dark in the moonlight.

Several more bones appeared, and then the prize he had been waiting for surfaced. Mansa almost lost his concentration when he saw it, almost failed in his attempt. But he held on, just barely, staring at the skull that had once been his. Encased in an eerie greenish glow, the skull danced on the water's surface. From where he stood, it looked like a skeleton was slowly rising out of the lagoon, for the skull faced him, its empty eye sockets watching the sorcerer work his strange magic.

Mansa reached out for the skull, drawing it toward him. Other bones followed. Tiny bones and big bones, floating on the water, drawn to him by his powers. Drawn back to the man they had once belonged to in the flesh long, long ago.

The last bone came to shore. The sorcerer sent his thoughts out to search for others, but there were no more to be found. His skeleton was now complete, now all that remained was its construction.

As the last bone, a tiny vertebra, washed up on shore, Mansa allowed his powers to wane. There was a moment of intense tingling, then a heaviness came over him, sending him to his knees. The little girl whose body he now used was too weak for such acts of magic. He had drained her of vital energy, and her physical body was now unable to stand.

Panic flared through Mansa Du Paul. Had he overdone it? Had he damaged the girl beyond all repair? Was she now nothing more than a helpless cripple, unable to even walk? He wiped his hand across his face, suddenly alarmed at the blood that continued to flow from the tiny nose.

"Stop it!" he commanded, angry at the physical limitations of his new body. He had never been so weak before; even as a boy he had always been strong. And when he started down the voodoo path, he had acquired strength few could even imagine.

But now he was weak. Though he was not as weak as a girl of Krissy's age would normally be, he was weaker than what he would have liked. He would have to be careful if he performed any more feats of magic. He didn't want to kill the child before he could gather the things he needed to reassemble his former body. The bones were just the beginning; he would also need a heart and a pair of eyes. Since his heart and eyes had been eaten by fish years ago, he would have to look for new ones.

Acquiring a pair of eyes and a heart might be difficult, for few people were willing to part with such organs willingly. Therefore, the things he needed would be taken by force, but Mansa knew the physical limitations of his new, borrowed body. If he wanted to get the things he needed, he had to rely on the element of surprise. He also needed a weapon. A knife.

Strength finally returned to the child's body, and Mansa was able to get back on his feet. Removing his sweatshirt, he laid the shirt on the ground and then placed the bones in the center of it. Tying the edges of the shirt together, he used it as a sack to carry the bones away from the lagoon.

He had to make two trips, hiding the bones in the same hollow log that already held those gathered by Krissy. His skeleton now complete, he covered the bones with twigs and dried leaves. Mansa then slipped the sweatshirt back on and made his way quietly through the forest.

He arrived at the Wekiva River a few minutes later,

pausing to look over his surroundings before venturing out into the open. On the other side of the river was the fish camp, a place that had been a beehive of activity for the past few days. The fish camp was now quiet, because the hour was late and the searchers had gone home for the night. Still, Mansa remained in hiding for a few more minutes, watching to make sure no one was around before moving out into the open.

Stepping out from behind a tree, he hurried along the edge of the Wekiva River until he reached the wooden footbridge spanning the waterway. Crossing the bridge, he made his way past the cabins to one of the larger buildings in the camp.

The body Mansa now possessed may not have been the strongest in the world, but it was extremely fast. It was also tiny enough to hide in even the smallest shadow, blending in with the night. Reaching the first of the two larger buildings, he pressed against the side, using the shadows for concealment. He paused there for a moment, motionless, making sure that he had not been seen. A minute or two passed, the silence reassuring him that all was well.

Mansa did not know what the building was used for, but his senses told him that he would find what he needed inside. Slipping from the shadows on the side, he hurried to the front of the building and tried the door. Unfortunately, the door was locked, and he wasn't strong enough, nor did he have the tools necessary, to open it.

It would be foolish to try to force the door open because the noise he would make would alert others of his presence. Nor could he use his magic to help him, for magic did not always work on things such as locks. And he dared not use his magic now, so soon after using it before, fearful of draining the body he wore. Drain the little girl's body any further and he may not be able to get away.

Frustrated at his inability to open the door, he moved from the first building to the second. The second building must have been a place for cooking, because he could smell the lingering odors of food. A pang of hunger shot through his stomach, caused by the smells that clung to the building. Mansa frowned. He had forgotten what it was to eat, and suddenly realized that the body he now used would need food in order to operate properly. He did not know the last time Krissy Patterson had eaten, but knew that he would have to eat soon or the body he rode would grow weak. Maybe he would find some food inside, something already cooked that would be easy to carry.

"This body is beginning to be a problem."

Moving to the front of the second building, he tried the door but found it locked. Determined to find a way inside, he circled the building to the back side. He found a second door, but it too was locked. Frustrated, Mansa was about to turn away when he spotted a large metal bowl on the ground beside the door. Inside the bowl, several eating utensils soaked in water. There were forks, spoons, and a large wooden-handled butcher knife.

Mansa smiled. Now this was something he could use. He reached in the bowl and removed the butcher knife, grasping it tightly in his right hand to get a feel for it. The knife was designed to be used by an adult, but its handle was not too large for a child's hand. He slashed the air a few times and smiled again. The knife fit just right in Krissy's tiny hand.

He felt better now that he had a weapon, more prepared to defend himself. It was true that the magical powers he possessed could also serve as a weapon, but those powers never came as quickly as the slash of a knife. The knife would also help him to gather the body parts he would need. It was far easier to remove a heart with a knife than it was to remove one with magic.

Mansa Du Paul studied the door in front of him, wishing there was a way to get inside to obtain food. He thought about using the knife to pry open the door, but was afraid of breaking the blade. The knife would be useless to him if it was broken.

Deciding that food would have to wait, he turned away from the door and started back across the fish camp. He had not been seen by anyone and wanted to keep it that way. If anyone saw him, twice as many searchers would come looking for the little girl. If they thought she was dead, or that she was no longer in the area, they might look elsewhere, or give up the search altogether.

He had just reached the other building, when he noticed a small wooden structure sitting beside it. The tiny structure looked like a little house, with a large doorway carved in its front wall. Mansa paused, wondering what the tiny building could be used for. Was it something for children to play in? If so, it was awfully small. Only one child at a time could fit inside the tiny house.

Two bowls sat on the ground in front of the tiny house. One bowl contained water, the other contained brown nuggets of some kind. The bowl containing the nuggets had the word PATCH written on it in large white letters.

"What's this?"

The sorcerer bent over and picked up the bowl with the white letters. The nuggets it contained were the size of walnuts, but they were soft as if made from dough. Perhaps they had once been hard, but they had gotten soft from exposure to the elements.

He held the bowl to his nose and sniffed. The nuggets gave off a strong food odor, though it was not like any food he had ever smelled before. Even the Seminoles had never made anything that smelled like that.

Along with the nuggets, there was something else in the bowl. Tiny white maggots crawled about the bowl, feeding on the brown food chunks.

Mansa smiled. If maggots fed on the brown nuggets, then they were indeed food. He could not imagine why someone had left a bowl of food lying on the ground. Perhaps someone had grown too full and simply wandered off. No matter. He was looking for food, and that's just what he found.

He popped one of the brown food nuggets into his mouth, trying to identify the flavor. It wasn't pork, or beef. Nor did it taste like chicken, or even fish. It tasted sort of like hominy cakes, but not quite. Mansa picked up another one of the nuggets, ignoring the fat maggot that clung to it. He popped both the nugget and the maggot into his mouth and chewed slowly.

The maggot seemed to bring out the flavor of the strange food. Perhaps that was why the bowl had been left on the ground: to draw maggots. Apparently the food was much tastier when served with the tiny worms. It was indeed a strange world that he had awakened into, but who was he to argue with changing times? At least now he would be able to feed the body he used.

Mansa had just swallowed the food chunk, maggot and all, when he heard a door slam, and the sound of approaching footsteps. Someone had just come out of the other building and was walking his way.

Panicked, afraid of being spotted, or caught, before he was back to full strength, Mansa ducked behind the little wooden house, hiding in the shadows. He had just gotten out of sight, when a bearded white man came around the corner of the other building.

The man must have been inside the building, and Mansa was surprised that he hadn't been heard when he tried to open the front door. As the man walked past, he glanced in Mansa's direction, but he obviously didn't see the girl that crouched in the shadows behind the little house.

Mansa remained perfectly still, watching as the bearded man walked on past. He thought about following the man, hoping for an opportunity to test out his new knife, but he quickly dismissed the idea. The body he rode was still weak from the magic he had performed earlier at the lagoon. He needed to eat first, then he could play.

Waiting until the bearded man had left the area, Mansa Du Paul slipped out from behind the little house and hurried toward the river. Carrying the bowl of food in his left hand and the butcher knife in his right, he left the fish camp and hurried back across the wooden bridge, disappearing into the darkness of the forest. Later he would come back in search of the things he still needed, but not now. It was dinnertime, and Mansa always did his best killing on a full stomach.

Chapter Nineteen

Captain Williams had joined the Palmetto County Sheriff's Department almost twenty years ago. Since that time he had been involved in stakeouts and drug raids, hostage situations, and had even single-handedly arrested a pair of bank robbers after a high-speed pursuit. He had been kicked, punched, and shot at, and had once been nearly run over by a speeding motorist.

Despite his experience as a law enforcement officer, this was the first time he had ever been in charge of a search for a missing child. It was quickly proving to be one of the most frustrating things he had ever done in his career, far more frustrating than trying to track down bad guys and criminals.

If Krissy Patterson had gotten lost in the forest, she could be injured and in need of immediate medical attention. The clock was ticking, and every hour that slipped past reduced the chance of the little girl being found in time to help her. And if, God forbid, she had been abducted, then they weren't dealing with hours; they were dealing with minutes. The longer it took to find clues to her whereabouts, or pick up the trail of her abductor, then the less chance they had of ever finding her again.

So far there had been few clues as to exactly what had happened to the missing child. The sheriff's department had run a thorough background check on her parents, but nothing had turned up. Neither Robert nor Janet Patterson had an arrest record, nor did they have a history of child abuse. Except for a speeding ticket acquired three years ago, they would appear to be model, law-abiding citizens.

The Pattersons were not suspects in the case, at least there was no reason to suspect them at the present time. As far as the sheriff's department could tell, they were not dealing with a case of parental abuse.

Normally, the parents would not be the first ones suspected when a child was missing, but over the past few years an alarming number of child abuse cases had happened in Florida. Horrifying cases of parents, and stepparents, abusing, torturing, and even killing their own children. Captain Williams had worked on several such cases, and it made him sick to think about them. He remembered how one father had burned his infant daughter with a hot oven rack; another father had gotten stoned on crack and thrown his two children out of a second-story window.

And then there was the father who had beaten and tortured his eight-year-old daughter to death. The little girl had shown up at school sporting suspicious cuts and bruises, yet nothing had been done to protect her. Family Services had not taken her out of the home, despite knowing that her father had a history of abuse. Instead, they had let her remain in the care of the man who would eventually kill her.

The captain shook his head, trying to clear the visions of child abuse from his mind. Why was it that all the sick people in the world seemed to migrate down to the sunshine state? Was the old saying true, did all the nuts roll downhill to Florida? One thing for sure, he would give a month's pay to be locked up for five minutes with some of the bastards who hurt their kids. Just five minutes. No more. He was quite sure that's all the time it would take to convince them never to lay a hand on another child.

He sincerely hoped Krissy Patterson's case didn't involve child abuse of any kind. Her parents seemed like nice people, and he would hate to find out that they had anything to do with their daughter's disappearance. He didn't think either of them were guilty, because there was too much hurt in their eyes. He had met a lot of people in his line of work, both good and bad, and he could usually tell if they were lying by their eyes. The eyes were windows to the soul, and what he saw in the eyes of Robert and Janet Patterson spoke of their innocence.

However, it wasn't that way for Jimmy Cypress. Captain Williams had taken a good look at Jimmy's eyes and had seen things he did not like. Jimmy had eyes that were cold and deadly, like those of a predator. Despite what Mr. Cypress had told him, the captain could tell that the Indian was lying or hiding something.

A book belonging to Krissy Patterson had been found at the cabin owned by Jimmy Cypress. A Dr. Seuss storybook. Jimmy said he had found the book in the forest, but he wouldn't specify where. He simply said that he had found the book while he was taking a walk.

Jimmy's story didn't hold up, because Robert Patterson was certain he had seen the book in his daughter's bedroom the day of her disappearance. He had also reported that Jimmy Cypress had earlier threatened his life, warning him to stay out of the forest or something bad would happen.

Had the crazy Indian kidnapped Krissy Patterson? Had he murdered her? A grave was found beside Jimmy's shack, but it only contained the body of a dog.

That was another mystery waiting to be solved. The dog in the grave had belonged to the owners of the fish camp, Ross and Mary Sanders. The dog had been noticed missing about the same time the little girl disappeared. Again Jimmy Cypress claimed complete innocence. He said he found the dog's body while out walking, and decided to bury him out of respect. That just didn't make sense. How many people would lug a dead dog back to their house for burial, especially a dog that didn't belong to them? Stranger still was how the dog had died. He hadn't died from sickness, old age, snake bite, or an attack by a wild animal. On the contrary, the dog's neck and spine had been broken.

Captain Williams slowed his unmarked patrol car as he passed the Blackwater Fish Camp. The hour was late and the camp was quiet, a pleasant change from the hustle of activity that had taken place earlier in the day. The searchers had gone home for the day, but they would return in full force first thing in the morning. The little girl had only been missing for a couple of days, so there was still a good chance that they would find her. None of them were about to give up on her so soon.

The captain had driven no more than fifty yards

past the fish camp when something darted across the road in front of him. At first he thought it was a deer and slammed on the brakes to keep from hitting it. But there she was, momentarily illuminated in the glow of his headlights, a little girl with mud-streaked blonde hair. And though her clothing and skin were stained and dirty, there was no mistaking that it was the same girl they had been looking for.

"Holy shit," Captain Williams said, swerving the car to keep from hitting the child. His patrol car came to a screeching halt, sideways in the road. "Shit. Shit. Shit."

He turned on his blue lights, unbuckled his safety belt, and jumped out of the car. But the girl was no longer on the road. She had vanished back into the darkness, disappearing as quickly as she came.

"Damn. Where did she go?" He turned and looked behind the patrol car, but she wasn't there either. And for a moment he wondered if he had even seen her at all. Maybe it was just a deer he saw, or maybe his imagination had played a trick on him.

"No. No. No. I know what I saw. It was her." Leaning back in through the open door, he switched on his spotlight and aimed it at the ditch bordering the right side of the road. At first he didn't see anything, but then the bright beam of the searchlight danced across the figure of a child standing in the shadows, watching him.

"Son of a bitch. It is her." Captain Williams was shocked. Here was the little girl that half the sheriff's department was looking for. She was there, no more than fifty feet from him. He had found her.

He wanted to get on the radio and call dispatch to

report the news, but he didn't dare take his eyes off the girl, fearful that she would vanish again. The radio call would have to wait.

"Now what do I do?"

Krissy Patterson had not moved. She still stood at the edge of the forest, trapped in the beam of the powerful searchlight. There was something odd about that, something not right about what was happening. The girl had run in front of his patrol car, as if running in fear from something, or someone. She had darted across the road and then stopped, hiding in the shadows to watch him. Now she just stood there, motionless, like a raccoon or some other nocturnal creature, frozen in place by the light.

Was she hurt? She might be in shock, completely unaware of what she was doing or where she was. Perhaps she had been abducted and was traumatized by the event. If so, then Captain Williams needed to be very careful about how he approached her. If she was in shock, or scared, she might run from him. She might disappear back into the forest, never to be seen again. It wouldn't look good to report that he had found the girl, only to lose her again.

Stepping away from his patrol car, he started walking slowly toward her. "Krissy, is that you?" He forced a smile, trying to look as friendly as possible. It wasn't easy because he was nervous, afraid the child might take off running. Although he was a fairly fast runner himself, there was no way he would be able to keep up with a frightened child in a dark forest.

"Krissy, my name is Captain Williams. I'm a police officer." He removed the badge from his belt and held it in front of him for her to see. "Are you okay?"

There was no response from the girl. She just stood there looking at him, her tiny body illuminated by the searchlight that was still focused on her. The light made her skin look far whiter than it should have looked, deathly pale, as if she were nothing more than a ghostly apparition.

The captain's pace momentarily faltered, and he almost allowed the smile to slip from his face. The little girl who stood before him did indeed look like an apparition, as if he were seeing a ghost and not a person of flesh and blood.

A chill walked down the big man's spine. He was a devout fan of television shows like *The X-Files* and *Sightings*, shows which often portrayed incidents of ghostly encounters. He greatly enjoyed that kind of program, but that was when viewed in the comfort, and safety, of his living room. It was an altogether different situation to think that a meeting with the paranormal might now be happening to him, in the middle of the night, in the middle of nowhere.

A cold sweat broke out on his forehead. He wanted to wipe it away, but he didn't want to make any sudden movements that might frighten the girl. If it was a little girl that stood silently watching him, and not her ghost.

Stop it. Stop it. Stop it. It's just a little girl. A frightened little girl. It's not a ghost. Quit scaring yourself.

"Krissy, are you okay?"

Again, she did not answer him. She only stood there, watching. No. Not even watching. There was nothing to indicate she even saw him. Her eyes didn't move, nor her head. She only stood there, looking in his general direction. Looking his way, but perhaps not seeing him.

He reached the edge of the road and started down into the ditch. He tried to move slowly, but the grass was slick with dew and his feet slipped out from under him.

"Shit!" he cried as he lost his footing and landed on his backside, sliding down into the ditch. He came to a stop at the bottom, quickly getting to his feet. He was afraid that his sudden movements, and the obscenity he had yelled, would frighten the child, causing her to run away. But she was still standing there, only now she was closer to him.

As Captain Williams got back up, he was surprised to see Krissy Patterson standing only a few feet away from him. Even though he had slipped and slid down into the ditch, she shouldn't have been so close. It was as if she had hurried to him while he was sliding out of control, only to freeze in place once he recovered.

"Krissy?"

Maybe she had hurried to him out of concern, a helpful child rushing to the aid of an adult in trouble. Maybe so, but now she was again standing motionless, a blank expression on her face. Again, he wondered if the little girl that stood before him was made of flesh and blood, or was she nothing more than a misty apparition?

The captain wiped the palms of his hands off on his pants. They had gotten wet during the fall. The seat of his pants had also gotten wet and was probably muddy. He tried to ignore the wetness, but the dew was cold and brought a chill to his legs.

"Krissy, don't be afraid. I'm here to help you. I'm

your friend. Your mother and father have been looking for you. We have all been looking for you. We've been very worried."

He stepped up to the girl and gently laid his hands on her shoulders, thankful to discover that she was indeed the real Krissy Patterson and not her ghost. She looked up at him, and he saw that something was not quite right about her eyes. They were not the eyes of a frightened child. Nor were they the glassy, vacant eyes of someone in shock. They had a strange bluish-green shine to them, like the eyes of an animal.

Captain Williams started to say something reassuring when he noticed a butcher knife clutched tightly in the little girl's right hand. He also noticed the smile that unfolded on her face like a flower. A cold, deadly smile.

There was a flash of movement, and the glint of light off cold steel, as Krissy Patterson whipped her arm around. Caught off guard, Captain Williams tried to jump back out of the way to avoid the knife. But he wasn't fast enough, and the blade of the butcher knife sliced deep into his groin.

The captain screamed in pain and dropped to his knees, grabbing his shredded testicles. Pain shot through him like burning fire, stealing his voice and forcing tears to his eyes. He knew the wound was serious, for he could feel blood rushing down his legs. The front of his pants turned wet and warm.

Before he could even think of defending himself against a second attack, the little girl slashed the knife's blade across the left side of his neck. The razor-sharp butcher knife sliced easily, laying open his flesh and severing his jugular vein.

His eyes went wide. He tried to cry out, but only a gargled hissing escaped his lips. He tried to draw a breath of air, but his throat was full of blood and he could not breathe. He was drowning in his own blood and knew he would be dead in a matter of seconds, but there was not a damn thing he could do about it. He placed the palm of his left hand against his neck and pressed tight, but it was a futile effort to stop the flow of blood. Even if a team of paramedics had been on the scene, it was doubtful they would be able to save his life.

He looked at the girl who stood before him, wondering why she had attacked him. He was only trying to help her, only wanted to reunite her with her parents. What in God's name had happened to her that would warrant such action? Had she been abducted and abused, did she look at him and see the man who had hurt her?

A thousand questions danced through his mind in those final moments, but they were questions that would go unanswered. As Captain Williams toppled sideways and fell to the ground dying, he heard a laugh. Cold. Harsh. Definitely not the laugh of a little girl.

Chapter Twenty

Mansa silently rejoiced as he watched the black man kneeling before him slowly bleed to death. It had been a long time since he had killed someone without the use of his magic or the aid of dark spirits. There was something extremely satisfying about taking a life with his own hands, even if his hands were actually now those of a ten-year-old girl named Krissy.

He glanced down at the tiny hands he now possessed, his grin growing wider. The small fingers which encircled the wooden handle of the butcher knife were covered with the soldier's blood.

The voodoo sorcerer looked at the dying man. At least he thought the man was a soldier. The black man wore no uniform, but he had identified himself as a captain. He had said his name was Captain Williams. Perhaps he wore no uniform because he was home on leave. Maybe he was a special kind of soldier and did not wear a uniform. Either way, uniform or not, Mansa was more than happy to take the man's life.

The captain gasped for air and toppled to his side, lying helpless on the ground. Though he wore a pistol, he made no attempt to reach for it. He was far too busy trying to stop the blood that spurted from his severed jugular. His efforts were foolhardy, however, for the knife had sliced deep into his neck. It would be only a matter of moments before he bled to death.

Looking around to make sure they were still alone, Mansa stepped forward and grabbed Captain Williams by the legs. He was worried that someone else might come down the road at any minute. Not wanting to be seen, he decided to drag the dying soldier into the forest. He expected the captain to kick at him as he grabbed his legs, but he was already too close to death to put up any kind of struggle.

The captain was heavy, and Mansa had to strain to get him out of the ditch. He slipped twice in the effort and had to put down his knife for fear of falling on it. Once the soldier was safely out of sight, he went back and retrieved the butcher knife.

Even in the forest, it was still light enough to see what he was doing. Mansa opened the captain's shirt, only to discover a second shirt beneath the first. The second shirt was heavy and stiff and appeared to be made of a protective material. It wasn't metal, but Mansa still suspected that the second shirt was some kind of protective armor. Perhaps the captain wore it for protection against Indians.

The sorcerer smiled, twisting his tiny mouth into an evil grin. He doubted if there were many Indians left in the area. At least he didn't think there were. Though he had been dead for over a hundred years, his spirit had been far from dormant. He had been aware of the people around the lagoon, and it had been a long time since he had felt very many Indians. As far as he knew, only one Indian still lived in the region.

His smile faded.

Since Mansa's death, there had always been a Seminole Indian living in the area. Just one. Not always the same Indian, but never more than one at a time. Since the time of his death, there had been a dozen different Seminoles living along the Wekiva River, each a man of medicine.

The Seminoles knew more about Mansa Du Paul than did the white men, and they had lived in fear that he would one day rise again from the dead. They had not been wrong. So the Seminoles had left a man behind when they moved their village farther to the south, one man to watch over the area and guard against Mansa's return.

At first he had been angry that the Seminoles were using their magic to keep him from returning, but over the years that anger had given way to bored amusement. The medicine men had powers, but their magic paled when compared to his dark gifts. Let them do their dances and sing their songs, let them smoke their pipes and wave their eagle feathers in the air. None of it meant a thing to him. They were merely children, playing with children's toys.

Now he had returned, and the Seminole who called himself the guardian had failed to stop him. Mansa was back in the flesh, even though the body he now wore was only temporary. Soon he would be back in his own body and at full strength once again. Then he would have to pay a little visit on a certain Indian. Wouldn't he be surprised?

The smile came again to the sorcerer's face as he thought of all the horrible things he would do to Jimmy Cypress. Yes, he knew the Indian's name, for the man had been foolish enough to say it aloud during one of his prayers. Mansa had been listening in on the prayer and clearly heard the name. It was unwise to let your enemies know your name, because it gave them power over you. Not that Mansa needed any more power, for he would soon have more than he could ever use.

Turning his attention back to the captain, Mansa removed the heavy protective shirt out of the way. There was another, thinner shirt beneath that, which he also removed. Finally, the captain's bare chest was exposed to him. Taking the butcher knife in his right hand, he carefully cut around the dead man's heart.

The work was difficult, and Mansa had to be careful not to slip and cut into the heart. There was also the problem of getting through the rib bones in order to get to the heart. He wished he had a saw, but he would have to make due with the knife. Nearly twenty minutes elapsed before he was able to work the heart loose from the soldier's chest.

"Finally," Mansa said, holding the heart up to the moonlight. He was delighted the heart had belonged to a black man. A very large, strong, black man. The heart was also large and strong. An excellent specimen. It would serve him well in his soon-to-be-resurrected body. He would have taken the captain's eyes, but the man wore glasses. Weak eyes would never do.

The sorcerer brought the heart to his nose and inhaled deeply, savoring the fragrance of fresh blood. It was such a wonderful aroma. There was nothing like it in all the world.

Unable to control his hunger, he allowed his tongue

to slip from between his lips to taste the bloody heart. Just a little taste, his tongue darting in and out of his mouth like a snake. And then he allowed his tongue to fully extend from his mouth as he licked the heart in one continuous motion, licking every drop of blood from the organ as he slowly turned it in his hand.

Bending over, he removed the captain's undershirt and carefully wrapped the still-warm heart in it. He still needed a pair of eyes, but Mansa wanted his vision to be strong, so he would just have to borrow a pair of eyes from someone else.

Mansa Du Paul smiled, knowing that he would have to kill again to get the eyes he needed.

Chapter Twenty-one

Robert Patterson sat in one of the oversized chairs in his cabin, staring at, but not seeing, the wall in front of him. The room was dark and that was good, because he did not want to see the walls or the simple paintings that decorated them. He wanted only the darkness, wanted only to stare but not see.

He was alone in the tiny sitting room. Janet had gone to bed several hours earlier, her sleep brought to her by the two tiny pills she had swallowed. Robert had not taken any sleeping pills, so he found himself, at three o'clock in the morning, sitting alone in the darkness, wishing for sleep to carry him away to a place without thoughts or memories.

But sleep refused to come to Robert Patterson. Instead, he was haunted by a thousand images and thoughts that floated through his mind like surrealistic cloud formations, formations that faded and slipped away as quickly as they came.

In the darkness, he thought back to the early days of planning for their Florida vacation, to the hours spent in their St. Louis home looking through countless brochures for the perfect spot to visit.

Janet had originally wanted to vacation in South

Florida, visiting the art-deco buildings of Miami, the wilds of the Everglades, and maybe even a quick trip to Key West. She was a big fan of Ernest Hemingway and wanted to pay a visit to his home. She also wanted to have a drink at the original *Sloppy Joe's*, a favorite haunt of the writer, and a place not to be missed by his devoted fans.

Krissy had warmed quickly to the idea of visiting Key West when her mother told her about the six-toed cats that lived at the Hemingway home. The cats were supposed to be the descendants of the six-toed felines the author had kept as pets when living in Key West, but that was probably nothing more than a myth. According to a published interview with the oldest son of the author, Ernest Hemingway had never even owned cats while living in south Florida. Janet had also promised her daughter that they would spend a day at the Dolphin Research Center in Key West. The thought of swimming with a dolphin had greatly excited the child, and it was all she had talked about for days.

Robert had also liked the idea of spending some time in Key West, but he wasn't too keen on paying a visit to Miami. Despite attempts to renovate the city into a colorful tourist destination, Miami still had a very serious crime problem. He had read about tourists being robbed and even killed when accidentally wandering into some of Miami's lower-income neighborhoods.

Nor had he been too keen on the idea of taking Krissy to the Everglades. A land of mosquitos, poisonous snakes, hungry alligators, and remote wilderness was not the kind of place he wanted to take his ten-year-old daughter.

But that's exactly the kind of place you brought her to.

Robert sighed, feeling a burning sensation settle deep inside his stomach. He had picked Blackwater as the perfect family vacation spot. It had been his choice. There was no one else to blame but himself. He had convinced Janet that central Florida would be much safer than the Miami area, had convinced his daughter that his vacation choice was the best by bribing her with a promised visit to Walt Disney World. That's all Krissy needed to hear to be on his side. A chance to shake hands with Mickey Mouse was much more exciting than visiting the home of a dead writer, even if that home did come equipped with six-toed cats.

Standing up, Robert crossed the room to where his shirt hung on the wall. He removed a pack of cigarettes and a lighter from the shirt's pocket, lighting one of the cigarettes. He had been trying to cut back on his smoking, but at that particular moment he no longer cared if he gave up cigarettes or not. He needed the taste of tobacco to kill the flavor of guilt that hung heavy on his tongue, needed the nicotine to steady his frayed nerves.

Slipping the pack of cigarettes back into the shirt pocket, he walked to the window and opened the curtains so he could see out. The hour was late and the fish camp quiet, all of the reporters and searchers having gone home for the night.

Though no one had actually said so, Robert was starting to have suspicions that some of the men in the search party felt that Krissy might never be found. It was the looks they gave him as they walked past, some of them deliberately avoiding eye contact. They were afraid he might ask them for encouraging news, and there was none to be given.

Perhaps they suspected him as a culprit in his daughter's disappearance. Maybe they thought he had done something terrible to her, and that he was now fabricating a story to cover his guilt.

But I'm not guilty. I didn't do anything wrong. I did not hurt my daughter. I did not murder her and then bury her body in the forest.

Feeling that anger and frustration was about to overcome him, fighting off the sudden urge to put his fist through the wall—even though he knew that he would surely shatter his hand in the attempt—he stared out the window and focused his attention on the night.

At first he saw only the trees, and the walking path that wound between them, but then he noticed a light reflecting off a neighboring cabin. It was the flashing blue light of a police car.

Stepping to his left to get a better view, Robert spotted an unmarked patrol car parked on the road with its blue lights flashing. Apparently, not everyone had gone home for the evening. Certain members of law enforcement were still on duty. He didn't see another vehicle, so it wasn't a traffic stop.

Curious, Robert turned away from the window and walked back across the room. A pair of binoculars sat in their case atop the small wooden table. They had brought the binoculars on the trip to do a little bird watching. So far, they had not gotten much use, as bird watching was the furthest thing from their minds.

Removing the binoculars from their case, he returned to the window and looked out. The moon was still bright; it cast a glare on the window and made using the binoculars difficult. But Robert was able to back up until the moon's light was partially blocked by a large oak tree. Adjusting the binoculars to his eyesight, he focused his attention on the patrol car.

The car was sitting in the middle of the road, partially blocking it, which struck Robert as odd, especially when he didn't see another vehicle. Surely the person driving the patrol car would pull over to the side, rather than risk causing an accident. Country roads were notorious for high-speed driving, and even the flashing blue lights might not be warning enough to keep the car from getting hit.

The second thing that struck him as odd was that the vehicle was empty. Despite the bright blue lights flashing in his eyes, he could clearly see that the driver's door was open and the patrol car unoccupied. He moved the binoculars to search the area around the patrol car, but didn't see anyone. Whoever was driving had gotten out of the car, not even bothering to close the door.

Robert lowered the binoculars and scratched the bridge of his nose with his free hand. Maybe the officer had come across some roadkill and was now dragging it out of the way. Maybe someone had hit a deer. Such things were not uncommon in rural areas, especially one as heavily forested as that around Blackwater. It probably happened all the time.

Maybe the officer had to make a nature call, due

to one cup of coffee too many, and was currently relieving himself behind a tree or bush. Robert smiled, thinking how funny it would be if the officer accidentally spooked a wild animal while in the process of doing his duty.

Raising the binoculars back to his eyes, he again searched the area around the patrol car, but didn't see anyone. He was about to look away when he caught a glimpse of movement.

Something darted out from behind the car and moved into the shadows beneath a clump of trees. Robert focused the binoculars in that direction and gasped in surprise.

A person was standing in the shadows, facing toward the fish camp. Even though it was dark, and the person in the shadows was covered with mud and filth, there was no mistaking her identity. It was Krissy.

"Dear God. Krissy!"

Robert started to drop the binoculars and run for the front door, but an uneasy feeling stopped him. Something wasn't right. Not right at all. Why was his daughter just standing there, looking his way? Why didn't she come back to the camp? Why didn't she come home? Was she afraid? Had someone in the camp done something bad to her?

Anger flashed through him as he thought about the other occupants of the camp. Although Ross and Mary Sanders seemed like nice people, he really didn't know anything about them.

What if Ross was some kind of deviant, a sexual predator, and had molested Krissy? Maybe he had sneaked into their cabin when they were sleeping.

Such a thing would have been very easy for the owner of the fish camp, because he knew who was staying in what cabin. He probably even knew which bedrooms they were sleeping in. He had the keys to all the cabins, so it would have been a simple matter to enter the cabin while they were out fishing or canoeing and unlock Krissy's bedroom window.

Neither Robert nor Janet had checked the window in their daughter's bedroom the night of her disappearance, prior to her going to bed, because it had already been checked the previous evening and found to be locked. No sense checking the window a second time when they were the only ones who had been in the cabin, or so they thought.

Had Ross entered the cabin and unlocked the window? Was he a sexual predator of some kind? Robert wished he had a computer with access to the Internet, because he knew that the Florida Department of Law Enforcement maintained a web site that listed all of the known sexual predators residing within the state. The site listed their names, the crimes they had been charged with, their last known address, even provided their photos. He had come across the site by accident while doing research for their vacation.

If he had access to the Internet, he could quickly find out if Ross had a history of molesting children. Unfortunately, he didn't have a computer, nor did he know anyone locally who did. Fishing gear he had access to, but not a computer, and you sure the hell couldn't log on the Internet with a rod and reel.

What if Ross was completely innocent? What if someone else in the camp had molested his daughter, making her afraid to come home? A couple of the cabins were rented by fishermen. What if one of them had harmed her? Maybe one of the men who had helped search for Krissy had actually been the person who abducted her. It would be a perfect cover story: kidnap a little girl, molest her, tie her up somewhere, and then come back and act like nothing had happened, going so far as to help the parents look for her, all the time making sure not to go anywhere near where she was hidden.

One of the fishermen could have done something to Krissy. It might not even have been one of the men staying in the cabins. The fish camp was a busy place during the day, with lots of people coming in off the road to use the river. Someone might have seen Krissy, might even have befriended her.

Robert frowned. There were times when he had let Krissy out of his sight, allowing her to wander freely around the fish camp. No one had been with her when she took her naps, or when he and Janet cooked up the bass they had caught. Krissy had been on her own then, helpless prey to a sexual stalker.

What about Mary Sanders? If her husband was some kind of sex offender she would know about it. Then again, what if she was actually the guilty one? It would not be the first time a woman had sexually molested a little girl. There were a lot of sick people in the world.

All the nuts roll downhill to Florida.

Robert suddenly remembered how uncomfortable Krissy had been around Mary Sanders the last time they had eaten in the restaurant. She had refused to look at Mary, as if she was terrified of her. Had Mary done something to his daughter? Had she hurt Krissy in some way?

Another thought suddenly popped into his mind. What if Krissy wasn't alone? What if someone was standing next to her, hidden in the darkness, someone who would not let the little girl return to her parents?

He focused the binoculars on his daughter, she hadn't moved, then moved them slowly to each side of her. If someone was standing there he, or she, was well hidden. He was still looking at his daughter when she turned her back on him and disappeared into the forest.

"Krissy! No!"

Robert dropped the binoculars and raced for the front door. Luckily, he was already wearing his jeans and a pair of tennis shoes, so he did not have to get dressed. Grabbing his shirt, he opened the door and ran out into the night. He didn't care that Krissy might not be alone, or that he was unarmed. He was not going to let his daughter get away from him this time.

Chapter Twenty-two

Robert ran through the campgrounds until he reached the road. The patrol car still sat empty in the middle of the narrow lane, its blue lights flashing like ghostly beacons. The driver's door stood open, and there was still no sign of the officer.

He passed the empty patrol car at a dead run, not even bothering to give it more than a quick glance. The road rounded a sharp curve just beyond where the vehicle sat, so it was doubtful if the patrol car, or its flashing lights, were visible to the patrons of the Blackwater Lounge, or anyone else in the main part of the fish camp.

To Robert's surprise, it turned out he had seen his daughter disappear into the forest on the same side of the road as the fish camp, just north of the cabins. Without hesitation, he navigated the ditch and plunged into the forest, following a small animal trail that Krissy must have used.

He thought the trail might lead back toward the camp area, perhaps it was a shortcut created by local hikers, but it turned away from the camp running in a northeasterly direction.

It was a clear night, and the moon was bright, but

the trail was narrow, the moonlight all but blocked by the branches of towering trees. Robert had to slow his pace due to the darkness, fearful of tripping over a vine or running into the pointy end of a hanging branch into his eyes. Having to slow his pace only added to his growing frustration. Somewhere up ahead was his daughter. Somewhere up ahead was the little girl he loved and had lost, and he was determined not to lose her again.

The path he followed changed directions, now heading due east, parallel to the fish camp. He could not see Krissy and wondered if she was still ahead of him. Was she following the same path as he was, or had she turned and gone a different direction? Several times he thought he saw movement up ahead, but it was probably nothing more than wishful imagination.

Robert wanted to call out his daughter's name, but was afraid that she might not be alone. If someone was with her, he did not want to alert them that they were being followed. If he called out he might be putting Krissy's life in even greater danger.

He thought about pausing for a moment to see if he could hear sounds of movement from up ahead. Surely, even the movements of a child would be loud enough to be heard. But if he stopped to listen then Krissy might get farther ahead of him, especially if she was running, or being dragged along by someone. No. It was better to keep moving and hope to overtake her.

He reached the Wekiva River, surprised to discover an old, little used footbridge spanning the water. The wooden beams and boards that made up the bridge were weathered and gray and looked in danger of falling down at the slightest touch. Still, it was a bridge and he needed to get across the river if he hoped to keep following his daughter.

Robert held his breath as he stepped onto the bridge. The wooden structure creaked loudly under his weight, but nothing seemed to give. At least the bridge didn't fall out from under him as he had feared. Hurrying across the bridge, he reached the other side of the river without getting wet.

He was now faced with a dilemma, for the path he followed forked. The left fork followed the Wekiva River north, away from Blackwater Fish Camp. The right fork followed the river south toward the camp.

"Damn it. Which way?" Robert said, frustrated. He was so afraid he might lose his daughter again that his stomach started to cramp, and he was suddenly in dire need of a bathroom.

"No. No. No. I don't have time for this." Pressing his palms against his stomach, he doubled over and waited for the pain to pass. Straightening back up, he again studied the paths before him.

He was about to choose the left path, because if someone was with Krissy they wouldn't want to go in the direction of the camp for fear of being seen, but then he spotted something in the soft earth by his feet. A footprint. Small. Delicate. A child's footprint.

Robert's heart thudded madly in his chest. The footprint had to be Krissy's. The odds of it belonging to another child were a million to one.

It had to be Krissy's, there were no other children living in the immediate area. Nor were any children staying at the camp. Besides that, the trail was not one that was regularly used. It was an old trail, replaced by the boardwalks farther to the south.

Choosing the right fork, he hurried along the trail. Despite the dangers of vines and branches, he felt that speed was necessary and moved as fast as he possibly could. Branches and brush snagged at his clothing and scratched his skin. Twice he nearly tripped and fell but managed to stay on his feet and keep moving.

He thought the trail would take him back to the fish camp, but it veered slightly to the east, away from the camp. It wasn't long before the narrow trail joined up with a wider path, which Robert recognized as being part of the camp's nature trail. But it was one of the older sections, because he soon came upon a section of boardwalk that had been burned by fire.

Robert suddenly recognized the trail he followed, and knew that it would lead him to the lagoon. A tingle of fear shot through him, for the last time he was at the lagoon his life had been threatened. A crazy Indian, named Jimmy Cypress, had warned Robert to stay away from the lagoon, otherwise something bad would happen to him.

Something bad had happened to him. His daughter had been taken.

The fear he felt was suddenly replaced by a surge of anger. The Indian had threatened him, then his daughter had disappeared. Krissy's favorite storybook had been found at Jimmy Cypress's cabin. Despite his protests of being innocent, the Indian had to be involved in the terrible things that had happened.

And now Krissy was found—well, almost found. Robert had seen her watching the fish camp. There was no mistaking who it was. Krissy was alive, and close by, but she was apparently afraid to come back. Or someone was with her, and they wouldn't let her come back to her family.

Was Jimmy Cypress with her? Robert thought the Indian had been arrested, and the police were holding him as a possible suspect in the case. He had to be a suspect. They had found Krissy's book in his house, had found a murdered dog in a shallow grave beside his house. And he had threatened Robert. Surely, that made Jimmy Cypress a suspect. The police would keep him in jail. They wouldn't just let him go. Would they?

A strong wind suddenly sprang up as he approached the lagoon, a wind that seemed to be blowing from the lagoon itself. Moments before the forest had been still; no breeze to be felt. But now the wind had suddenly whipped up, as if a thunderstorm drew near. The night sky, however, was clear, the moon full and bright.

"What the hell?" he said aloud, turning his head to keep dirt from being blown into his eyes. Around him bushes and branches danced and swayed, casting eerie shadows. The wind grew stronger, causing leaves to cascade down upon him like a feathery rainfall. He ignored the falling foliage and pushed on.

He finally emerged from the forest into the clearing that surrounded the lagoon, leaving behind shadows and darkness for a world cast in silvery moonlight. The moonlight reflected off the surface of the water in fiery brilliance, making the lagoon look like a giant gemstone.

The first thing he noticed upon stepping into the clearing was that the Indian's staff was gone. The strange staff with the skull and feathers had stood at the water's edge, directly in front of the place where the path emerged from the forest. That staff was now missing. Perhaps it had been taken by the Indian, or the police. Maybe it had been stolen by a tourist far braver than Robert.

The second thing he noticed was Krissy. She stood at the edge of the lagoon, her back to him, staring down into the water. She was alone and apparently oblivious to everything around her, looking at something only she could see.

Robert looked quickly to the left, then right, searching to see if anyone else was around. He had suspected that his daughter was in the custody of an abductor, but it now looked as if she was alone. If anyone was nearby, watching her, then he was well hidden. Turning his attention back to his daughter, he watched in disbelief as she slowly waded into the lagoon.

"Krissy, no!" Robert yelled and rushed forward. He stopped at the water's edge, reluctant to wade in for fear of quicksand. He didn't know if there was such a thing as quicksand in Florida, but he did not want to take the chance. Still, he had to stop his daughter. The water was already up to her waist.

Again he called out Krissy's name, but she acted as if she did not hear him. Perhaps she was in shock. Frantic, he snatched up several pine cones and threw them at her.

The first two pine comes missed. The third struck Krissy between the shoulder blades. She turned and stared at him, looking right through him. And then she spoke.

"Dad-d-y"

The voice was not his daughter's. There was no sunshine and warmth in the voice. No happiness. The words were icy cold, like the wind blowing through a graveyard at night. A chill danced up Robert's spine and touched his heart.

And even from ten feet away he could tell that her eyes were different, even in the dark. They were no longer the soft brown eyes of the little girl he loved so much. On the contrary, her eyes now shone with an unholy bluish-green light, reflecting the glow of the moon like the eyes of a nocturnal animal.

Sweet Jesus, what have they done to you?

Fear suddenly swept over Robert, stealing his voice. The little girl that stood before him was his daughter, there was no doubt about that. He knew every inch of her body, every mole and scar. It was his daughter all right, but there was something terribly alien about her. It was his daughter, and yet it wasn't.

Images from the old science fiction movie *Invasion of the Body Snatchers* sprang to mind. His daughter looked the same on the outside, except for her eyes, but this was not the Krissy he knew and loved. She was now a pod person, her spirit taken over by aliens.

Nonsense. She's your daughter. How can you think otherwise?

But look at her eyes. Damn it, look at her eyes. They're glowing like an animal's. And her voice. What about her voice?

It's just the night air. Maybe she's thirsty. She's been out here in the woods for two days, naturally her voice is going to sound funny. Maybe she's sick, or has a cold.

A thousand arguments danced through his head, a

thousand questions. But no answers came to him. He did not know why his daughter sounded different, or why her eyes were shinning like twin candles in the moonlight. The not knowing scared him, scared him half to death.

Confused and frightened, Robert stumbled back from the water's edge. He had only taken two steps, however, when he slipped on the leaf-covered ground and fell. He scrambled to get back up, but before he could get to his feet something grabbed his left ankle.

A flash of pain shot up Robert's left leg. He lifted his head to see what had grabbed him, and was shocked to see that it was Krissy. The little girl stood knee deep in the water, grabbing his ankle in the vice-like grip of her right hand. A grin unfolded on her face, a grin that stretched far too wide at the corners of her mouth.

"Let's play a game, Dad-d-y."

She squeezed his ankle tighter, bruising his flesh and nearly cracking bone. Robert howled from the pain; his bladder suddenly emptied, causing him to pee in his pants. He tried to sit up and pry the tiny fingers from around his ankle, but she squeezed again and the world swam around him in a hazy fog.

Kick her. Kick her. Kick her.

His mind screamed the command, but he just couldn't bring himself to kick his daughter. Despite what he saw and felt, he refused to believe that it wasn't Krissy who stood before him. It had to be her. But why was she trying to hurt him?

She must be in shock. That's it, she's in shock.

He had heard about people in shock performing amazing feats of strength, like the story about the woman who had lifted a car off of her son. He had always thought such stories were nothing more than urban myths, but maybe some of them were true. That would explain Krissy's sudden strength and the reason why she did not recognize her own father.

The grip around his left ankle grew tighter, and then Krissy started moving back, dragging him into the water.

"Krissy, no. . . !" He clawed at the ground, digging furrows in the layers of dead leaves and soft earth. He was already halfway in the water. Any second he would be pulled all the way in. Desperate, he grabbed a root and held on. Krissy pulled harder, fingernails digging deep into his flesh.

Robert cried out in desperation, hoping someone would come to his aid. "No. No. No. Please, somebody help me!"

There was a sudden rustling from the forest behind him, and the sound of someone running. Robert looked and saw a man racing toward him. He couldn't tell who it was at first, but then he saw that it was Jimmy Cypress, the same Indian who had threatened his life—the man who was probably responsible for the abduction of his little girl.

Oh, no.

Jimmy was running toward him, probably intent on stopping Robert from rescuing Krissy. The Indian was crazy, deranged; in his hands he carried the same skull-topped staff Robert had seen earlier and mistakenly touched. The Indian was going to attack him with the staff, and there wasn't a damn thing Robert could do to stop him. He was unarmed, and he couldn't even stand up because Krissy was still dragging him into the water.

But Jimmy Cypress didn't hit him with the staff, as Robert feared. Instead he stopped at the water's edge, and, muttering words of an ancient dialect, touched Krissy's hand with the tip of the beaded staff.

A blue spark jumped from the staff to the little girl's hand. Bright blue. As bright as lightning on an August night. Krissy released her hold on Robert's ankle and jumped back. Hissing in rage, she turned to the left and ran along the water's edge, then turned back toward the shore and raced up the bank to the forest. At the tree line she paused to look back at them, then disappeared into the night.

Robert watched his daughter disappear into the forest, too stunned to even call out her name. The pain in his ankle, and his struggle to keep from being dragged into the lagoon, had taken a lot out of him. He could only lie there and pant, trying desperately to catch his breath. A few moments passed before his heart began to quiet. Rolling over on his back, he saw that Jimmy still stood beside him.

"You!" Robert said, sitting up. "This is your fault. What have you done to my daughter?" He tried to stand up, wanting nothing more than to throw himself at the Indian, but his left foot and ankle would not support his weight. He could only sit there and point at Jimmy Cypress.

"I have done nothing," replied the Indian.

"Liar. This is your fault. You kidnapped my daughter. You did something to her. Did something to her mind. What was it? What did you do?"

Jimmy Cypress frowned. "I did not take your little girl. Nor did I do anything to her."

"Liar!" Robert shouted. "They found her book in your house."

Jimmy nodded. "There are many books in my house. I am a collector. I found your daughter's book here, by the lagoon, and added it to my collection. The police don't think I kidnapped your daughter, at least they have no proof, which is why they let me come home."

"What about the threat you made to me? What about that?"

"I told you to stay away from this lagoon for your own safety. There is a great evil buried beneath these waters, and I did not want you coming here. You stayed away, but your daughter did not. She came here, perhaps drawn by the voice of the evil one."

"Voice?" Alarm bells sounded in Robert's head. He remembered Krissy telling him how she heard a voice. Supposedly it was the voice of her special friend, a friend that could be heard but not seen.

"My daughter said she heard a voice, but I thought she was just making it up. I thought it was only a game."

"Did this voice have a name?"

Robert nodded. "She said his name was Mansa."

Jimmy's eyes opened wider, as if the name he heard surprised him. He started to say something, but stopped and shook his head. Instead of speaking, the Indian held out his hand, offering to help Robert stand up. Robert looked at the hand for a moment, then accepted the offer and slowly got to his feet.

"We will go to my cabin," Jimmy said. "I need to

take a look at your ankle, and the light is better there. Can you walk?"

Robert placed his weight gently upon his left leg and nodded. "I can walk."

"Good. I didn't want to carry you." Jimmy Cypress grabbed Robert around the waist, helping him to keep the weight off his injured ankle. "At my cabin we will talk about your daughter, but not here. This place isn't safe. I will tell you this: the voice your daughter heard is only too real. And what is happening is not a game."

Chapter Twenty-three

Robert's left ankle was beginning to swell, and he had to grit his teeth every time he put weight on it. Walking was a nightmare, and he wanted nothing more than to sit down and rest for a few moments, but Jimmy Cypress wouldn't allow it. The Seminole insisted they had to hurry to his house; time was a key element to saving Krissy, and time was not on their side.

He wasn't sure he believed the Indian. Wasn't sure he even trusted him. He still had suspicions that Jimmy was somehow involved in the abduction and strange behavior of his daughter, but he didn't know how. Maybe he had drugged her, given her a hallucinogenic chemical of some kind. He had heard that Indians used peyote and magic mushrooms; maybe Jimmy Cypress had slipped Krissy some Kool-Aid laced with mind-altering drugs.

Robert stepped on his left foot and winced as pain shot up his leg. His ankle was severely bruised, and he was damn glad that it had not been broken. Krissy had grabbed him in a grip tight enough to leave the impressions of her tiny fingers tattooed upon his flesh, exerting far more force than was normal for a child her age. That was another indication she might be on some kind of drug. He had read how junkies and speed freaks were sometimes stronger than normal men, able to snap leather restraints and withstand gunshot wounds that would easily kill an average person.

Casting a sideways glance, Robert looked at the man who was now helping him hobble along. If Jimmy Cypress was guilty of Krissy's abduction and strange behavior, then why was he helping him now? Could the Indian be doing a bit of playacting, trying to throw suspicion off himself by pretending to help? If so, then why was he taking Robert back to his cabin? Why go through such a charade, unless he had some ulterior motive in mind.

Unless he's trying to get me alone.

The thought sprang into his mind, causing him to stop suddenly. Did Jimmy Cypress have some kind of sinister plan in mind? Was he trying to get Robert back to his cabin so he could hurt him more than he already hurt? He remembered the threat the Indian had made and wondered if it really was a good idea to go to the cabin.

Jimmy turned and looked at Robert, wondering why he had stopped. He studied the other man's face for a moment, then smiled. "Don't worry. I am not going to hurt you. I'm taking you to my home so I can take a look at your ankle. There's medicine there. The lighting is also better."

Robert didn't move, which caused the Indian to laugh. "Trust me. I am not going to kill you. Had I wanted to do so, you would have already been dead."

"What about the threat?"

"As I said before, that was for your own protection.

If I killed every white man I threatened, there wouldn't be too many of you guys left to bother me."

Jimmy reached into his pants pocket and pulled out a tiny pocket knife. Opening the blade, he said, "Here. Take this. If I try to kill you, you can stab me."

Robert looked at the pocket knife. The blade was only about an inch long, far too small to be much of a weapon. "That's okay. You keep the knife."

"Suit yourself." Jimmy closed the knife and put it back into his pocket.

"If you wanted to be really nice, you would let me use that staff to help me walk."

Jimmy looked at the medicine staff he held, then looked at Robert. "Who said I wanted to be nice?"

Robert frowned. "I thought you were in a hurry to get back to your house. The staff would help me walk faster."

"I am in a hurry," Jimmy replied, "but I cannot let you use this staff for support. It's a medicine staff. You saw what it did at the lagoon."

Remembering the blue spark that had jumped from the staff's tip to his daughter's hand, Robert asked, "How did you do that? Is it electric?"

The Indian shook his head. "Not electrical. Magic. Strong medicine. The staff is a weapon against evil."

"I don't believe in magic," said Robert.

Jimmy grinned. "I bet you also didn't believe that your daughter could have glowing eyes, or that she could be strong enough to ever hurt you."

Robert tried to come up with an argument but couldn't. "All right. You win. For now anyway."

"Good. Now let's get going. We're wasting time standing here."

Fortunately for Robert, it wasn't far to the cabin. Reaching their destination, Jimmy pushed open the door and entered the tiny dwelling. Once inside, he lit one of the candles that was sitting atop a folding card table.

"Are you going to stay out there all night?" Jimmy asked, turning to find Robert still standing in the doorway.

Robert remained in the doorway, astonished by what he saw. Instead of a dirty, dingy squatter's shack, the cabin was neat and clean. Jimmy Cypress may have been poor, but he obviously took great pride in the few possessions he owned. Inside the cabin was a sofa, a folding table and chair, and numerous bookshelves filled with books. A pair of purple lace curtains hung over the windows, while a wooden orange crate served as a coffee table. A wood-burning stove sat in the corner of the room, providing a source of heat on cold nights, as well as a place to cook simple meals.

Jimmy turned and looked behind him, surveying the contents of the room. "At least they didn't tear it up too badly this time."

Entering the room, Robert closed the door behind him. "What do you mean?"

"The cops. They always tear up the place during a search. But this time it looks like they put most of the stuff back, although I'm sure all of my books are now in the wrong place. At least they didn't cut up my sofa, like they did last time."

"Last time?"

Jimmy nodded. "The police thought I was a suspect the last time a kid was missing. They tore up my place looking for clues, really made a mess of things. They didn't find anything of course, because I was not guilty. They trashed my place and then left, without even bothering to say sorry."

"Why didn't you complain to someone?"

"Who am I going to complain to? I'm an illegal squatter, at least according to the authorities. I'm not even supposed to be here. The only reason they haven't torn this place down is because this house was here long before the area was turned into a state park. The last guardian lived here before me."

"Guardian?"

He nodded. "But we'll get to that in a minute. Here. Sit down. Get your weight off that ankle. I'll get my medicine kit."

Robert hobbled over to the couch and sat down. Jimmy crossed the room and removed a small cedar box from beneath the stove. He carried the box back over to the sofa and sat down beside Robert.

"I'm surprised this is still here."

"What is it?"

"It's my first-aid kit. Seminole style. Nothing but natural ingredients, straight from Mother Earth. Roots. Leaves. Better than anything you can get in a drugstore. I figured the cops would have taken it. The police are bad about taking herbal medicines from Indians. They think everything is a narcotic, and that we run around smoking marijuana in our prayer pipes."

"What do you smoke in your pipes?"

The Indian gave Robert a dirty look. "When your daughter squeezed your ankle she must have cut off the circulation to your brain. We smoke tobacco in our pipes. The same thing you white guys smoke in yours. We try to avoid using store-bought tobacco whenever possible, and sometimes we mix other things with it: sage, cedar. None of it will get you stoned. We smoke a pipe to pray, not to get high. Most people seem to forget that marijuana was brought to this country by the Europeans."

Robert rubbed his chin, as if deep in thought. "Gee, I guess you learn something new every day."

"Only if you listen," Jimmy replied. "Now, let's take a look at that ankle. Take your shoe and sock off."

Robert removed his shoe and sock and rolled his pants leg up out of the way. His ankle was swollen, but not nearly as bad as he suspected. Krissy had grabbed him just above the anklebone, and there were purple marks where her tiny fingers had sunk into the flesh. There were also claw marks from her fingernails.

"Looks like you got off lucky," Jimmy said, examining the ankle. "An inch or so lower and she might have broken the bone. We still have to worry about infection. No telling what kind of germs got into those scratches."

"You sound like a doctor."

"I've done my fair share of doctoring. It's something you learn in combat."

"You were in combat?"

Jimmy nodded. "I was in the army, part of an all American Indian platoon. We spent two years in Nam, but that's still classified. The official record says we never left Guam."

"Why's that?"

"It's because we were assassins, and the government doesn't like to admit they have such people on the payroll. I came back from overseas with a purple heart, a couple of silver stars, and a deep mistrust for authority."

The Indian stood up and crossed the room, retrieving a jug of water and a facecloth from near the front door. Returning to the sofa, he wet the cloth and applied it to Robert's ankle. Cleaning the wound, he removed several green leaves from the cedar box. He wet the leaves and applied them to the injured ankle, holding them in place with the facecloth.

"What are those?" Robert asked, watching as Jimmy applied the leaves to his ankle.

"Seminole home cure, taught to me by my grandmother. The leaves will take the swelling down. They will also keep you from getting an infection. While we're waiting for the swelling to go down we'll talk. Actually, I'll talk; you listen."

"Got any aspirins in that box?" Robert winced as he straightened his leg. "I listen better when I'm not in pain."

"No aspirins, but I do have something for pain." Jimmy leaned forward and reached under the sofa, pulling out a half-full bottle of Wild Turkey. He set the bottle on the orange crate in front of them. "If you don't like drinking out of the bottle, I'll see if I can find a cup."

"No. No. This is fine." Robert picked up the bottle and uncapped it, taking a sip of the whiskey. He took another sip, then recapped the bottle and set it on the orange crate before him.

"Feeling better?" Jimmy asked.

"Much."

"Good. But you might want to keep that bottle

handy, because you're not going to like what I'm about to tell you."

"What's that?"

"Your daughter is not on drugs, if that's what you're thinking."

Robert looked surprised. "How did you know what I was thinking?"

"I know a lot of things." Jimmy smiled. "And she wasn't bitten by a rabid animal, nor is she in shock."

"Then what's wrong with her? Why did she attack me?"

"She's possessed."

Robert's mouth dropped open. "What? Possessed by what?"

Jimmy leaned forward and grabbed the whiskey bottle off the orange crate. "She's possessed by an evil spirit."

"That's ridiculous," Robert said, shaking his head. "I don't believe you."

"No reason you should believe me." Jimmy opened the bottle and took a sip. "But you should believe your own eyes. You saw your daughter tonight. Did she look like your little girl, or was she different? What about your ankle? Could your daughter do that?"

"Well, I . . ."

"I didn't think so." Jimmy took another sip, then recapped the bottle and set it back on the table. "Now, let me tell you a little story. It's sort of a tribal legend. When I'm done maybe you will understand what has happened to your daughter. You will also know what we have to do to help her."

Jimmy Cypress told the story how long ago, back

when the Seminoles still lived in the area, a voodoo sorcerer by the name of Mansa Du Paul established a village on the banks of the Wekiva River, not far from where the fish camp was now located.

"Mansa? Did you say Mansa?" Robert asked, nearly jumping off the couch when he heard the name. "That's the name of Krissy's invisible friend."

Jimmy nodded. "They're one and the same. Now, may I finish my story?"

The Seminole continued his story, telling how Mansa used black magic to call upon spirits of darkness. He also had a strange fondness for human flesh, especially that of young children.

For years the neighboring Seminole tribe had suspected Mansa Du Paul of committing terrible deeds, but they were never able to catch him in the act. Then one day two of Mansa's servants kidnapped the children of a tribal chief. An old woman, who had been cleaning at the river, witnessed the kidnapping. A war party of the bravest warriors was quickly formed. They had had enough of Mansa and his evil ways, and were determined to do away with him and his village once and for all.

That night they slipped quietly through the forest, attacking the village of Blackwater before anyone could sound an alarm. As the Seminole warriors attacked the residents of the village, the tribal chief and several of his best men rushed into the cabin Mansa occupied. They caught the sorcerer red-handed with the children. Dragging Mansa Du Paul outside, they tied him to a cypress tree and shot him full of arrows. They then cut his body into little pieces and threw the pieces into the river. The village was also burned, and the residents who were not killed outright fled for their lives into the forest.

What the Seminole chief and the others didn't know was that Mansa was far too powerful to be killed by conventional methods. They killed his body, but his evil soul remained, trapped in the waters of the lagoon. That evil had been there all these years, watching, waiting for a chance to be free again, hoping someone would come along to help him.

"Krissy," Robert said.

Jimmy Cypress nodded. "Your daughter is young, and children are more receptive to the ways of spirits. Some children can see spirits. Others can hear them. I think Mansa reached out and touched your daughter, made contact with her. Maybe she heard a voice. Maybe she saw him. He might also have used a disguise, appearing before her as a bird or animal."

"I thought you said his spirit was trapped in the lagoon?"

"In the lagoon, and the area around it. That is why my staff was at the lagoon. I was trying to use the staff's medicine to keep Mansa from reaching out any farther. I don't think Mansa was able to reach very far beyond the lagoon, which is why I think your daughter must have met him there."

"But we never took Krissy to the lagoon," Robert argued.

"Never?"

"No. Never." Robert shook his head, then paused. "Wait. We did go to the lagoon once, by accident, but only for a moment. We went canoeing and made a wrong turn. We ended up at the lagoon, but only long enough to turn around."

"That was more than enough time for the sorcerer to touch your daughter's mind. Once he made contact, he could have lured her back to the lagoon at his leisure."

"But she didn't go back to the lagoon."

"Are you sure? There was no time when your daughter wasn't with you?"

"We were with her at all times . . . except when she was napping." A sick feeling settled in Robert's stomach. "We left her alone when she was sleeping. The cabin was locked. I thought she would be safe."

"How long did you leave her alone?"

"Not long."

"Long enough for her to sneak out and go to the lagoon?"

Robert nodded.

"Did you notice anything unusual about your daughter after you went to the lagoon that first time?"

Again Robert nodded. "She told us that she had a new friend. A special, invisible friend that only she could hear."

"Your daughter told you this? What did you do?"

"Nothing. My wife and I thought she was making it up. Children sometimes have make-believe friends. It's normal."

"Make-believe friends might be normal when a child is at home, playing house or having an imaginary tea party, but they are not normal when you're vacationing in the middle of the wilderness."

"Krissy has always had a very active imagination," Robert said. "We just thought it was a stage she was going through. Correction, I thought it was just a stage. My wife wasn't too happy about Krissy having an imaginary friend, but I said it was okay."

Jimmy looked at him and nodded. "Your wife must be the smart one in the family."

"I'm beginning to think so." Robert reached for the whiskey bottle. "If my daughter is possessed, what can we do about it? Call a priest?"

"You'll never get a priest to believe you. It's not like *The Exorcist*, where you can call up a priest and have them rush over to save your daughter. Those who preach the words of God are usually the least likely to believe in spirits, evil or otherwise.

"Nor do we have time to sit around and wait for a priest to show up. Mansa Du Paul is using your daughter right now. I believe he is using her to gather up his remains."

"How do you know that?"

Jimmy shrugged. "Sometimes I just know things. Call it an occupational fringe benefit. Once Mansa has all of the bones gathered together, he is going to perform a ceremony to bring his former body back to life."

"Can such things be done?"

Again Jimmy shrugged. "Maybe. I don't know. Mansa's spirit is very powerful, far more powerful than you or I will ever be. It's so strong he's almost a demon. If there is a way to raise his body again, then I'm quite sure that Mansa will know how to do it. But a ceremony like that is evil, and he will need to make a blood sacrifice. The blood of an innocent."

Robert sucked in air. "Krissy."

Jimmy Cypress nodded. "I feel your daughter is in great danger, and time is running out. Once Mansa has gathered together the things he will need for his ceremony, he will use your little girl to make his final sacrifice."

"We have to stop him before it's too late."

"Can you walk on that ankle?"

"We're talking about my little girl, I'll fucking run on it if I have to."

Jimmy opened up the cedar box and took out a small leather pouch fastened to a leather cord. He handed the pouch to Robert. "Here, put this on."

"What is it?"

"It's a medicine pouch. We're going up against evil, and you can use all the help you can get."

Robert slipped the cord over his head, allowing the pouch to hang in the center of his chest.

"Wear it under your shirt," Jimmy instructed. "Wear it against your skin."

Robert sniffed the pouch before slipping it under his shirt. "It stinks. What's in it?"

"You don't want to know." Jimmy grinned. "Now, let's go find your daughter."

Chapter Twenty-four

The Blackwater Lounge had closed several hours earlier, but not all of the customers had gone home. Charlie McGee still sat at the bar, nursing a long-neck bottle of Budweiser. It was his fifth beer of the night, or maybe his sixth. Charlie was never very good at keeping track of how many beers he drank in an evening. Not that it mattered much one way or the other. He wasn't married, so he didn't have a wife to fuss at him about having too many beers. And he didn't have a job, so he didn't have to worry about getting up early in the morning to go to work.

The truth was Charlie didn't have to worry about too many things anymore. He was in his mid-seventies, living on social security and the pension checks earned from working over twenty years as a newspaper reporter. The money wasn't much, but then again he really didn't need all that much. His mobile home was paid for, as was the old Ford pickup truck he drove. Even his beers were usually free, bought by Ross in exchange for him watching the bait and tackle shop, or the lounge, when such things were needed.

It was the promise of free beer that usually kept Charlie at the lounge later than he should be. Not that he had anywhere else to go. He could go home, but there was nothing to do there but drink a couple of more beers and watch the idiot box. There wasn't much on television late at night that he liked watching, except for those commercials that featured sexy women asking you to call them.

Charlie smiled. He had always thought about calling one of those numbers, just to see what the women would say to him. Would they promise to smother him with kisses? Would they tell him what they were wearing, or what they weren't wearing? Would they promise to make sweet love to him? Or would they somehow know he was seventy-three years old, and slam the phone in his ear? After all, there wasn't much a seventy-three year old man could do with his penis, except get drunk and piss on his shoes. But would those women even care how old he was, as long as he was paying $4.95 per minute to talk to them?

Yep, Charlie had often thought about calling up one of those numbers, but he had never done so because he didn't have a credit card. He didn't have a phone either, which was another reason why he couldn't make phone calls to sexy women who appeared on the television late at night.

He chuckled, took another drink of beer, then wiped his mouth with the back of his hand.

"What are you laughing at, old man?" Ross called, appearing from the back room with a case of bottled beer. He set the case on the floor and then slid open the door on the drop-box cooler. Checking to see how many bottles were left in the cooler's first bin, he opened the case of beer and started restocking the cooler. Budweiser was the best seller, so it took up two bins in the cooler: one bin for bottles, the other for cans. After that came Miller, Miller Light, and an assortment of other brands. The last bin was reserved for imports, with Corona being the best seller of the foreign stuff.

Ross emptied the case and looked up at Charlie. "I said, what are you laughing at?"

"You've got awfully big ears to hear me laughing in the back room." Charlie grinned.

"Maybe you've got an awfully big mouth," Ross retaliated. "What are you doing, talking to yourself again? You know that's a sign of being senile, don't you?"

Charlie shook his head. "I wasn't talking to myself. And I'm not getting senile! I was just thinking about some of those commercials they show on television late at night. You know, the ones with the pretty women in them who want you to call them."

"The nine hundred numbers?"

"That's the ones."

"What about them?"

"I was just thinking about them, that's all. Thought it might be fun to call one once. Wonder what they would do if they found out they were talking to an old-timer like me?"

Ross smiled. "They wouldn't do nothing but keep you talking. That's all. They don't care how old you are, as long as you have money. Hell, some of those women who answer those calls are probably as old as you are. Maybe even older."

"You don't say?"

"I do say. The women you see on television aren't the ones who take the calls. Those are just models they hire to do the commercials. The women you talk to aren't beautiful, or sexy. And they probably wouldn't fuck you, no matter how much money you have. Oh, they'll talk dirty to you, just as long as you want them to talk to you. But it wouldn't be much of a turn-on if you knew you were talking to a three-hundred-pound woman, with six kids, and two teeth missing."

"You don't get to talk to the women in the commercials?" Charlie asked, disappointed.

"Nope," Ross replied. "But why you worried about it? You don't even have a phone."

"I know, but I was thinking about sneaking back in here and calling them on your phone."

Ross laughed. "Old man, you start calling nine hundred numbers on my phone and there will be hell to pay."

"It was just a thought." Charlie finished his beer, setting the empty bottle down on the bar. "You ever call one of those nine hundred numbers?"

"Nope. Never have. Mary would kill me if I called one of those numbers."

"I bet it would be a real hoot."

"Probably would."

Ross reached down into the cooler and fished out a cold bottle of Budweiser. He opened the bottle and set it in front of Charlie. "Here, have another beer. I've got to finish stocking this cooler." He grabbed the empty beer case and started toward the back room. "And leave my phone alone!"

Charlie picked up the full bottle of beer and took a sip. He should be going home, but he wasn't in much of a hurry. And Ross didn't mind him hanging around, because it gave him someone to talk to while he was cleaning up the place and restocking the cooler.

The drop-box cooler was almost empty, because there had been so many people at the fish camp the past few days: police officers, firemen, reporters, people just showing up to watch the show. Ross would be carrying twice as many cases of beer out of the back room. Charlie offered to help him, but it really was a one-man job. Two men would just get in each other's way.

Charlie thought about how busy things had been lately. And he thought about the little girl that was still missing. That was a damn shame; it had to be really tough on her parents. He didn't think they were ever going to find that little girl. If they were going to find her, they would have done it already. He didn't think she was anywhere around there to be found. Nope. That girl was somewhere else, long gone from Blackwater. Someone had taken her. She was either long gone, or she was dead. It was as simple as that.

He had just started to take another sip of beer when the lights when out, casting the room into darkness. "Hey! What the hell are you doing back there?"

"It wasn't me," Ross called back. "Must have blown a fuse."

"Well, fix it."

"I will. Give me a minute. I've got to find my flashlight first."

The room wasn't completely dark. There was an emergency-exit sign over the front door that ran off batteries in case of a power outage. The red letters of the sign marked the location of the door, so customers could find their way out. The sign also had two spotlights that were supposed to come on during a power failure, but those spotlights hadn't worked in years. The local fire marshal didn't know the spotlights didn't work, so Ross had gotten by without having to replace the sign.

The letters of the exit sign cast a dim red glow over the front entrance. The letters would probably be brighter if Ross ever bothered to clean the sign. Years of dust and cigarette smoke had dulled the letters. Customers could still see the sign and could probably figure out how to get to the front door, but the room was pitch black when the power went out.

A crash sounded in the back room, and Ross said out loud, "Son of a bitch."

"What you doing back there?" Charlie laughed, turning in the direction of the noise.

"Breaking my fool neck," Ross answered. "What do you think I'm doing?"

"Did you find a flashlight yet?"

"Not yet. I'm working on it."

"Well, hurry up. I don't like drinking in the dark."

"If you don't shut up you'll be drinking your beer in the parking lot."

Charlie laughed again. He started to take another drink of beer, but he suddenly felt a draft on the back of his neck. Turning on his bar stool to look toward the front entrance, he saw the door slowly inching closed.

The old man sat looking at the front door, not sure if he had really seen it move. The darkness and the beers could be playing tricks on him. The draft he had felt on his neck could only be caused by the door being opened, but no one had entered the bar. At least there was no one standing in the doorway. He glanced around the room, but didn't see anyone in the darkness.

Maybe someone had opened the door, looked in, and closed it again. Maybe it was a deputy making the rounds, or one of those reporters. He was probably hoping to have a beer, but saw that the room was dark and figured the lounge was closed. Perhaps it was Mary who had opened the door. The electricity in her cabin might also be out, and she had come over to see how things were in the lounge.

"The least she could have done was say howdy," Charlie said aloud. But Mary might not have seen him sitting there in the darkness.

Wondering if the whole camp had lost power, Charlie got up and made his way to the front door. He opened it and stepped outside. The camp was dark, but it usually was at nighttime. Ross knew that a lot of his campers liked looking at the night sky, so he burned as few lights as possible. There were no lights set on poles to distract from the stars, but he did keep a light burning in the bait and tackle shop at night. He also kept a yellow bug light burning above the door to his cabin, so people would know where to find him in case they needed anything. Those lights now burned as normal, so the whole camp was not without electricity.

The camp still had electricity, so that would mean that it wasn't Mary who had opened the door. She was probably already asleep, and would have no reason to come to the lounge so late at night. If it wasn't Mary, then who had opened the door?

Charlie looked around but didn't see anyone. There

were no strange vehicles parked in the parking lot, so that ruled out deputies or search team members. Even the last reporter had finally gone home. The wind must have opened the door. That sometimes happened if you didn't close it tight. He had told Ross that he needed to get a new door, but Ross was slow about getting things fixed.

"Enough of this. My beer's getting warm." Charlie opened the door and stepped back inside. The bar was still dark, which meant Ross hadn't found his flashlight yet. That, or he had found the flashlight, but hadn't found the spare fuses.

"What's the holdup?" Charlie called. "You on some kind of break?"

"Shut up, old man. I'm working on it."

Charlie laughed and made his way back to his bar stool. He was about to reach for his beer when he noticed that the beer was no longer sitting on the bar. He turned and looked down the bar, figuring that he had just sat down on the wrong stool. But there was no beer bottle sitting anywhere on the bar, full or otherwise. He turned and looked back toward the front door, thinking he had set the bottle down on one of the tables on his way outside, but there wasn't a bottle there either.

He started to call out to Ross when a peculiar noise got his undivided attention. It was the chunk-chunk sound of a glass bottle rolling across a hardwood floor. Looking down, he was surprised to see his full bottle of Budweiser roll across the floor in front of his feet, splashing beer on the floor as it passed.

"What the hell?" The bottle came to a stop a few feet beyond where he sat. He looked at the bottle, then turned his attention toward the opposite end of the room. Someone had rolled that bottle at him. Someone who could not be seen in the darkness.

"Who's there?" Charlie called out, getting up off of his bar stool. There was no answer.

"Who did that?" He took a step forward and stopped, trying to see to the far end of the room. But the lounge was still dark, and the beers he had drank made his vision fuzzy. Not that he had the best eyesight to begin with; twenty years of newspaper work had taken its toll on his vision, and he wore glasses more often than not. There could be a dozen people standing at that end of the room and he would not be able to see them.

Someone had to be playing a joke on him. That was it, a joke. One of the regulars must have slipped inside the bar when he wasn't looking, and was now trying to have a bit of fun at his expense. That must be it. One of his drinking buddies was trying to scare him to get a laugh. They were going to scare him, then make fun of him. Charlie didn't like people making fun of him, and he wasn't about to fall victim to any stupid joke.

"It's not going to work. I'm not scared." Charlie pulled a pair of prescription glasses out of his shirt pocket, hurrying to put them on. But even with the glasses, he still couldn't see who was hiding from him.

"You're wasting your time. I'm not afraid." He called out to the darkness, but there was no reply. No snicker of laughter. Nothing. The old man took a few more steps forward, then stopped again.

It might have been a joke, but it was no longer funny. Maybe it was the alcohol talking, but he was starting to get a little nervous about the whole thing. His body broke out in a thin sheen of sweat, causing his shirt and pants to stick to him.

"Joe, is that you? John? Come on guys, you've had your laugh. Ha. Ha. Ha. Now quit fooling around and come out where I can see you."

There was no response. No hardy laughter, followed by the appearance of his friends. Nothing but the darkness. He turned and looked toward the back of the building, wishing that Ross would hurry up and get the lights back on.

"Ross, have you found that flashlight yet?"

Charlie suddenly realized that there was no noise coming from the back room. Nor did he see the soft glow of a flashlight. That meant Ross had not found the flashlight he was looking for and had probably gone to his cabin to get one. It also meant that Charlie was alone in the lounge.

Not alone. Someone was in the lounge with him. Someone who liked to play scary games.

Charlie was suddenly afraid. The fear killed the beer buzz he had been enjoying only moments before, leaving a bitter metallic taste in his mouth. He didn't think any of his drinking buddies were playing a trick on him. They all had wives and had gone home hours earlier. They also had jobs and would not be returning to do any more drinking. That meant someone else was in the lounge with him. Someone he didn't know.

"This isn't funny. If someone's hiding there, you had better come out. I've got a gun." He didn't really have a gun, didn't even have a pocketknife, but Ross kept a pistol somewhere behind the counter. "If you don't come out I'll shoot."

Charlie thought that saying he had a gun might be a pretty good bluff, but he was apparently wrong. From the darkness in front of him came a laugh: a cruel, deep-pitched laugh that sounded more animal than human. The laugh grew louder, growing higher in pitch, until it sounded like the laughter of a child. It sounded like the laugh of a little girl, only there was something about it that was pure evil.

He took a step back and thought about running for the front door, but then he saw the eyes. Two bluish-green eyes beneath the table closest to him, glowing in the darkness like the eyes of an animal. The eyes watched him for a moment, then came toward him at a rush.

Charlie screamed in fear, something he had never done in his entire life. Before going to work for the newspaper, he had served several years in the army. He had seen combat in World War II, had even been wounded, but he had never screamed in fear. Never. But now he cried out in terror, for there was something about those eyes that scared the hell out of him.

As the eyes rushed toward him, Charlie got to see the body they were attached to. It was a small body, not much bigger than a child. As a matter of fact, it was a child: a little girl. It looked like the little girl everyone had been searching for, but there was something wrong about this little girl. Something very, very wrong.

Charlie started to say something to the little girl, but his words were stopped short by the pain that ripped through his right thigh. Instead of words, he could only scream.

He screamed and staggered back, reaching down to

the source of the pain. He didn't need a light to know that he was bleeding. He could feel warm blood spurting from a deep cut just above his right knee. The little girl had stabbed him with something. He was bleeding bad enough to need a doctor.

"Ross, help me! Please, help me!" His cries for help went unanswered, because Ross had not returned. Charlie looked up, but the little girl was no longer in front of him. She had moved. He started to turn around to defend himself, but he was too late. The girl had slipped behind him and was on the attack again.

Another bolt of fiery pain shot through Charlie's right leg. He had been stabbed again in the thigh, this time just beneath his right buttocks. She must have severed his tendon, because his right leg collapsed beneath him like an accordion.

He fell to the floor and the girl jumped on him. She stabbed him again and again, driving a knife deep into his back. Charlie tried to scream, but he could not find his voice. He tried to get back up, but his body refused to obey his command. He could only lie there, whimpering like a whipped pup, as the long steel blade of a knife sank deep into his body. He died a few moments later, his face only inches away from the beer he would never finish.

Ross banged his shin against a wooden shelf and bit his lip to keep from crying out. He knew Charlie McGee would laugh at him if he heard him cry out, so he remained quiet despite the pain. He did, however, mutter a few choice words under his breath.

Rubbing his shin to take away some of the hurt, he reached around on the shelves in search of his flashlight. It was there the other day, but now, when he actually needed it, the flashlight seemed to have vanished. Without a light it would be nearly impossible to check the fuses in the fusebox, which was mounted on the back wall in the beer storage room. He could probably use a lighter, but it was hard to hold a lighter steady while he did the checking. The beer storage room was also the darkest room in the place, and the most cluttered, and he would probably trip over something and break his neck if he didn't have proper lighting.

Since he couldn't find the flashlight that he kept in the bar, he decided to go get the one from his cabin. He called out to Charlie, to let him know that he was leaving for a minute, but the old man didn't answer. He either didn't hear him, or he didn't feel like answering. Hell, knowing Charlie, the old fool had probably fallen asleep at the bar again. Or he was in the bathroom, trying to hit the urinal in the dark. Not that he could hit it much better in the light. Old Charlie, bless his heart, could be rather messy at times, especially when it came to pissing with a drunk dick.

After making his way slowly to the back door, Ross unlocked it and stepped out. He saw that the light above his cabin door still burned, and knew that he had indeed blown a fuse. Blown fuses were nothing new. The wiring in the lounge was old and overloaded, especially with the coolers and air conditioning running at the same time. It was really bad in the summertime, when the equipment was doing double duty to keep everything cold. He could expect a blown fuse at least once a week during the summer months.

Closing the back door, he made his way across the

campgrounds to his cabin. The lights were off inside the cabin, which meant Mary had already gone to bed. Unlocking the front door, he slipped in as quietly as possible.

He found the flashlight in the kitchen, in a cabinet drawer on the left. Checking to make sure the batteries were still good, he closed the drawer and started back toward the front door.

"What are you doing?"

Ross stopped and turned around. Mary stood in the bedroom doorway, watching him. "Sorry. I didn't mean to wake you. I've blown another fuse at the lounge. I couldn't find my flashlight, so I came here to get this one."

"You didn't wake me," Mary said. "I was having trouble sleeping. You sure it's just a fuse?"

"Yeah. None of the other lights are out."

"You going to be long?"

"Not long. I've just got to replace the fuse, then finish filling the cooler."

"Anyone still over there?"

"Just Charlie, and I'm going to send him home in a few minutes."

"Okay then." Mary nodded. "With any luck I'll be asleep by the time you get here."

"I'll be quiet when I come in."

Ross left the cabin and hurried back to the lounge. He had just entered through the back door when he heard a crash from the front.

"Charlie, are you okay?"

There was no answer.

"Charlie, what was that noise? Are you okay?"

Still no answer.

Ross headed for the front of the building to investigate the noise he heard. "Aw, hell. What did you do now, old man? I told you to sit still until I got the lights back on. Don't tell me you tripped over something, or knocked something over. If you knocked one of my beer mirrors off the wall I'm going to kick your butt."

He pushed through the swinging double doors, entering the front room directly behind the bar. Shining his flashlight from left to right, he saw that Charlie McGee no longer sat at the bar. "Where did you go? I don't have time to be playing games."

Ross turned left and walked past the drop-box cooler and draft beer taps, stepping out from behind the bar. He kept the flashlight aimed at the floor in front of him as he went. He had heard a crash and didn't want to trip over something in the darkness.

The first thing he saw as he stepped out from behind the bar was that one of the square wooden tables had been turned over. The table had obviously made the crash he had heard from the back room. The second thing he saw was a pair of legs lying on the floor just beyond the table. The legs were dressed in faded blue jeans, with feet covered with Timberland work boots. The legs, jeans, feet, and shoes all belonged to Charlie McGee. The old man was sprawled on the floor just beyond the overturned table.

"Oh, Jesus. What did you do?" Ross took two steps forward, the beam of the flashlight he held sweeping up Charlie's legs to his back. He froze when his light illuminated the still-widening puddle of crimson beside the old man's body.

It only took one glance to know that Charlie McGee

was dead. He lay on his stomach, his head turned to face Ross, eyes open and staring, his eyeglasses on the floor in front of his face. Charlie's shirt, once white, was now bright red with blood, and there were tears in the back of the shirt that looked like stab wounds.

"Sweet Jesus. No." Ross stood staring at the old man, unable to tear his gaze away from the carnage that lay before him. Charlie McGee, the lovable elderly drunk, was as dead as a doornail, stabbed to death, his blood forming a huge pool around his body. Old Charlie had just been murdered.

"Murdered."

The word snapped Ross out of his daze. If Charlie McGee had been stabbed, then somebody had to do the stabbing. It had only been a few minutes since the old man was still alive, so that meant the murderer was probably still around. He could be in the camp. Hell, he could still be in the lounge.

"Shit." Knowing that he was also in danger, Ross turned and swept the flashlight around the room. He didn't see anyone, but that didn't mean he was alone. The lounge was cloaked in darkness, creating a hundred places a killer could hide. He could be in one of the restrooms, in the storage room, in the closet just off the kitchen, hiding in the walk-in cooler, even crouching in the shadows beneath one of the tables. He could be anywhere.

"Shit," Ross said again as he turned on his heels and raced behind the bar. He kept a loaded .38 revolver on a shelf beneath the cash register. He had never needed the gun before, but he damn sure needed it now. For a moment he was afraid the gun might not be there, but it was still lying on the shelf where he always kept it.

He picked up the revolver and switched off the safety. There was no need to check to see if it was still loaded. If the pistol had not been moved, then it was. A quick glance showed him that the cash register had not been touched either. If robbery was the motive behind the murder, then the thief had not gotten to the register yet. Perhaps he heard Ross coming back and had taken off.

God, I hope so.

A dark thought crossed his mind. What if it was more than one person behind the killing? Even with a loaded gun he was ill equipped to go up against multiple bad guys. Hell, he wasn't really equipped to go up against just one bad guy. His hands were shaking so bad he wouldn't be able to hit what he was aiming at. If he missed in the close confines of the lounge, then he too could end up as a bloody victim, especially since he was apparently up against a psychopath.

Okay, I've got the gun. Now what do I do?

Call the police. That's what he had better do. Dial 911 and get some help. Someone had just been murdered in his place of business, and the killer could still be around.

Ross held the pistol in his right hand, and the flashlight in his left. He was reluctant to set either of them down long enough to pick up the phone. Knowing he had to let go of one of them, he laid the flashlight on top of the bar and grabbed the telephone.

He had just picked up the receiver when he heard a noise coming from a row of booths just to the left of the front door. Ross froze, the phone halfway to his left ear, his blood turning to ice.

What was that?

He heard the noise again, a strange whimpering sound that sent chills marching down his spine. The noise sounded like someone softly crying.

Ross hung up the phone and picked up his flashlight. He aimed the light at the booths, his mouth going dry with fear. There was something in the booth closest to the door, but he couldn't tell what it was. He hadn't seen it before, because the high back of the booth's seat had hidden it from view.

He was suddenly very afraid, almost too afraid to move. He thought about running out the back door to his cabin, worried now that Mary was all alone. But he was afraid to take off, fearing that whatever was in that booth might not be there when he got back. Was it a person? Was it the killer? Surely not, because it wasn't big enough.

The sound coming from the booth grew louder, causing the skin at his temples to pull tight. It was a strange sound, almost animal, like the whimpering of a small dog. But it wasn't a dog in the booth, he could tell that much. The thing in the booth wasn't hairy.

Knowing he had no other choice but to take a closer look, Ross slowly moved out from behind the bar. The thing at the booth didn't move; it remained an unidentifiable lump of darkness lying on the seat. He wished it would move so he could see what in the Sam hell it was, but if it did move he would probably shoot it out of fear.

As if in a strange dream, Ross suddenly became aware of everything around him. He became aware of his footsteps, the sound of his breathing, even the beating of his heart; the sounds seemed to be magnified by the fear that enveloped him. He was aware of the brightness of his flashlight, and the tiny motes of dust that danced hypnotically in the light's beam. Even the wood floor he walked on seemed different, as if he had never truly seen it before.

He was getting closer to the front door, and still the thing in the booth had not moved. Thirty feet. Twenty. Ten. It wasn't an animal, he was certain of that now, for he could make out the fabric of clothing. Dirty. Mud-caked. But clothing nonetheless.

A horrifying thought crossed his mind, nearly causing him to turn around and flee in fright. What if the thing at the booth was a dead thing? What if it was something that had crawled out of a graveyard, like the things they showed on those late-night zombie movies? Or what if it was a creature like nothing anyone had ever seen before, some kind of monster that had come out of the woods?

"Ain't no such thing as monsters," he whispered, trying to gather his courage. That may be true, but there were such things as killers that murdered old men, and things that hid in bar booths and whimpered.

He was only a few feet away from the booth, close enough to make out the form of what lay on the seat. It was human, and it was small. The tiny form was huddled up on the seat, facing away from him, knees drawn up to its chest. He could see mud-crusted tennis shoes that might have once been red, and long hair that might have been blonde but was as muddy as the shoes. He could also see the crimson stains of blood splattered on small legs and arms. The tiny person in the booth was apparently hurt and in need of medical attention.

Ross stood staring at the figure for a few more moments, suddenly realizing what he was looking at. It was the little girl everybody was searching for. Krissy Patterson was in his lounge, and she was obviously hurt.

"Krissy, is that you?" Lowering his pistol he stepped forward. The little girl had obviously been hurt by the same sick bastard who had killed Charlie. She was covered in blood and was probably in danger of dying on him. He had to do something to help her.

He set the flashlight on the booth's table, aiming it so the beam pointed in the girl's direction. Reaching out with his left hand, he gently touched her shoulder and attempted to roll her over.

The little girl rolled over easily at his touch, and as she did Ross knew that something was very wrong. She was splattered with blood, but there didn't appear to be any wounds on her body. And even though she had been whimpering in pain only moments before, she was now smiling. It was a hideous smile that stretched her mouth far too wide. Then Krissy Patterson opened her eyes, and Ross knew he was in serious trouble.

It may have been a little girl lying there on the seat, but she didn't have the eyes of a little girl. She had the eyes of an animal, glowing a strange bluish color in the darkness. Ross looked at those strange, terrifying eyes, and then he noticed the object she held in her left hand, an object she had kept cradled to her body so he would not see it.

Ross tried to jump back, but he wasn't quick

enough. The object the girl held was a butcher knife, its blade stained with the blood of Charlie McGee. Before he could back up, she uncoiled like a snake and stabbed him in the stomach.

The blade sank deep into his abdomen, the pain sending a shock wave through his body. The muscles in his right arm spasmed, causing the pistol to fire. The gun was pointed away from the girl, the bullet striking the floor near the front door.

Stumbling backward, out of control and off balance, Ross felt his legs go out from under him. He landed on his butt, hitting the floor hard enough to make his teeth clack together, causing the pistol to fly out of his hand. The gun skidded across the floor, disappearing into the darkness.

He watched the pistol vanish from view, and then he looked down and was aware of the blood spurting from his body. He placed his left hand over the wound, but could not stop the flow. The wound was deep, and a major organ had obviously been hit. Already he was becoming woozy and light-headed.

A strange laughter split the night. Ross looked up and saw Krissy slide out of the booth and move toward him. She was still smiling, and she still held the butcher knife. He suddenly recognized the knife. It was Mary's favorite butcher knife: an Old Henry he had bought for her years ago. The knife had been used to cut beef, veal, pork, chicken, even venison. It was now being used to cut a different sort of meat.

Ross tried to stand up, but he could no longer feel his legs. He had already lost too much blood, and was on the verge of passing out. He actually wished that he would pass out, so he wouldn't have to feel what was about to happen to him. But he had no such luck. Ross Sanders was still very much awake when the butcher knife sank into his flesh again and again and again.

Chapter Twenty-five

Mary Sanders was still awake when the sound of a gunshot split the night. The sound was close, but it was somewhat muffled, as if it came from inside a building. Sitting up in bed, she listened carefully but the gunshot was not repeated.

Knowing that her husband kept a loaded pistol at the lounge, she climbed out of bed and hurried to put her clothes on. Ross kept the gun for protection, though there had never been need for him to use it. Most of the customers who frequented the bar were regulars, and fairly well behaved for drunks. Even the rednecks and troublemakers had enough respect for Ross to take their fights outside. The gun was only there in the event they were ever robbed, and that had yet to happen.

Still, the gunshot had come from the direction of the lounge. Not that she thought there was any trouble. Not really. Ross had just been over to grab a flashlight, complaining that the electricity was off. He had probably been fumbling around in the darkness and knocked the pistol off the shelf, causing it to fire. She was worried now that her damn fool husband might have accidentally shot himself in the foot.

Slipping on her blue jeans and blouse, she pulled on a pair of sneakers and hurried to the front door. The night was quiet, no sounds of shouts or screams. That was a good sign. Had her husband shot himself in the foot, or had there been an attempted robbery, she was quite sure she would be hearing six kinds of hell.

Looking around, she noticed that no lights burned in any of the other cabins, so the gunshot had not disturbed any of the guests. Actually, the Pattersons were the only guests still staying at the campgrounds, and their cabin could not be seen from where she stood. The other guests, two pair of fishermen from somewhere up north, had grown tired of all the recent chaos and confusion and had cut their vacations short to go back home.

Closing the cabin door, she crossed the campgrounds to the lounge and entered through the back door. The electricity was still off, and the interior was as dark as a tomb. She had to slow her pace, being careful where she stepped, fearful of tripping over a beer box or mop bucket. Ross was real bad about leaving things lying in the way, and the electricity being off would not mean he had suddenly changed his habits.

She called out to her husband as she entered the back room, but did not get a reply. Figuring he just didn't hear her, she called out again. "Ross, was that a gunshot I heard?"

Mary closed the back door and took two more steps, then stopped. She was suddenly aware of how quiet everything was inside the lounge. Too quiet. With the electricity off, the noticeable hum of the coolers had been hushed. Still, there should have been some noise. Ross said Charlie McGee was drinking at the bar, his truck was still outside, and she knew that Charlie was the talkative sort. He should have been chatting up a storm, even while sitting in total darkness.

But Charlie wasn't talking. Neither was Ross. As a matter of fact, from the sounds of things, she was completely alone in the lounge. Were they out front somewhere? Maybe that's why she had heard a pistol shot. Maybe her husband had been shooting at an animal. A stray dog maybe. Not that he had ever been much for shooting at animals, any animal. He didn't even like to hunt. Fishing was his pastime, not hunting.

One thing for sure, she was definitely the only one in the lounge. That made her mad, because her husband was supposed to be checking the fuses. He was not supposed to be goofing off with Charlie, target shooting in the middle of the night.

Shooting a gun wasn't a very smart thing to do, not with everything that had transpired during the past few days. The police were still looking for Krissy Patterson, which meant there were probably patrols in the area. The sound of a gunshot would have been heard, and it might be only minutes before the cops showed up in force to investigate. They would not be happy to learn that two old fools like Ross and Charlie had been shooting off a gun just for the hell of it.

"I swear I'm going to put a lump on Ross's head before the night is through."

She made her way from the back rooms to the swinging doors that separated the front of the lounge from the back. She paused before stepping through the doors, feeling for the shelves that stood just to the right of the doors. On the bottom shelf was a metal coffee can containing pencils, pens, magic markers, and nails. The can also contained several books of matches that she kept handy for emergencies.

Finding the can in the dark, she fumbled around with the contents until she found one of the books of matches. Tearing a match from the book, she lit it and pushed through the double saloon doors.

The soft glow of the match didn't cast much light, but it did light things up enough so she could move around without tripping over something. The area directly behind the bar was free of beer boxes and other obstacles. Also absent were her husband and Charlie McGee.

"Ross, where are you?"

She turned to the right, making her way toward the cash register. She punched the "no sale" button, which caused the cash drawer to slide open. The drawer still contained the evening's profits, so there had not been a robbery as she first feared when hearing the gunshot.

Mary breathed a sigh of relief. They hadn't been robbed, which had always been a fear of hers. The fish camp was quiet and peaceful, but it was also rather remote, making it an ideal target for robbers. A person could rob the place and be long gone before the sheriff's department showed up. So far nothing like that had ever happened, but she was always concerned about such things. Times were changing, with robberies becoming more commonplace.

The match was burning dangerously close to her fingertips, so she dropped it into one of the metal ashtrays sitting on top of the bar and lit another one. Closing the cash drawer, she looked beneath the register for her husband's gun. He usually kept it on the shelf, hidden from view beneath one of his old shirts. The shirt was still there, but the pistol was not.

"That old fool. What's he up to now?"

Mary turned away from the register and walked out from behind the bar. She had only taken a few steps when she noticed that one of the wooden tables had been knocked over. Curious, she took a step toward the table, stopping when she spotted a pair of legs. Someone was lying on the floor, just beyond the table, but she couldn't see who it was from where she stood.

"Ouch!" Mary had not been paying attention to the match she held, and the tiny flame burned the fingertips of her right hand. She dropped the match to the floor and hurried to light a new one, fearful now to be in total darkness for even a moment.

Lighting a new match, she stepped slowly forward to see who was lying on the floor. She prayed that it wasn't her husband, worried that the gunshot she had heard earlier meant that something bad had happened to him. But it wasn't Ross on the floor. It was Charlie McGee. The old man lay on his stomach, his face turned toward her, eyes open and staring.

On first impression, she thought Charlie McGee might have had a heart attack and died, for he was definitely very much dead. Then she saw all the blood, and knew that old Charlie had met a fate far more violent than a heart attack. He had been murdered, stabbed to death by the look of things.

Stabbed. Murdered.

Alarm bells sounded in her head. One of their best customers lay dead on the floor, and there was no sign of her husband. The gunshot she had heard earlier was no accident. The pistol had not been knocked off the shelf; nor had her husband been fooling around, or shooting at an animal.

Ross had been shooting at someone.

It suddenly made sense to her. Ross had come home to grab a flashlight. While he was at the cabin, someone had murdered poor old Charlie. Perhaps they were attempting to rob the place, and Charlie had tried to stop them. They must have already killed him, or were still in the process of killing him, when Ross returned to the lounge. Seeing what was going on, he had grabbed his pistol and fired. Perhaps he had hit the killer. Perhaps not. He must have chased someone out the front door. That would explain his absence.

Unless . . .

A dark thought crossed her mind. She had heard only one gunshot. Just one. And now her husband was nowhere to be seen. Nor did he answer her. Maybe he hadn't shot the killer. Maybe the killer had . . .

"No. No. No. Don't think such thoughts."

Mary lit another match, suddenly afraid that something bad had happened to her husband. She turned away from the body of Charlie McGee, determined to find Ross at all costs. Thinking he might have chased a bad guy out the lounge, she headed for the front door. She had only gone a few feet, however, when she noticed a second body lying on the floor.

"Oh, dear God. No."

Even from several feet away, she knew that it was her husband. He lay on his back, a few feet from the booth closest to the door, his legs crossed in an eternal figure four. He had been stabbed several times in the chest and stomach, and his throat had been cut from ear to ear. The deep cut in his throat made it look like his neck was smiling. Ross's eyes had also been cut out and removed, leaving behind deep dark holes where his baby blues had once been.

"No. No. No. No. No."

Mary hurried to light another match, but her hands shook so hard it took several fumbled tries to get another one lit. The match's flame was tiny and did little to push back the darkness, but it was enough to see the ghastly sight that lay before her. Her husband was quite dead, murdered and mutilated by some sick bastard.

She had just lit the new match when she spotted a flashlight lying on the floor by her feet. It was the same one Ross had gotten from the cabin. She picked it up and worked its switch, but the light did not come on. It must have been damaged when Ross dropped it.

"Come on, you stupid thing. Come on." Mary worked the switch again, slapping the flashlight against the palm of her hand. She was delighted when the light suddenly came on.

With the flashlight, she no longer needed the matches. Dropping the lit match to the floor, she stuffed the book into her pants pocket and swept the beam of the flashlight around her.

The dull gleam of metal instantly caught her attention. Turning, she saw Ross's pistol lying on the floor not far from his body. He had obviously taken at least one shot at his murderer, might even have hit him. She started to take a step toward the gun to retrieve it when there came the sounds of movement from behind her.

Mary spun around, her heart starting to jackhammer. She had been so shocked by the bloody sight of Ross and Charlie that she hadn't even thought about her own safety. She had never even considered the possibility, not even for a moment, that the killer, or killers, might still be inside the lounge.

She aimed the flashlight toward the far wall and was startled to see that someone was standing there. Someone small. A child. Mary looked at the child for a moment or two before realizing that it was Krissy Patterson.

"Oh, my God."

The little girl was covered with mud and grime, her long hair plastered to her head. She stood with her back to the wall, watching Mary with a pair of eyes that glowed a strange bluish-green.

Mary felt her blood turn to ice. She had seen many things in her life, but she had never seen a child with such eyes. The little girl's eyes burned with a strange glow that was evil beyond description.

"Krissy, is that you?"

The girl made no reply. She only stood there, watching with eyes that were as cold as a wintry tomb. Both of her hands were behind her back, but, as Mary watched, the child removed her left hand from behind her back to reveal what she was holding.

Krissy Patterson held a small plastic bag in her left hand. It was the same kind of Ziploc bag that Ross kept in the lounge, perfect for storing nuts, bolts, washers, and other odds and ends. But the bag that Krissy held did not contain nuts and bolts. Instead, it contained a pair of human eyeballs: blue human eyeballs. The same color of blue as Ross's eyes.

Mary felt bile burning a path from her stomach to her throat. She opened her mouth to gag, but nothing came out. Krissy must not have felt the same revulsion for the eyes she held, because she smiled. Then she showed Mary the bloody butcher knife that was in her other hand.

"Oh, God. No!" A million messages shot through Mary's brain all at once, confusing her. But she finally got the signal she needed to get her feet moving. Turning, she raced toward the pistol lying on the floor.

She now knew what her husband had been shooting at. It hadn't been a robber, or a band of desperate outlaws. On the contrary, he had been shooting at a ten-year-old girl. A little girl with the face of an angel, and the eyes of the devil.

Mary had just reached the pistol when she heard a sound behind her. It was a strange rumbling, like the deep-throated growl of a dog. The sound was accompanied by the noise of tiny footfalls on a wood floor, and the rushing of air as something came at her at a dead run.

She tried to turn, but something hit her from behind, taking her feet out from under her. Mary went down hard, a scream tearing from her throat. Then the pain began. Pain beyond description and words. Pain that left the walls splattered with blood and brought the blissful darkness of death upon her.

Janet Patterson had been sound asleep when a gunshot split the night. Even then she did not come fully awake because she was in the throes of a deep sleep aided by a prescription medicine. She became partially aware of the sounds around her, but she still dozed, unable to open her eyes and wake up. A few minutes later she was brought to full awareness by the sharp, terrified screams of a woman.

She sat up in bed and listened carefully, startled by the sound she had just heard, but not altogether sure that it wasn't just part of a dream. Janet tried to remember if she had been dreaming, but no nocturnal images floated around in her mind. If she had been, then the dream had completely disappeared on the moment of her waking.

Sitting tense in her bed, she reached out to the other twin bed to wake her husband, only to find that the other bed was empty. The bed's emptiness disturbed her, but for only a moment. Robert was sometimes a night owl, especially when his mind was troubled. He had probably stayed up to drink a few beers, falling asleep in one of the chairs in the sitting room.

Getting out of bed, Janet crossed the room and switched on the light. Her husband was definitely not in his bed. Nor, from the looks of things, had he ever gone to bed. His bed was still made, the covers neatly tucked in. Frowning, she slipped a robe on over her nightgown and left the room.

She left the bedroom and entered the cabin's tiny sitting room. It was dark, the only light being the moonlight that filtered in through the front window. Even in the darkness, she could tell that Robert was not in the sitting room either. She turned and looked toward the bathroom, thinking he might be making a late night nature call, but the bathroom door stood open and there was no one sitting on the throne.

A thought entered her mind, and she crossed the sitting room to the bedroom Krissy had occupied. Opening the door, she entered the room but found that it too was empty.

Janet stood in the doorway, looking at the bed her daughter had slept in. For just a brief moment, as she entered the room, she thought she saw a tiny lump beneath the covers, but it was only the shadows playing tricks on her. The bed was empty; her little girl had not come home.

Robert wasn't in the room either. She thought he might be sitting there, his mind troubled with thoughts of Krissy. She thought she might find him in the room, because that's where she had spent several hours earlier in the day.

She had come into the bedroom to be alone with her thoughts, also wanting to be near the place where her daughter was last seen. At first she had just stood in the doorway, looking around, hoping to see something the detectives might have overlooked, some clue that might help them get her little girl back. But the room had already been gone over several times, and there was nothing that could unlock the mystery of Krissy's disappearance.

Still, Janet was not going to give up. There had to be something overlooked that might help the police with their investigation. She had gone to the dresser and opened the drawers, searching through her daughter's clothing.

As she'd inspected the clothing she'd lifted each item to her nose and inhaled—shirts, pants, socks, even panties—smelling the sunshine sweetness of her baby girl, her mind filling with a thousand images that brought bitter, burning tears. Here was the shirt Krissy had worn to Six Flags St. Louis. Here were the socks she had used to mop up spilled Kool-Aid. Here was her favorite pair of blue jeans, still sporting the yellow "happy face" patch Janet had used to cover a tear.

Finished with the clothing, she had gone over to the bed and lain down. She had wanted to lie where her daughter had slept, wanted to feel what presence the child had left behind. The pillow had still smelled of Krissy's Herbal Essence shampoo, but already the scent was fading.

Janet had lain on the bed for several hours in an attempt to feel closer to her daughter, wondering what had happened the night Krissy disappeared. Had someone entered the room through the window, tiptoeing across the floor to stand over the child's bed? Had they awakened her by placing a hand tightly over her mouth? Had they pressed a knife to her throat, or a gun to her head?

And what had Krissy thought when these terrible things were happening to her? Had she waited in vain for her mother and father to rush through the door to rescue her? Had she felt betrayed by her parents as the kidnapper dragged her from the bed, carrying her off into the night? And what if the worst had already happened? What thoughts had gone through Krissy's mind as her precious life was brutally taken from her?

Janet had stayed on the bed that afternoon and cried like she had never cried before, great wracking sobs that left her weak and heartsick. She and her husband had failed their child, and there was nothing they could do to change that. Krissy might be badly hurt, might even be dead, and it was all their fault.

She had lain on the bed and cried until she was unable to cry any more. Then she had gone back into her bedroom and retrieved several prescription sleeping pills from the bottle she kept hidden in the bottom of her purse. The pills had come from Janet's mother, a gift to help her get through sleepless nights. She only took them when she absolutely needed one, making sure to keep the bottle hidden from Robert. Her husband didn't like her taking drugs, so she kept the pills a secret. It was wrong for her to take sleeping pills, but it was quite all right for him to drink himself to oblivion when he felt stressed.

Janet remained standing in the doorway, looking at the empty bed. She felt no desire to lie down or go through her daughter's clothing. She was all cried out, and felt only numbness. As she stood there, the last of her nocturnal fogginess slowly lifted, and she remembered what it was that had awakened her.

She had heard a scream, at least it sounded like a scream. Maybe Robert had heard it too and had already gone to investigate. Maybe something had happened. Perhaps the scream had something to do with Krissy.

With this thought in mind, she left Krissy's room and hurried back into her own bedroom. Discarding the robe on the floor, she slipped out of her nightgown and into a pair of khaki pants, and a pullover shirt. A pair of running shoes came next. Once dressed, she headed for the front door.

It was quiet as she stepped outside the cabin, the silence marred only by the distant hooting of an owl. She didn't know the time, but the moon was already low in the western sky so it must be early morning. The silvery moonlight made the dew-laden ground luminous, causing shadows to look darker than they normally would.

Janet stepped out on the tiny porch and closed the

door behind her. The campgrounds were quiet, and it didn't look like anyone else was up, which meant that only she had heard the scream. If there had been a scream. She still wasn't convinced that she had actually heard something; it had probably been just part of a medicine-induced dream.

No sooner had she stepped outside the cabin than a flashing blue light got her attention. On the narrow road beyond the fish camp was parked an unmarked patrol car, its emergency lights flashing. Something was going on. Maybe they had found Krissy. Perhaps Robert was already there, talking with the officers.

Stepping off the porch, Janet hurried through the camp to the road. She expected to find people clustered around the patrol car, but no one was there. In fact, she didn't even see a deputy. The patrol car sat in the middle of the road, with lights flashing, but it was empty. The driver's door stood open, and the little light in the ceiling lit up the empty interior of the car.

Curious, Janet approached the car and looked inside. A small notebook lay on the front seat, obviously placed there by the driver. On the passenger seat lay an empty soda can, and a half-full pack of cigarettes. The keys to the patrol car were still in the ignition.

She stepped back and looked around. It wasn't normal for a law enforcement officer to go off and leave a patrol car sitting in the middle of the road, especially with the door standing open and the keys in the ignition. She didn't know who was driving the car, but such things were not done. Even she knew that.

But maybe there was a reason for the officer's actions. Perhaps he had to exit the vehicle quickly, and there wasn't time to take the keys or close the door. He might be chasing a bad guy, or he might have seen someone he was looking for.

Krissy.

Janet looked around, suddenly hoping that her daughter had been found and this was the reason for the officer's careless actions. Maybe he had seen her, or the person who had taken her. Perhaps he saw them both, alongside the road, and had stopped the car to give chase.

She studied the forest on the opposite side of the road. There was no sign of her little girl, the officer, or the big bad man who might have taken her. If the deputy had seen someone, then he had given chase into the forest. He had apparently not called for backup, as proper procedures dictated; instead, he had decided to do the pursuit by himself.

"If there was a pursuit," she said, aloud. "For all I know he's behind a bush taking a whiz."

That might also be true. The officer might only be standing somewhere in the shadows, relieving himself. If that was the case, then it was stupid to leave the patrol car in the middle of the road. Country roads were notorious speedways, and even the flashing lights of a patrol car might not be enough to keep it from getting hit by a fast driving redneck.

Wondering if the deputy was somewhere nearby, Janet looked around and called out, "Hello? Is anyone here? Officer?"

There was no answer. Surely, if a deputy had been standing behind a bush, relieving himself, he would have heard her calling. That meant something else was going on. Perhaps the deputy was following someone. If that was the case, he might need help. At the very least someone ought to call the sheriff's office to tell them about the empty patrol car and the missing officer.

There was a phone in her cabin, but Janet didn't feel like walking all the way back across the camp to use it. There was also a phone in the Blackwater Lounge. She didn't know what time the lounge closed, but if it was still open she could use the phone there. If the lounge was still open, then that's where she would probably find her husband. She could ask him if he had also heard a scream.

Leaving the roadway, she cut across the campgrounds to the lounge. The lounge might already be closed, but she knew some of the locals always stayed later than closing time. Finding the front door unlocked, she opened the door and entered the lounge.

The lounge was dark, real dark, and at first she didn't think anyone was still inside. Everyone must have already gone home, but if that was true then they had forgotten to lock the front door.

"Hello?"

No one answered.

"Hello? Mr. Sanders, are you still here? I wanted to use your phone."

The interior of the Blackwater Lounge was quite dark, even the beer signs above the bar had been turned off. The emergency exit sign above the door was still lit, its red letters casting a pale crimson glow over the area directly in front of the door. It wasn't much light, but it was enough to see the bodies.

"Oh, my God."

Three people lay on the floor just inside the doorway, two men and a woman. She recognized two of the people as Ross and Mary Sanders. They lay in separate pools of blood, not far from each other. An older man lay on the floor farther back from the door. She didn't recognize the third person, but suspected he was probably a customer. Or he had been a customer. Like Ross and Mary, the older man was also dead.

"Oh, my God," she said again, her lips barely forming the words. Something terrible had just happened inside the tiny lounge. Someone had just murdered the owners of the Blackwater Fish Camp and one of their customers. From the looks of things, they had either been stabbed repeatedly with a knife or shot with a large-caliber gun.

Janet remembered the gunshot that had awakened her, and the scream she had heard, and a chill came over her as she realized those sounds were associated with the murder of people she knew. While she had slept peacefully, someone had been killing three innocent people no more than two hundred yards from her cabin.

A sudden fear came over her. She looked quickly around the lounge, fearful that she might also find the body of her husband. But there were only three people lying on the bloody floor.

She also remembered the empty patrol car sitting on the road and wondered if the officer had responded to a call for help. Surely not, for a call about a shooting, or a stabbing, would have summoned more than just one car. Perhaps the officer, just driving by, had seen the murderer running from the lounge, and had given chase. If so, he was up against a dangerous psychopath and would need backup.

She thought about hurrying across the room to use the phone behind the bar, but stopped herself for fear of disturbing a crime scene. She was also afraid to enter the lounge, fearing the killer might be hiding in the darkness.

Hiding in the darkness.

Her mouth went dry. She had been standing there, a witness to a bloody crime scene, and she had not considered the possibility that the killer might still be around. If he was, then she too could end up as a victim.

Get out of here. Now!

She turned on her heels and fled back out the door, running for her cabin. She had just rounded the corner of the building when she almost collided with someone coming from the other way.

Janet screamed, startled by the sudden appearance of another person. She thought it was the murderer, but the person she nearly collided with was much too small to be a killer.

She stopped and jumped back, her hands automatically going to her face for protection. But the other person made no move to attack, just stood there, looking at her. A tense moment passed, and then Janet recognized the person standing before her.

"Krissy?"

The little girl was covered with filth and mud, and her long blonde hair was so dirty it was almost black. She would have been unrecognizable, had it not been for the familiar shape of her body and face. Even her eyes looked different in the darkness, appearing to glow with a strange bluish-green light.

"Krissy? Oh, my God, it is you. Oh, my God." She took a step toward her daughter, then stopped. Krissy didn't seem to recognize her. She just stood there looking at her, looking right through her.

"Krissy, it's okay baby. It's Mommy. You're safe

now. No one is going to hurt you." Janet wanted to rush forward and scoop her daughter up in her arms, but she held back. Krissy might be in shock, and any sudden movements might terrify her. There was no telling what she had gone through during the past couple of days, what someone might have done to her. She might have severe psychological damage. It might take years of therapy for her to recover.

"Krissy, it's okay. You're safe now," Janet repeated, trying to keep her voice from quivering with emotion. It wasn't easy, because she was fighting hard to hold back the tears. She wanted nothing more than to rush forward and smother her little girl with hugs and kisses.

The girl gave no indication that she recognized her mother. She just stood there, looking at her, standing still as a statue, with both hands behind her back.

"Would you like some hot cocoa, honey? How does that sound? We have some cocoa back at the cabin. I'll have Daddy make you some, with little marshmallows." Janet looked around, hoping that Robert would miraculously appear now that she needed him most, but her husband was nowhere to be seen.

She turned back to Krissy, surprised to find that her daughter had moved a few feet closer while she had been looking away. As she watched, the little girl moved her left hand out from behind her back. In her left hand she held a plastic bag that contained something, though it was much too dark to see what was in the bag. A dark liquid leaked from one corner of the bag. It looked like blood.

"What's that you have there, sweetheart? Is it something for me? A present?"

The little girl looked at her for a moment longer, then smiled, finally recognizing her mother.

"Yes, Mom-m-y. A present for you."

Janet was startled by her daughter's voice, because it didn't sound normal. She was probably parched with thirst. Or she might have a sore throat from exposure to the elements. It didn't matter what her voice sounded like. Krissy now recognized her, and that was the important thing.

Still holding the plastic bag in front of her, Krissy started walking toward her mother. Janet opened her arms wide to embrace her baby. Krissy's smile widened. Janet smiled back. It was the happiest moment of her life.

Chapter Twenty-six

The pain in Robert's ankle had diminished considerably. The herbal concoction Jimmy Cypress had used on it had obviously done some good. Chalk up one for traditional Indian cures. The swelling in the ankle had gone down, and it only hurt a little when he placed his full weight upon it. Now all he had to worry about was getting an infection in the scratches, and, according to Jimmy, that was now not likely to happen.

With his ankle wrapped with moist leaves and an Ace bandage, and with his courage fortified by half a glass of whiskey, they had left the cabin of Jimmy Cypress and headed back toward the lagoon. Jimmy thought that Krissy might return to the lagoon, guided by the spirit of the voodoo sorcerer that now possessed her, but the little girl was nowhere to be seen. Knowing that time was running out for them, they decided to make their way toward the fish camp in hope that someone else might have seen the child.

They followed the boardwalk through the forest, Jimmy's black cowboy boots making a hollow clomp-clomp sound as he hurried along the wooden path. Robert's ankle was better, but it wasn't perfect, and he still had to remind the Seminole man to slow down so he could keep up.

Arriving at the Wekiva River, they crossed the wooden footbridge to the back side of Blackwater Fish Camp. Robert remembered how he had previously seen an owl sitting on the sign marking the beginning of the nature trail, and how he had thought at the time that it might be some kind of evil omen. Little did he know that the owl's appearance would indeed mark the beginning of what seemed to be a never-ending nightmare.

Entering the camp, they made their way toward the Blackwater Lounge. They both knew that Ross Sanders kept late hours at the lounge, and they were hoping they could find a few people to help them search for Krissy. Of course, they couldn't tell the others what they knew. No one would believe them. How could you convince someone that a ten-year-old girl was inhabited by the evil spirit of a voodoo sorcerer?

Robert wasn't even sure if he believed it. His daughter had acted strange, that was a given. She had even attacked him. Still, everything he had been taught in life made him doubt that such things as possessions were possible. The story had sounded convincing enough when being told by Jimmy Cypress in his tiny cabin, especially after a few shots of bourbon whiskey. But now, out in the fresh air, with the whiskey starting to wear off, he was starting to have his doubts about what had been said to him. His little girl couldn't really be possessed. Could she?

What about the way she acted?

She was probably in shock. Maybe Krissy had not recognized him. Maybe she thought he was her abductor, and had attacked him out of fear.

But she called me Daddy.

That she had. Which meant his daughter had recognized him, and had not thought that he was her abductor coming back to hurt her some more. Maybe she had only recognized him for a moment, long enough to call him Daddy, before her mind slipped back into a delusional world caused by pain, fear, and a traumatic experience. That was possible. Or maybe someone had given her drugs, and she was in the midst of a hallucination.

What about her voice? She didn't sound like Krissy.

The gravely voice was easy to explain. She had been missing for days and exposed to the elements. She could have been thirsty, her throat dry and parched. She might even had been tied up, a rope wound tightly around her neck. Such things could easily affect her voice. Hell, there might even be permanent damage to her vocal cords, especially if she had been choked by someone. Drugs too could alter her voice. If Krissy was under the influence of some powerful hallucinogen, or narcotic, that would explain why she was talking funny.

Okay, smart guy. What about her eyes? How do you explain how her eyes had looked?

Again drugs. That was how police could tell if a person was stoned, by their eyes. Marijuana made a person's eyes look shiny, while LSD and amphetamines made the pupils dilate. Drugs could have made her eyes look big and shiny, appearing to glow in the light of a full moon.

Bullshit. You know better. You've been there, done that.

Robert had come of age during the seventies, a decade when drugs were very easy to obtain and used by just about everyone. During his college years, he and his roommates had smoked, snorted, and swallowed just about every kind of illegal substance they could get their hands on. He knew what it was like to be stoned, and he knew what a person looked like when they were tripping on the hard stuff. Krissy did not have the eyes of a drug user. And there wasn't a drug made that would change the color of a person's eyes, other than make them red. Krissy had brown eyes, but when he had seen her at the lagoon her eyes had glowed a strange bluish-green.

Her eyes had glowed.

Krissy had the eyes of an animal, there was no other way to describe them. Her eyes had shone with the strange reflective glow of a nocturnal predator, like the eyes of a wolf caught in the bright beam of a car's headlights. No drug he knew would make a person's eyes look like that.

He didn't want to think about how his daughter's eyes had looked, for it made him go all rubbery in the legs. It also made him want another drink real bad, made him want several drinks—hell, he wanted the whole damn bottle. He wanted a bottle of the strong stuff and a place to hide, allowing himself to get so drunk that all the hurt and pain of the past couple of days would go away. Maybe when he woke up things would be back to normal, with Krissy sleeping safely in her bed.

Robert frowned. Getting drunk was not the answer. It was up to him to find his daughter. Up to him and a Seminole Indian named Jimmy Cypress. A Seminole with a box of leaves and a magic staff.

The camp was quiet when they arrived. No lights burned in any of the guest cabins. They had just passed the bait and tackle shop when Robert spotted Janet in the shadows near the lounge. She was kneeling, her arms outstretched before her as if to give someone a hug. He took a few steps toward his wife, and saw that she was about to hug Krissy.

"Janet, no!" Robert yelled a warning, running toward his wife. "No. Stay back. That's not Krissy!"

Janet turned to look at him, obviously confused by his sudden outburst. Krissy also turned to look at him, her facial expression becoming almost animal as she spotted the two men running toward her.

"Robert, what. . . ?" Janet was still looking his way, so she did not see the knife that suddenly appeared in Krissy's right hand. The little girl had been hiding the knife behind her back, but now held it in front of her.

"Look out!"

Janet turned and saw the knife in her daughter's bloody hand. Her mouth dropped open in shocked surprise. Hissing in anger, Krissy lunged at her mother but missed. The deadly blade sliced only air. And then Krissy was past her mother, running away toward the front of the camp.

"Krissy, no!" Robert yelled, but the little girl did not slow down. She raced away into the night, disappearing from view.

Robert reached Janet's side. "Are you okay?"

Janet nodded. "Yes. I think so."

"Are you sure?"

She looked down, checking to make sure she had not been hurt. "Yes."

"Thank God."

She got to her feet. Her eyes were wide with a mixture of shock and horror. "Krissy tried to stab me."

Robert nodded. "I know. I saw it."

Tears formed in her eyes. "But why? Why did she want to hurt me? I'm her mother."

"Krissy's different now."

"Different? How? What do you mean?"

Jimmy Cypress arrived next to them. He had started to chase after the fleeing child, but had stopped and turned back. "Your daughter's actions are not her own. She has been possessed by an evil spirit."

She turned to look at the Indian man, apparently not comprehending what he had just said. "Possessed?"

The Seminole nodded. "Your little girl is no longer your little girl. She is a thing of evil, possessed by the spirit of Mansa Du Paul. He is inside her, controlling her."

Janet shook her head and turned to Robert. "I don't understand. Isn't Mansa the name of Krissy's make-believe friend?"

Robert put his hands on his wife's arms. "Mansa Du Paul was a voodoo sorcerer who used to live in this area. He was an evil man that performed black magic ceremonies. He also ate children. The Indians living in this area killed him. They cut his body up into little pieces and threw them in the river, but they couldn't kill his spirit."

She stared into her husband's eyes, trying desperately to understand what he was saying. Turning her attention back to Jimmy Cypress, she asked, "And you think the spirit of this sorcerer is now inside Krissy?"

Jimmy nodded.

"Do you believe it too?" she asked Robert.

"I'm not sure what to believe. All I know is that our daughter is no longer the same little girl we know and love."

"Maybe she's in shock. Maybe she has been hurt, or molested."

He shook his head. "Being in shock would not make her mean. She just tried to stab you. Earlier she tried to hurt me."

"Stop it. I don't want to hear this." Janet put her hands over her ears. "I don't believe in possessions. It can't be true."

Jimmy Cypress stepped closer. "My people have known about the evil in this area for a long time. That is why I'm here. I am the guardian, and it is my job to make sure that Mansa Du Paul never returns. But I have failed. His spirit is now inside your daughter, and he is using her to gather together his bones. He wants to bring his former self back to life, and he will accomplish this unless we stop him."

"His bones?" Janet asked. "Krissy's gathering his bones?"

Jimmy nodded. "Yes. Once his bones are together in one place, he will use his black magic to bring his body back to life. If that happens he will again have all of his powers. He may be even stronger now, because he has lived in the land of spirits for many years, learning their ways."

"This ceremony. What else is needed for it?"

"I'm not sure. The ways of voodoo and black magic are not the ways of my people. Still, I would imagine that some sort of sacrifice will be needed."

"What kind of sacrifice?"

The Indian looked at Robert, then back to Janet. "A blood sacrifice."

Janet's eyes widened. "Oh, my God. Then it's true. The knife Krissy had. She did it. She killed them."

"Killed who?" Robert asked.

"Ross and Mary. Someone else. They're in the lounge. They've been murdered. She must have done it. They must have been sacrifices."

Jimmy shook his head. "Not sacrifices. Perhaps something else. The blood must be fresh; it must be spilled during the ceremony for the magic to work. Maybe they were killed for some other reason."

Janet put a fist to her mouth. She started to sway, but Robert held her tighter. "Something else? They were killed for something else?"

She looked at Jimmy. "You said this Mansa Du Paul is using our daughter to gather his bones. Is that all he needs for the ceremony? What about the internal organs? Would he need those too? What about the eyes? Would he also need eyes?"

"Maybe." Jimmy shrugged. "I'm not sure. My way is not his way. Some cultures believe there is power in the heart and eyes. Some believe we have three spirits: one in the eyes, one in the heart, and one in the top of the head. Why?"

"Krissy had a bag, a small plastic bag. In it were a pair of eyes."

"Are you sure?" Robert asked.

She nodded. "Yes. I saw them. I didn't know what they were then, but I do now. They were eyes. She had them in a small plastic bag."

"My God," Robert said.

Jimmy turned and looked toward the lounge. "I had better take a look inside. Maybe someone is still alive. You stay here."

"No way. I'm going," Robert said.

"Me too," added Janet.

"No. You stay here," Robert said to his wife.

"Why? I've already seen the bodies. I'm not staying here by myself."

Robert looked at her for a moment, then nodded. "Okay, let's go."

The three of them circled around to the front of the lounge. The door stood open, and it looked like all the lights were off on the inside. Stopping in the doorway, Jimmy reached into his pants pocket and removed a tiny flashlight.

"You came prepared," Robert said, seeing it.

"I used to be a Boy Scout."

"Really?"

"No. I'm just kidding." Jimmy turned on the tiny flashlight and pointed its beam in through the doorway. There were three bodies on the floor inside the lounge: two men and a woman. All three of them had been brutally murdered, their bodies and the floor around them covered with blood.

"Sweet Jesus," Robert said, looking over Jimmy's shoulders. "Could Krissy have done that?"

Jimmy nodded. "Remember, she is no longer Krissy. The spirit of a grown man is inside her body. A very powerful spirit."

The Indian stepped through the doorway, being careful not to walk in any blood. It was obvious, without touching them, that the three people inside the lounge were dead. They had been stabbed too many times to survive. Janet nearly screamed when the flashlight's beam swept over the face of Ross Sanders. Not only had Ross been murdered, but his eyes had also been cut out.

"Oh my God," Robert whispered, his voice catching.

"She took his eyes. But why Ross? Why not one of the others?"

Jimmy Cypress looked around. "The old man was wearing glasses, so Mansa knew that his eyes were weak. I'm not sure why he didn't choose the woman; maybe she didn't show up until the others were already dead. Perhaps Mansa just killed her and the old man for the fun of it.

"We have seen enough here," Jimmy said, backing up. "There is nothing we can do for them now."

"We should call the police," Robert suggested.

"Later perhaps. Not now."

"Why not now?"

The Seminole turned to face him. "If we call the police there will be questions to be answered. Lots of questions. We do not have time to answer questions, not if we want to find your daughter in time to save her life. And do you want the police here now, knowing that it was your daughter who held the knife? Do you think they will believe that she is possessed by an evil spirit? Or will they just look upon her as a murderer?"

Robert thought about it a moment. "You're right. They'll never believe us. They'll think Krissy is a killer."

The three of them stepped back outside, Jimmy left Robert to comfort his wife while he walked across the parking lot to the road.

"We may be too late," he said, returning. "The police are already here. There's a patrol car parked down the road, with its lights flashing."

"That car was parked there earlier," Robert said. "I checked it out, but there's no one inside."

"I also walked over there," Janet added. "The driver's door is open, but I didn't see an officer anywhere."

"Maybe the officer is no longer with us," Jimmy suggested. "He might have tried to help the wrong person."

"Do you think he's dead?" asked Janet.

"I don't think he would have gone off and left his car sitting in the road."

"What do we do now?" Robert asked.

Jimmy Cypress glanced back toward the lounge. "We have to stop Mansa Du Paul from performing his ceremony. He is already collecting body parts, which means he has already found all of his bones. All he needs to do now is put everything together and say the right words. He will call upon dark forces to help him, paying with a fresh sacrifice of blood."

"But everyone's already dead, and you said the blood had to be spilled during the ceremony," Janet said.

Jimmy looked at her a moment before replying. "Everyone is not dead. There is another."

"But you said . . ." Janet stopped, her eyes going wide with fear. "You don't mean . . ."

Jimmy nodded. "Once Mansa Du Paul recreates his former body, he will no longer have a need for your daughter. Despite what has happened here tonight, your little girl is still an innocent. Her blood, and her spirit, will be the perfect offering to the evil ones. That is why we have to stop the ceremony from ever happening."

"But where will the ceremony be held, and when?"

The Seminole stood silent for a moment, his head cocked slightly to the left, as if listening for something only he could hear. "Mansa's place of power is at the lagoon, so I think that is where he will perform the ceremony. I think also that he will do it soon. Very soon. Maybe even now."

"Now?" Robert asked, surprised. "Now? Then why are we standing here? Let's go."

Jimmy stood silent for a moment longer, then nodded. "Let's go save your daughter, if it is not already too late."

Chapter Twenty-seven

Robert, Janet, and Jimmy Cypress raced along the nature trail to the lagoon. Leaving the boardwalk behind them, they had to slow their pace as they followed the narrow path that wound between the dense foliage. In the pale light of the moon, the trees and brush around them seemed to shimmer and dance. It was only when he slowed his pace that Robert realized the greenery was indeed moving, and it was not merely an illusion caused by the shadows. The movement around them seemed to increase as they drew closer to the lagoon.

"Look at that!" Robert said, stopping to point at a palmetto bush growing along the trail. The bush was shaking, vibrating as if some maddened animal was hiding beneath it. The plant was also bending toward the trail, as if reaching out to grab them as they passed. It wasn't the wind that caused the movement, for there was no wind to speak of.

"What the hell is that?"

Jimmy Cypress stopped to look where Robert pointed. "It's magic. Evil magic. This is a bad place, for the spirit of Mansa Du Paul is one with the land. He is using his powers to stop us."

Janet stopped to look at the trembling palmetto bush.

The plant's shaking had grown more frantic, as if the bush was literally trying to tear itself free from the ground. She was so absorbed by the sight before her that she didn't notice the slender root by her feet. As she stood there, that root slithered across the ground and wrapped itself around her left ankle like a snake.

Feeling something caress her ankle, Janet jumped back in alarm. But the root held her tight and she fell. "Robert, help me!"

Robert spun around, seeing his wife sprawled on the ground. He also saw the black root wrapped around her ankle. At first he thought it was a snake of some kind, but then he noticed that the root stretched from his wife's leg to a nearby tree.

"Son of a bitch!"

Robert rushed forward to help his wife. He grabbed the root and attempted to pull it off of Janet, but the root was hard and wrapped tight, and he could not tear it free.

"Help me!" Janet cried out, terrified by what was happening to her.

"I'm trying. I'm trying. It's not easy."

"Use a knife or something."

"I can't. I'll cut you."

Two more roots suddenly exploded out of the ground. One of the roots grabbed Janet around her right wrist. The other circled her waist.

"Do something!" she shouted, her voice etched with fear.

"I am. I am," Robert answered, trying to tear the roots from his wife.

Seeing that the situation was now out of hand, and fearing for the woman's safety, Jimmy Cypress rushed forward to help. Grabbing the root that encircled Janet's waist, he pulled his hunting knife and began sawing at the root. It took a few moments of frenzied work, but he was finally able to cut through the root, freeing her waist.

Stepping forward, Jimmy grabbed the root that encircled Janet's ankle. Luckily, the root wasn't as thick as the others, and he was able to pry it off of her without using his knife. He had just freed her ankle when Robert was able to get the root off of her wrist.

Janet jumped up and fled to the other side of the trail. Her encounter with the animated roots had been terrifying, but she wasn't hurt.

"I suggest we keep moving," Jimmy said, backing away from the roots he had just done battle with. The roots continued to slither across the ground, searching for someone else to grab.

Robert looked at the roots, then turned to the Indian. "That day we first met in the woods, when you yelled at me, there were kudzu vines wrapped around my legs. I thought you had done that, but you didn't. Did you?"

Jimmy shook his head. "The vines were under Mansa Du Paul's control. Had you slept any longer they might have wrapped around your neck and choked you."

"Then you saved my life?"

"Perhaps." Jimmy nodded.

"All this time I thought you were trying to hurt me."

Jimmy grinned. "There will be plenty of time for you to apologize later. Maybe you can even shed a few tears. Right now, however, we have work to do."

Robert frowned, angered by the sarcasm in Jimmy's voice. But the medicine man was right, they had to keep moving if they wanted to help Krissy. There would be plenty of time to talk later.

Their pace through the forest was now considerably slower because they were on the lookout for roots and vines that didn't act like normal roots and vines. Twice they had to step off the trail and detour around where the foliage grew too thick, rather than risk wading through it. Several times they were delayed by kudzu vines that fell from the treetops in an attempt to grab them, but the vines were thin and easily cut with Jimmy's knife.

"Mansa's medicine is getting stronger," Jimmy said, cutting through several kudzu vines. The vines he cut continued to move, quivering on the ground like a lizard's tail. "It was never like this before."

"What does that mean?"

"It means we may be too late to stop Mansa. He may be too strong for us to fight."

"What if we can't stop him?" Robert asked. "What will happen then?"

"I don't know," Jimmy replied, "but I don't want to be around to find out."

"What about Krissy?" Janet asked. "What about our daughter? You said we could help her. I thought you knew what to do."

Jimmy glanced at her but did not slow down. "I will do everything I can to help your daughter. But to save her I will have to defeat Mansa Du Paul, and he may already be too strong for me. His power is that of the darkness, of worlds beyond worlds, while mine comes from much humbler sources. We will see what happens."

Despite the vines and roots that tried to stop their

progress, they finally reached the lagoon. They emerged from the forest into the clearing, only to discover that Krissy had already laid Mansa's skeleton out on the ground.

"Krissy, no!" Janet started to rush toward her daughter, but Jimmy grabbed her arm and held her back.

Janet wheeled on the Indian. "Damn you, let me go. That's my daughter. She needs me."

"She is no longer your daughter. Not now. She is a wild animal, ridden by the spirit of one who is pure evil. She will kill you without so much as a second thought, maybe even drink your soul. You will not do your little girl any good if you are dead."

Janet stopped struggling and turned back around to look at her daughter.

Krissy stood in the middle of the clearing, halfway between the lagoon and the forest. On the ground before her was the skeleton of a man, the bones brown with age. The skeleton had been carefully laid out so that all the bones were in their proper place, with the top of the skull facing toward the west.

Mansa Du Paul appeared to have recovered all of his bones, for the skeleton seemed to be complete. Placed within the chest of the skeleton, with rib bones carefully laid over top of it, was a human heart. The heart glistened wetly in the moonlight. Along with the heart, the eyes of Ross Sanders had been placed in the eye sockets of the skull.

"Dear God," Janet whispered, noticing the eyes. "That poor man."

"Shhhh. . . . She'll hear us."

But Krissy made no notice of their presence. Or if she was aware of them, then she didn't care. Instead, the little girl circled the skeleton, making final adjustments here and there. Once satisfied that everything was in place, she positioned herself by the skeleton's side and raised her hands toward the night sky.

Robert did not understand all of the words that his daughter spoke, for she spoke them in several different languages: English, something African, and a dialect so ancient it was long forgotten by man. He didn't need to know all the words to be terrified, because what he did understand was enough to make his flesh crawl.

Speaking in the voice of Mansa Du Paul, the girl called upon the dark forces of nature to aid her. She also called upon the *bacas*, the demons, to come from their hiding places in hollow trees and from beneath the ground. She called upon the guardians of the spirit world, upon the gate keepers, and upon Legba. She called upon them all, asking them to send their powers to her.

Jimmy grabbed Robert, turning him around to face him. "Listen to me, and listen good. That is not your daughter standing there. Not anymore. Not now. If we are going to save her, we may have to hurt her."

"Hurt her. What do you mean?"

"We have to stop this ceremony, and to do so we will have to fight Mansa. Your daughter may get hurt."

Robert shook his head. "I will not hurt my daughter. Nor will I let you hurt her."

"There may be no other choice. If we do not stop Mansa, your daughter will lose more than just her life. She will also lose her soul."

"It may be too late to stop her," Janet said, pointing.

The others turned to see what she was pointing at, mesmerized by the sight before them. Krissy still stood with her hands raised toward the night sky, calling upon the forces of darkness. The forces must have answered her prayers, because there was movement at her feet.

As the three of them watched in awe, muscles and veins slowly started to form over the skeleton. The transformation started at the feet and worked upward. Veins and thin strips of muscles seemed to grow out of the bones themselves, flowing from the toes to heels, over the ankles and up the legs. As the veins reached the chest the heart began to beat, its movement clearly visible beneath the yellowed rib bones.

The veins and muscles flowed up the chest and back, and down the arms, up the neck to the skull, pulling everything tight as they went, joining together the spine and other bones. The eyes moved in their sockets, an image so hideous it was beyond words. Beyond madness. The lower jawbone opened and closed, but no sound was heard.

The skeleton of Mansa Du Paul was slowly disappearing beneath a layer of muscles, and miles of veins. The reincarnation of the voodoo sorcerer was almost complete. All that was needed now was a sacrifice to the dark gods.

They had been so mesmerized by the sight of the body forming before them that none of them had noticed that Krissy had stopped her chanting. The little girl let her arms drop as she bent over to pick up something lying on the ground beside her. When she again lifted her arms to the sky, she held a butcher knife in her right hand, blade pointed toward her unprotected neck. It was Janet who first noticed the knife.

"Oh, my God. Look!"

"Krissy, no!" Robert yelled. He started to move

toward his daughter, but Jimmy Cypress was already in motion. The Indian had dropped his staff and was racing toward Krissy at a dead run. The little girl had stopped talking, and Robert knew that Mansa Du Paul was about to spill her blood in sacrifice. Before the sorcerer could make the child thrust the knife down into her own throat, she was tackled by the Seminole.

Jimmy tackled Krissy around the waist, taking her to the ground. Over and over they rolled, the Indian trying desperately to get the knife away from the girl before she stabbed him. He was lucky, for he was able to tear the knife from her grasp without losing any blood in the process.

Getting back to his feet, Jimmy tossed the butcher knife into the lagoon. Even without the knife, the little girl was still dangerous. The spirit inside her body was powerful and was willing to fight to the death. Mansa did not care if he injured, or even killed, the body he rode. Knowing this, Jimmy decided to directly challenge the sorcerer, hoping to bait his pride.

"Mansa Du Paul, you are a coward," Jimmy said, shouting to be heard. "You hide yourself inside the body of a little girl. Why not come out here and fight me like a man? Are you afraid? I thought your power was great, but I think it is no stronger than the little girl you now ride."

Krissy stood up and looked at him, her eyes glowing. She hissed at him in anger, and then she spoke with a voice more animal than human. "Stupid Indian. I am not afraid of you. Your people are weak and foolish. I will kill you, then I will feed on your flesh, as I have fed on the flesh of your people many times in the past."

Jimmy threw his head back and laughed. "Words.

Words. Words. Still, I see nothing but a little girl. Where is the Mansa Du Paul I have heard so much about? Where is the mighty voodoo sorcerer who can summon spirits and demons? Do not tell me that I have waited all this time just to fight a child. Show yourself, Mansa. Come out and fight me, if you are not afraid."

There was a hiss of anger from Krissy, then the glow in her eyes faded and she slumped to the ground. Seeing his daughter fall, Robert started to rush forward.

"Stay back," Jimmy warned.

Robert stopped dead in his tracks. "What's happening?"

"I'm not sure, but I think Mansa just accepted my challenge."

"That means he is no longer in Krissy," Robert said. "We have to get her out of here."

"His spirit may not be in her, but it hasn't gone far. It would be dangerous to touch her now."

"But—" Robert started to argue, but he was interrupted by a disturbance in the middle of the lagoon. The water in the lagoon was suddenly bubbling, as if an air line had ruptured beneath the surface.

"What the hell is that?" Robert asked, very afraid.

Jimmy turned to watch what was happening out in the middle of the lagoon. He pulled his hunting knife from its sheath. "It looks like we have company."

"Is it Mansa?"

"That would be a good guess. Maybe I shouldn't have called him a coward."

"You think?"

The bubbling grew stronger, churning up the water. Then something slowly rose to the surface, rising up out of the water. A shape, almost human in nature, but bigger. Much, much, bigger.

Mansa Du Paul had accepted Jimmy's challenge, rising up in a body made from the muck and mire that lined the bottom of the lagoon. The creature was sculpted in the shape of a man, but it stood eight feet tall and probably weighed over four hundred pounds, its body a mass of slime, mud, stones, and slithering things. The thing was faceless except for its eyes, and they glowed a strange bluish-green, like Krissy's had glowed only moments before.

Jimmy Cypress backed up, watching in dread as the towering mud-thing slowly lumbered out of the water. All his life he had been preparing for this fight, but now that it was upon him he felt that he wasn't up to the challenge.

No man could ever be up to such a fight. Jimmy was no exception. And even though he was a man of medicine, he suddenly doubted that his medicine was strong enough to help him.

"Grandfather, I'm going to need all the help you can send my way. Not just for me, but for the little girl. Mansa Du Paul has to be stopped."

Could the voodoo sorcerer be stopped? The Seminoles had tried to stop him before, and they had failed. Even cutting his body into little pieces had not been enough to kill him. So what chance did Jimmy have now, one man against such odds?

The mud-man reached the shore and came toward him. Jimmy wanted nothing more than to turn and flee, leave the area as quickly as possible. After all, why should he give his life for the white man and his family? What had they ever done for him? They were the ones who had spoken against him, getting an innocent man arrested for the abduction of their daughter. They had laid their faults upon an Indian's shoulders, as their ancestors had done throughout time.

Why should his people even give a shit about Mansa Du Paul? So what if the sorcerer came back and killed a few thousand white people? It was no skin off their noses. The white men claimed the land as their own now, so they should have to deal with their own problems. Why should they help them?

Jimmy sighed. Mansa Du Paul was evil, and his people had always been opposed to evil in its many shapes and forms. It was as simple as that. And he had taken a sacred vow to fight evil, no matter what size or shape it came in. No matter how ugly, or how big.

He looked up at the mud-man. "Damn if you're not both ugly and big."

Shouting his best rendition of a war cry, Jimmy Cypress rushed at the creature of mud. Coming in low beneath its grasp, he stabbed his knife deep into its left leg. But the blade of his knife had absolutely no effect on the creature, sinking deep into the mud but causing no harm.

Jimmy stabbed its leg a second time, hoping to make it fall. Again his knife had no effect. The creature was solid, but it was solid mud.

He was about to stab it again when the creature struck him across the back of the head. The creature may have been made from mud, but its punch was anything but soft. The blow sent Jimmy flying, nearly landing him in the lagoon.

Jimmy Cypress hit the ground and rolled. He was dazed from the blow but still able to stand back up. He had just gotten to his feet when he realized that he no longer had his knife. He had dropped the hunting knife when he hit the ground.

"Shit!" Jimmy looked around, but the knife lay hidden in the darkness. Nor did he have time to look for it, because the mud-monster was already upon him.

He tried to get out of the way, but the creature grabbed him by the face and lifted him high into the air. Jimmy struggled to draw a breath as he fought to get loose. But no matter how hard he struggled, he just couldn't break free from the thing's grasp.

"Do something!" Janet shouted.

"What?" Robert asked.

"I don't know, but do it quick. He's losing."

Robert looked around for a weapon of some kind, his gaze falling upon the medicine staff of Jimmy Cypress. He remembered how the Indian had used the staff on Krissy, and wondered if that magic would now work for him.

Snatching up the staff, Robert raced toward the mud-monster. The creature had its back to him and didn't notice his approach.

Holding the staff as he had seen Jimmy hold it, he reached out and struck the mud-creature on the back. Nothing happened. There was no magical blue spark. No flame. No thunder. Nothing. The staff sank a few inches into the muddy flesh of the creature, but that was it. There wasn't even enough damage done to get the creature's attention.

Robert knew Jimmy Cypress was a goner if he didn't do something to help him, but what could he do? There were no other weapons to be had. He needed a rocket launcher, and all he had was a stupid stick.

Frantic, terrified, Robert thought about tossing the staff aside and getting the hell out of there. Mansa Du Paul was occupied with Jimmy Cypress. Now was the time to get Krissy and his wife to safety.

But he couldn't leave Jimmy, knowing he would be leaving him there to die. The Indian had helped them, risking his life to help people he didn't even know. Robert could not turn his back on a man like that. He had to help him. There had to be something he could do.

"But what? Damn it. What?"

He looked around and saw the unfinished body of Mansa Du Paul, an idea suddenly forming in his mind. The staff had no effect on lagoon mud, but maybe it would have a different effect on flesh and bone, especially if that flesh and bone was pure evil.

Turning his back on the fight taking place, Robert rushed forward to Mansa's half-formed body. Raising the staff above his head, he struck the body across the chest. As he struck the flesh of the sorcerer, a blue spark jumped from the tip of the medicine staff.

"That's it. That's what I'm talking about." Robert hit the body a second time. And a third. With each blow of the staff against the sorcerer's body, pieces of the mud-man broke away and fell to the ground. He was striking the body at his feet, yet it was the creature of mud that was breaking apart. Two more blows and the creature released its hold on Jimmy Cypress. Another blow after that and it literally crumbled to pieces.

Jimmy Cypress was quite surprised when the creature let go of him. Hitting the ground, he rolled and quickly got to his feet, only to find that the mud-man was no longer a threat. It was now nothing more than a pile of muck and squiggly things.

Looking away from the creature, he saw Robert striking the body of Mansa with the medicine staff and knew what had happened. He also saw Robert's daughter, Krissy, push herself up off the ground, her eyes starting to glow with a strange bluish-green light.

"Robert, your daughter!" Jimmy yelled. "Quick, Mansa is trying to get back inside of her. Put your medicine pouch around her neck. It may stop him from getting back in."

Hearing the warning, Robert turned and saw that his daughter was starting to wake back up. He also saw the strange evil light come back into her eyes. He dropped the staff and sprinted to her side, taking off his medicine pouch and slipping it over her head.

The light in Krissy's eyes glowed for a moment more, then faded back out. Apparently they had kept Mansa's spirit from reentering the little girl's body.

"It worked!" shouted Robert. "Look at her eyes. They're normal."

But the sorcerer had not given up the fight, for suddenly the eyes of Mansa's half-finished body began to glow. Robert had his back to the body and did not see the glow, and didn't know what was happening until the half-finished body rose to its feet.

"Robert, look out!" Janet cried, unable to believe what she was seeing.

Robert turned and saw Mansa Du Paul coming at him. He tried to get out of the way, but he wasn't quick enough. The voodoo sorcerer was already upon him, grabbing him around the throat in a vicelike grip.

Seeing Robert being attacked, Jimmy started forward to help. He had only taken a few steps, when he saw

Krissy get to her feet. The little girl's eyes no longer glowed with a strange bluish light, like those of an animal. Her eyes were normal, even though they were now wide with fear. Apparently she had regained full consciousness and was now terrified by the sight of a half-formed man attacking her father.

Jimmy expected to see Krissy run away in fear, but instead she bent over and picked up the fallen medicine staff. Then the ten-year-old girl did something that surprised him.

Instead of running away, Krissy stepped forward to help her father. Holding the medicine staff like a baseball bat, she struck the half-formed body of the sorcerer across the back of the head.

There was a brilliant flash of blue light, and a hideous scream, as the skull of Mansa Du Paul shattered into hundreds of tiny fragments. The rest of the body collapsed upon itself, leaving Robert standing there in amazement. He looked down at the headless body that had just attacked him and then turned to see his daughter holding the medicine staff.

"Krissy, is that you?" Robert took a step forward, but stopped, fearful that the girl standing before him might not be his child.

Krissy looked at him a moment, then smiled. "Daddy, don't be silly. You know it's me." She looked down at the body at her feet. "Who was that, Daddy? And why does he look all funny? Why was he trying to hurt you? Was he a bad man?"

"You don't remember?"

She shook her head. "Uh-uh."

"Thank God," he whispered.

She looked up at her father. "You're not mad at me, are you, Daddy? I'm not in trouble. Am I?"

Robert smiled. Stepping forward, he grabbed his daughter in his arms and hugged her tight. "No, sweetheart. You're not in trouble."

Krissy hugged her father, then pulled back. "Where's Mommy?"

"Right here, baby," Janet said. She had been keeping back, fearful that Krissy might still be possessed, but now she knew that her little girl was back to normal. "I'm here, baby."

Janet hurried forward and gave Krissy a hug. "We're both here."

"But why are you crying, Mommy?" Krissy asked, looking at her mother.

"I'm just happy. That's all."

"Oh, okay." Krissy allowed her parents to continue hugging her, apparently unaware of the things that had transpired during the past few days.

"Who's that?" Krissy asked, looking past her parents.

Robert turned his head and saw Jimmy Cypress standing there, watching them. "He's a friend, Krissy. A good friend. His name is Jimmy."

Robert patted his daughter on the head, leaving her in Janet's care. He walked over to where Jimmy stood and shook his hand. "I don't know how we can ever thank you."

"No need to thank me. You have your daughter back, and that makes me happy." Jimmy smiled. "If it wasn't for her, we might not have beaten Mansa Du Paul. Your little girl is still innocent, and the innocence of a child is stronger than the greatest evil."

Robert looked to where Mansa's body lay. "What do we do now? Should we call the police?"

"What will you tell them?"

"The truth."

"What? You will tell them that the spirit of a voodoo sorcerer possessed your little girl, using her to murder several people? Do you think they will believe you?"

Robert dropped his head. "No. I guess not. But we have to tell them something. Three people have been murdered. Maybe four. The police will want answers."

"Not if they don't know about the murders," Jimmy said.

Robert was shocked. "Not know about the murders? How will they not know?"

The Indian stood silent for a moment, as if thinking things over and trying to come up with a plan. He turned his attention back to Robert. "Are there any other people staying at the fish camp?"

Robert shook his head. "No. They all left. We're the only ones still staying there."

"Good." Jimmy nodded. "Then there were no witnesses to what happened earlier tonight. And there will be no witnesses to what is going to happen."

"Why? What's going to happen?" Robert was suddenly concerned. "What are you planning on doing?"

"Your daughter is innocent. You know that, and I know that. But the police might think differently, especially when they start investigating the murders. They may find her footprints at the crime scene, in the blood. They may also find her fingerprints on the bodies, or other evidence to suggest that she was somehow involved in the killings. Maybe one of the victims fought back, and trace elements of your daughter are now under their fingernails. I can promise you that the police will use every scientific method available to investigate the crime.

"But what if no one else finds out about the murders? What if all evidence linking your daughter to the crime is destroyed? Instead of a crime scene, what if the police think that three, maybe four, people died in a terrible fire?"

"Burn the lounge? Is that what you're suggesting?"

Jimmy nodded. "It won't be hard to do. I have burned parts of the boardwalk to keep people away from the lagoon, so I can easily burn the Blackwater Lounge to cover a crime scene and protect your daughter."

"I don't know," Robert hesitated. "It just isn't right."

"What's not right?" asked the Seminole. "The three people in the lounge are already dead. I suspect the missing police officer is also dead. There is nothing we can do to bring them back, and we have already avenged their deaths by destroying Mansa Du Paul. We must now think only of your daughter. You do not want her to be part of a murder investigation, especially after all she has already been through. There will be questions enough when the authorities learn that she has been found."

Robert turned to look at his wife and daughter, thinking over what Jimmy Cypress was telling him. "What about Krissy? What will I tell the sheriff's department when they ask about her?"

"You will tell them that you have your little girl back. Tell them the kidnapper let her go."

"But she wasn't kidnapped."

"They will think she was, especially when they can't find me."

"Why? Where are you going?"

"The police will never believe that I wasn't somehow involved in your daughter's disappearance. They will always suspect me, looking for any excuse they can think of to take me in for questioning. Maybe they will even find a reason to lock me up. I am too old for jail, so I will be returning to south Florida. There are places on the reservation to hide, places where they will never find me." Jimmy smiled. "I am no longer needed here, and I am rather tired of living in a shack."

He pointed at the body of Mansa Du Paul. "I will be taking that with me. I will chop it up into tiny pieces and scatter them over a hundred miles of swampland. I will scatter the pieces so far apart the evil one will never be able to return. Mansa Du Paul will be no more."

Jimmy patted Robert on the arm. "Now go. Take care of your daughter. She needs a hot shower, and maybe some food. Wash her clothes so no one sees the blood. Get her cleaned up and fed, then call the police to report that she's back. There will be lots of questions, but you will get through them. Tell them she came home, and remembers nothing. That is the truth.

"But wait until after I start the fire before you call," Jimmy instructed. "I still have a missing police officer to find, and a voodoo sorcerer to chop up."

Robert smiled and nodded. "I'll wait until after I see the flames."

Jimmy smiled back, shook Robert's hand, and walked off into the night. Robert watched him go, knowing that he would never see him again. Jimmy Cypress would disappear into the Everglades, taking with him the evil that was Mansa Du Paul. Before he left, he would help a little girl one final time by destroying all evidence of a multiple homicide.

As for the Patterson family, Robert was hoping he would soon have a chance to take his wife and daughter to a different kind of jungle. He was taking Krissy to Disney World.

Epilogue

A fine spray of water drifted over Robert Patterson and his family as the boat drew close to the falls. He would have steered away to save himself a partial drenching, but he wasn't steering the boat. As a matter of fact, nobody was steering the boat. It moved along under its own power, following a metal track that was hidden beneath a few feet of water.

Not that he really wanted to steer the boat away from the falls, because there was no danger from the jagged rocks, or from the herd of elephants that played beneath the cascading water. The rocks weren't real rocks, and the elephants were mechanical, props and animated robots carefully created by the people at Walt Disney World to excite those brave enough to face the dangerous waters of The Jungle Cruise.

Krissy squealed with delight when she spotted the elephants, especially the cute baby elephant that played in the water with its mother. Robert smiled at his daughter, quickly snapping a photograph of the elephants as the boat continued down the river.

To look at his daughter, you would never suspect the terrible ordeal she had endured during the past few days. She was like all the other kids in the park: happy, wide-eyed, and full of endless energy. Even the scratches on her face and arms had healed and were starting to fade. A purplish bruise was still visible on her neck, but Janet had covered the bruise with a layer of makeup so it barely showed.

Krissy's visible scars were fading, and it would seem that any mental scars she may have had were already gone. The little girl had no memory of the things that had transpired while she was under the control of Mansa Du Paul. She had been spared painful memories of murder and mutilations, images guaranteed to unhinge the mind of someone so young and innocent. Even the strange things she had seen upon waking from her trance were no longer a part of her memory. Krissy did not remember seeing the half-formed body of the voodoo sorcerer, nor did she remember hitting it in the head with Jimmy Cypress's medicine staff. Robert was extremely grateful that that memory had also faded from his daughter's mind, because he would have been hard pressed to explain such things to her. Lord knows, he had already done enough explaining during the past few days.

After defeating Mansa Du Paul, Robert and Janet had taken Krissy back to their cabin. They had cleaned her up and fed her, taking time to thoroughly wash her blood-soaked clothing. Several hours later, Robert had spotted flames leaping through the roof of the Blackwater Lounge. He had waited a few minutes after seeing the flames, then he had called 911 to report both the fire and the safe return of his daughter.

The lounge was a serious inferno by the time the fire department arrived at the fish camp, the flames fed by numerous bottles of alcohol and several storage rooms filled with flammable materials. Since the lounge and restaurant shared the same building, both businesses were a total loss. The flames were so intense that the fire department could do little more than stand back and watch the building burn to the ground, taking care to keep the flames from spreading to the other buildings or to the forest.

Jimmy Cypress must have found the missing sheriff's department officer, because four bodies were found in the smoldering ruins of the lounge. All four bodies were little more than blackened skeletons and had to be identified by their dental records. The fourth body was identified as Captain James Williams of the Palmetto County Sheriff's Department. The evidence indicated that the captain had given his life in a brave attempt to rescue three other people trapped in the burning building.

As the flames engulfing the Blackwater Restaurant and Lounge slowly died out, the authorities turned their attention to Krissy Patterson. They were delighted to see that the little girl was safely back with her parents, but they also wanted to know where she had been for the past few days. Unfortunately, Krissy could not answer any of their questions, because she had no memories of the events. She was questioned by four different detectives, and by several child welfare officers—she was even questioned by a child psychologist—but no one was able to get any answers from her.

According to the medical experts that also examined Krissy, the little girl was suffering from an acute case of amnesia due to her ordeal. While it was suggested that she be kept in a hospital under observation until her memory returned, it was finally decided that she would be much better off in the custody of her parents.

In addition to the questions, and the mental evaluation, Krissy had undergone a series of physical examinations. She had spent two days in the hospital, being poked, prodded, and studied under a microscope. Except for being a little malnourished, she appeared to be in excellent health. She had not been raped, or sexually abused, as many of the examining doctors had first feared. Nor did she have any injuries, other than a few scratches and bruises.

Robert and Janet had also spent their time under a microscope. They had been questioned at great length about their daughter's return, explaining that they had found Krissy in the parking lot a few minutes after they had seen flames leaping from the roof of the lounge. They had no idea why their daughter had shown up at that time, but suspected that she had been guided back to camp by the flames, or by the smell of smoke.

While the Palmetto County Sheriff's Department was suspicious of the situation, they did not suspect Robert and Janet of any wrongdoing. On the contrary, the person they suspected of being involved in Krissy's unexplained disappearance, and her mysterious reappearance, had vanished from the area, leaving behind a collection of used books and little else. They also suspected the same person of starting a fire that claimed the lives of four people.

Though still under investigation, several official statements had already been made suggesting it was arson that destroyed the restaurant and lounge. It was also openly speculated that Jimmy Cypress was the person who started the fire, and that his sudden disappearance was an admission of his guilt. A warrant had been issued for Jimmy's arrest, but it seemed the Seminole was nowhere to be found. He had vanished without a trace, leaving no clues to his whereabouts.

The authorities were not wrong, because Jimmy Cypress had started the fire. But they were mistaken in labeling him as a murderer. Jimmy had not killed anyone. Instead, he had gone to great lengths in protecting an innocent little girl from what would have been another bad situation. He had destroyed all evidence connecting her to a crime scene, protecting her from the police, and the press, and ensuring that she would once again have a normal childhood.

Robert lowered the camera and turned to look at his daughter. Krissy's eyes were again shining, but they did not glow with a strange bluish-green light—as they had glowed when she was possessed by the evil spirit of Mansa Du Paul. Instead, they sparkled with happiness, as she waited to see what kind of animal lurked around the next bend in the river. Would it be another elephant? A hippopotamus? Or a hungry crocodile? Whatever mechanical creature appeared next, it was certain to bring a smile to her lips.

Raising the camera to his eye, Robert snapped a picture of his daughter as that smile unfolded. And as he took the photograph, he quietly whispered, "Thank you, Jimmy Cypress. Wherever you are."